MISERABLE LIES

MISERABLE LIES

NOLON KING

STERLING & STONE

To YOU, the reader.
Thank you for your support.
Thank you for the wonderful emails.
Thank you for the thoughtful reviews.
Thank you for reading and loving our stories.

Chapter One

QUENTIN

EVERY MAN IS guilty of all the good he did not do.

Quentin replayed the line in his head. Again. Just in case he was asked.

He smiled at Luther Gregory, the Flix producer who had talked him into an interview he should probably never have granted. Luther was looking over at him, and like every other time, the large man with small glasses had stolen a glance without trying to hide it.

Luther was taking visual inventory of Quentin's office, ostensibly looking for possible angles to shoot, but fixing his gaze on the subject for several seconds out of every minute. Peering at him through some of the cleanest lenses Quentin had ever seen.

Glasses were an opportunity for those who wore them to express themselves. There was always a story told by a person's chosen frames. Some suggested the owner didn't care, and of course, indifference itself had a narrative. People who saw themselves as creative often preferred color. A cheerful person might opt for patterned frames.

Aviators were for adventurers, browlines for the business-minded, big and round for suited folks who liked to see themselves as "quirky."

Luther's frames were simple and clean. Pragmatic lines without any waste, lenses gleaming like they'd just seen a bottle of Windex.

"How are you doing this morning?" His voice rumbled through the room.

"I'm good. Same as last time." He nodded at Luther, wondering what it was about this man that made him feel so disarmed. He was the cop here. More than that, Quentin Porter was the deputy chief of this precinct in the coastal city of Las Orillas, just south of Los Angeles.

"You feel ready?"

"For twenty years now." Another smile, but Quentin wasn't feeling it. "How much longer until we get started? I need to—"

"Just another minute or so, Deputy Chief Porter. We're setting up our last camera now." Luther smiled, though there were still too many questions in his eyes.

Quentin understood, and couldn't complain. Different professions, but they were still hacking axes on opposite sides of the trunk. They were both searching for truth. Difference was, cops like Quentin put bad guys behind bars while the Luthers of this world were looking to hand those same offenders a microphone.

He understood that so much better than he used to. He would have gladly given the bird to Hollywood back before this all started. But the industry had been good to him ever since *The Magistrate Murders* tore through Las Orillas, and Quentin quickly learned to let the industry work for him. In the last twenty years, it had never truly clocked out.

Things had cooled down, but he still lived in Little

Venice, where the homes were too close, but the canal was spitting distance from his front door. And cooling down was a good thing. For a while, they were out of control. In a good way. The documentary, its follow-up docuseries, and the eventual feature film, all changed his life. He'd never been recognized in public before the flurry of national attention that followed his appearances on the talk show circuit, sitting next to Angus Doyle, the man perfectly cast to play him. An unknown at the time, the blockbuster turned Angus into a star, and Quentin into a very minor celebrity. For a year after the movie came out, he couldn't go to Provisions without getting recognized and accosted. And prior to all the attention and opportunities, Provisions wasn't even a place Quentin could really afford to shop.

Yes, he felt ready.

He was mic'd up and waiting to start. Luther was working with Trauma, documentary filmmakers who'd landed an exclusive deal with Flix, developing a series that somehow managed to be taken seriously by critics while also being somewhat sensational. Their first series, *Murdering History*, had come out of nowhere and become one of the platform's juggernauts, starting with the pilot episode, *George Washington: Serial Killer*, which constructed an extremely loose narrative suggesting that several prominent people in the first American president's past had perhaps been murdered to make way for many of the fortunes that came the war hero's way. An excellent hook, but also a fairytale. And that's the truth that kept Quentin so nervous.

What story did Luther Gregory want to tell?

There had already been a few suggestions that Quentin Porter was more an actor than an officer these days, and those accusations consistently pissed him off. He shouldn't be made to feel guilty about the opportunities he had earned through diligent police work. Actor or not, Quentin was the cop who had put Linus Cole away.

He looked over at Luther and saw that the producer turned interviewer was still looking right back at him. He nodded toward Quentin's office chair, directing the man to sit.

"You need any water or coffee before we get started?" Luther asked.

He took his seat. "I'm good. I didn't get any questions ahead of time, so——"

"Did you think you were supposed to?" Luther raised his eyebrows.

"You haven't exactly been clear about the topic of today's interview."

Luther took a seat directly across from him. "We're talking about Linus Cole. Is that a surprise to you?"

"No, of course not. But I know how these things go, and I think it's fair to ask what kind of documentary you're making."

"That is fair, but you're in good company." Luther gave him a knowing smile. "You've been on this ride-along before, a few times now. You know that the best documentaries are born in the editing room."

"You must have some idea of the angle you'll be taking."

"Should that matter, Deputy Chief Porter? Will the angle of this documentary affect the quality or veracity of your answers?"

"Of course not." Quentin shifted in his seat, glancing around at the crew, every one of them looking at him. "Just let me know when we're rolling."

"We've been rolling since you took your seat."

"Great." He shifted again, offering the camera a smile that was supposed to appear confident but was surely awkward instead. "What would you like to know?"

"Let's start with Cole's book, *An Innocent Man*."

"What about it?"

"I'm assuming you've read the book …"

Quentin shook his head, looking uninterested, waiting for Luther to ask a better question. "Sorry, but I haven't."

Though, of course, Quentin had devoured it. The best way to ensure his side of this story held up was to monitor the only person alive who could ever contest it.

Luther looked incredulous. "I find that hard to believe, Deputy Chief Porter."

"You should get used to calling me Port if we're going to do this thing." Quentin leaned back and folded his hands, trying to look a lot more relaxed than he was. "Is this an interview or an interrogation?"

"An interview, of course. Port." He produced Cole's book like a magic trick and waved it in front of Quentin's face as though he'd never seen it. "I'm surprised you're not more interested in reading a firsthand account of the case that made you so famous."

Luther held it out but Quentin didn't accept the offering so he dropped it on the desk with a thud.

"I'm hardly famous. And that book's a firsthand account from the man I put away. I've heard his bullshit plenty. Why would I want to waste any more of my time reading the same crap 'in his own words'? His are the *last words* I want to read in my story."

"*Your* story?"

"*The* story," Quentin corrected himself.

Why had he agreed to this bullshit again?

Oh, right. Because Quentin felt like he didn't really

have a choice. Sure, he enjoyed the attention, but the real reason he accepted this "opportunity" was that by doing so Luther agreed to keep Emilia and Danica both out of it. Two decades ago Emilia was in the middle of a meltdown, and Danica was a child. He had managed to steer them clear of the media onslaught so far. Emilia wasn't exactly chatty these days, or especially coherent holed up at Morning Tide. But still, twenty years had made both women fair game for the vultures.

Luther's smile faded. "The Magistrate Murders brought you an awful lot of attention. It's easy to see how that amount of recognition could cast you as the star of this story."

Quentin shook his head. "That's now how I see things."

Luther nodded, clearly not believing him. "And who would you say *is* the star?"

"Justice," Quentin answered before the question was fully out of Luther's mouth.

Another light nod. "You've said that a lot: *It's not about the fame, it's about the justice.* Can you elaborate on that statement?"

"Sure." His first word came out terse, so Quentin chuckled to himself and delivered a more pleasant response. "I've never cared about the money or the fame, though yes, the nature of this case gave me my share of both. Regardless of the benefits, it's *always* been about the truth."

"That's what Cole keeps saying."

"What?" Quentin sensed a trap. "What does Cole keep saying?"

"He said something awfully similar in his prison interview with Abraham George last month."

Quentin waited. Luther clearly wanted to tell him the

rest. No need to dignify his interrogator with an unnecessary prompt.

Luther looked down at his tablet, tapped the screen a couple of times, paused for drama even though he wasn't the one on camera, then said, "Here it is: 'I can't make any money in here, and I'm already more famous than I ever wanted to be. Writing *An Innocent Man* has always been about the truth.'" Another pause. "Do you think that's interesting that both you and the man you put away are expressing such similar thoughts?"

"Linus Cole has always been an excellent marketer."

Luther pursed his lips, looking thoughtful. "Can you elaborate?"

"Of course." Another well-oiled smile. "Customers don't want to hear about the labor pains, they want to see the smiling baby."

Luther looked at him, waiting.

"Linus Cole is surprisingly likable. That's one of the reasons he's always managed to mine so much attention from the media. He stares right into the camera and makes everything sound like the truth." Quentin shifted in his seat while shaking his head. "But that doesn't mean it is. You'll never hear about the labor pains from Cole because he doesn't want the jury to picture his victims. But I was there. I still see those burned-out corpses sometimes when I'm trying to sleep. Even now I have nightmares, seeing the word *GUILTY* written in blood on an innocent victim's forehead. Who is Linus Cole to judge anyone?"

Still smiling. Still only pretending. Still waiting for a softball.

Every question was a landmine, and Quentin could never forget that despite this being his office, Luther was the boss here. He could cut these interviews to tell whatever version of the story he most wanted the world to see and hear. In that way, there wasn't much difference between the producer of a docuseries and a defense attorney. Both warped the true narrative for their personal gain.

Difference was, the last few producers Quentin had dealt with felt more like friends than cross-examiners. It wasn't that they threw him softballs, though they had, it was that they seemed more interested in seeing justice ultimately served, in making sure the murderer paid for his crimes. Luther, on the other hand, seemed keen on ensuring that his work was seen as appropriately sensitive, often siding against the establishment in his prior work.

Quentin had no problem taking down demonstrably racist or sexist systems of oppression. The system was rigged against marginalized people, and things did need to change. But Luther's take too often started with the argument that the establishment, and anyone in power, was always wrong, even when it wasn't. It seemed a cynical view, playing to an audience's biases with little if any regard for the truth. Sometimes the bad guy was just the bad guy and not a victim of the system. To pretend otherwise was a disservice to both the victims and to the legitimately wrongly accused.

"What about you, Deputy Chief Porter? Do you think the audience finds *you* likable?"

Quentin appeared to think, though the answer required thought. "I think they find me relatable."

"And what is it they relate to?"

"I'm an honest guy, going to work every day. Doing his job."

"What kind of car do you drive? If you don't mind my—"

"I do mind you asking," Quentin said, sharper than he meant to. "I don't see what that has to do with anything."

"My apologies." Luther raised his hands, palms out. "Question withdrawn."

But Quentin knew what he was thinking, and what the man was doing, a bullshit tactic used in court by prosecutors and defenders, trying to slip something inadmissible into the jury's minds. Or, in this case, the viewers.

Yes, Quentin had made more money than most men in his position, but it still wasn't about the dollars and it sure as hell never had been. Same for the fame. This was about leveraging attention to do something good for Las Orillas. The better he did in his career, the more bad guys he would be able to put away. And that was a boon for the city.

Quentin understood the cycle by now. The docuseries would nab him some extra attention, and in this instance, he'd be able to leverage that recognition into a promotion to chief when the current chief announced his retirement. Even if Luther was coming off as adversarial, his finished project would still remind everyone that Quentin Porter had been the man to finally catch the Magistrate.

"You sure you haven't read the book?" Luther looked down at *An Innocent Man*, sitting on Porter's desk.

"I've read a lot of books about the case, but if you're asking me about Cole's again, then the answer's still *no*."

"Mind if I ask why not? The man is about to be executed, and you're the one who put him on death row. I can imagine my own curiosity, were I in your position."

"I thought I answered this question already?" Still holding his smile. "I've heard Cole's story. Plenty of times. And I didn't 'put him on death row.' I arrested a serial killer for killing."

"Even now, twenty years after his arrest, Linus Cole still maintains his innocence. Do you have *any* doubt about the conviction? Does his insistence give you *any pause whatsoever?*"

"None. Cole is facing execution, his motives are clear and easy to understand. I was there, and the man is unequivocally guilty."

"He says *you're* guilty, and that you know it."

Quentin was ready for this one. He chuckled, then said, "Every man is guilty of all the good he did not do. I could have found Cole faster, and I'm sorry I didn't. The best partner and friend I ever had would still be alive if I'd been better at my job. So yeah, I feel guilty as hell, but I live with it every day as best as I can, knowing I did my best."

"*Every man is guilty of all the good he did not do.*" Luther nodded appreciatively. "That Voltaire?"

The lights were too bright in his office, hot and getting hotter.

The camera crew made the place feel like it'd lost half its square footage.

He really wished the walls would stop closing in.

"It is," Quentin managed to say without gritting his teeth, again shifting in his seat but now feeling under duress. "Let me be clear about one thing: I have zero malice toward Linus Cole. In truth, I can't read the book because doing so would deeply depress me, and that makes my job a lot harder to do. Being a cop puts you in a front-row seat to witness some of the worst shit a person can imagine. I'm always saddened by the depths to which a human can fall ... but when it's a case that's already so personal?" He shook his head. "The candle's not worth the wax."

"'The candle's not worth the wax'?" Luther repeated.

"I don't need to read the book. I'm a hundred percent sure that he's guilty. And as for the execution, Cole is getting what he deserves. You break the law, you get punished. That's how the system works. That's how it's *supposed to work.*" Quentin shrugged, to signal the conflicted thoughts of a decent man, over an empty gesture from someone overly dismissive. "I'm just hoping people won't fall for his sympathy play, and remember the innocents he slaughtered."

"Like Detective Tate?"

"Yes," Quentin agreed, still burying his annoyance. "Like Detective Tate."

It was an interviewer's job to get their subject emoting, but he wasn't used to it happening so early in an interview, or anywhere near this aggressively. Fortunately, these were the questions he was most used to answering. Everyone wanted to know how it felt to lose their partner and best friend to a monster. It made the story of Cole's eventual takedown that much more personal.

Quentin could say this next bit in his sleep. "Miles was a good man and terrific partner. He always had my back, and never gave up until he got his man. His being taken from his wife and daughter was — *is* — an unforgivable crime."

Three sentences that once felt like a mantra, back when Quentin was using them to salvage his sanity while grieving the loss of his partner and Emilia's descent into madness. His turmoil had been a constant, fretting to ulcers that the so-called Magistrate's charm would be enough to convince a well-meaning jury to hang itself.

But those sentences now felt stale on his lips. Quentin probably would have hated the sound of them anyway, but the way Luther was looking at him made it impossible not to.

"Let's talk about Emilia and Danica."

Quentin narrowed his eyes at the interviewer: *We talked about this. Emilia and Danica are off-limits.*

"What do you want to know?"

Luther shouldn't have brought them up, and Quentin should have had some talking points prepared, just in case he got interrogated by a double-crossing cocksucker, willing to betray his trust, which he obviously was.

"What impact has Tate's death had on each of them?"

Another knowing look for Luther to remind him of their deal, but the producer still didn't respond. So Quentin gestured around the room, surveying the crew before turning back to their fearless leader. "We agreed to leave them out of this."

"No, Deputy Chief Porter, we did not. I promised not to interview either woman, and I won't. But Miles Tate had a wife and a daughter. Whether or not you see them as needing your protection, they are both a significant part of this story. If you don't want me talking to them, fine, but that means you will need to talk about them. There's no other way this works."

"Of course." The smile was actually hurting his face. "That makes perfect sense."

"So ..." Luther repeated, "how has Miles' death impacted—"

Quentin's phone began to ring.

"Sorry." He pulled it out of his pocket, surprised. He'd left it on *Do Not Disturb* for the interview. This had to be an emergency.

"Port."

Quentin listened in disbelief as Detective Simpson relayed the impossible. He couldn't imagine the expression on his face as Simpson delivered the news, and desperately wished that the cameras weren't still rolling.

"You're positive?" Of course, he had a hundred other questions, but Quentin wasn't about to ask any of them with Luther and his crew in the room. He turned away from Luther, and held the phone even closer to his face, listening to Simpson's response, at first paranoid that the producer might be able to hear what they were saying, then numb after realizing that he'd know soon enough.

"I'll be right there." Quentin hung up without saying goodbye, then swallowed twice before looking back up at Luther in a stupefied fog. "We'll have to pick this up later."

"Police business?"

"Police business," Quentin repeated, disconnecting the lav mic from his belt as he stood.

He dropped it onto his desk, giving the worried-looking crew an apologetic half-smile on his way out of the office.

Luther kept pace right behind him. "Mind if we ride along? It would be great to get some footage of you on the job."

Quentin answered without looking back, walking faster. "I can't let you film anything related to an open investigation. We can't let details leak to the public."

"I wouldn't dream of—"

"Listen, Luther …" Quentin finally turned around, just on the other side of the precinct entrance, with him on one side and Luther still on the other. "This isn't about what you will or won't do, it's about protocol, and you're subject to the same rules as every other journalist. So that means I'm asking you to please stay away."

He didn't wait for Luther's response. Quentin offered him another camera-ready smile, because of course there was at least still one rolling, then turned around and marched toward his car.

He opened the door — it was the first time he'd ever regretted having a Tesla, though fuck anyone who wanted to judge him — then got inside, turned the engine, and sped off with a whisper, stomach-churning with all the questions he'd have to answer tomorrow when *The Las Orillas Herald* broke the news.

He never should have agreed to this.

Quentin kept driving, gripping the wheel, chewing his bottom lip, and telling himself that Detective Simpson had to be wrong.

The Magistrate Murderer couldn't be back.

Chapter Two

QUENTIN

QUENTIN LOOKED DOWN at the lifeless body hidden behind the tarps set up around the crime scene near the marsh outside the Agora shopping center, trying to swallow the knot of bilious phlegm before it bubbled too far up in his throat. He could sense the other officers trying not to stare, giving him enough space to observe the scene that filled him with a macabre feeling of déjà vu.

Judge Eleanor Engle had presided over the trial of Linus Cole, whom the media had dubbed the Magistrate Murderer, early and often. Some serial killers were barely a blip on the radar, while others had branding worthy of Madison Avenue. Cole had been lucky enough to earn the latter, through a cancerous charisma that Quentin felt bitter about.

But at least he understood now what he didn't back then. The *why* behind it all.

Americans were obsessed with serial killers, despite the nightmares that obsession invited into their lives. There was a reason shows like *Murdering History* were so insanely popular. People loved to watch brutality recreated and played out in real time. Seeing such things was a way to understand what they couldn't otherwise comprehend, to look the devil in his eyes, and maybe believe that evil didn't triumph in the end. Because the killer was usually caught in such shows, and people had a need to know that if true evil existed, at least it wasn't unstoppable.

Quentin swallowed again, still trying not to vomit. The sight was always harder to accept when he knew the victim. He had to talk himself down, remind himself that the scene was an aberration, and that his loved ones were safe.

But doing so was never easy, and this time, looking down at Judge Engle it felt next to impossible.

He should be in control of the scene, but instead he was losing it. He'd been crouched down, pretending to study the body for a while now. Smelling the corpse and ignoring his gooseflesh, Quentin felt grateful that Emilia was too far gone to understand the implications, even if someone at Morning Tide were to mention the horror. But his heart pounded hard enough, thinking about what this would do to Danica.

No way to keep it a secret. By morning, all of Las Orillas would know, and so would she.

Murder scenes were always disturbing, and grisly displays like this doubly so. But a member of the justice system? That made it all so much worse. And the reality of it being the twentieth anniversary of the Magistrate's initial killing spree made it a nightmare brought to life.

Linus Cole was nearing his execution date, and this copycat — because it *had* to be a copycat — could complicate things. Maybe bring the wheels of justice to a grinding, agonizing halt.

Quentin had been looking forward to this door finally closing, and now some copycatting asshole had kicked it wide open. He needed it shut again, and soon. Danica deserved to preserve the life she had built for herself after suffering such unmitigated atrocity. The media's nickname had not only given Cole a more powerful identity, it had also gifted him with a quiet yet undeniable air of authority for those who preferred to see him as an outsider who questioned the rules or raised his fist on behalf of the disenfranchised.

That was all bullshit and always had been.

The man was a monster, and so was his human stain of an echo.

Like all of the Magistrate's prior victims, Engle's eyes were wide open, her mouth gaping in a silent O of agony. Clothes shredded and scattered about her, the mess of a corpse looking like leftovers scraped off a plate.

But also like the others, Quentin was sure there wouldn't be any signs of sexual assault. Cole wasn't that kind of killer; the monster saw himself as an artist.

The body had been split open from the center of her chest, with a gash running down the middle of Engle's body, her insides lit on fire, and the word *GUILTY* stamped in her blood, caked and flaking off her slowly rotting skin. There was only one difference between the original and the copy: this time, the victim's fingers had been burned.

Quentin finally stood, walked away from the body, and surveyed the scene. He heard a ruckus near the perimeter. He spun around and saw the last thing he wanted to deal with right now — Luther and his crew pulling up.

"You've gotta be fucking kidding me," he muttered to himself, marching over.

Alderson — a beat cop fairly new to the force and eager to prove himself — spread his arms to block the producer and his small but clearly determined crew. "You can't go in there. You need to stay back."

Luther looked his way but Quentin averted his gaze, walking over to Detective Simpson instead. He could see the producer waving at him from the corner of his eye, trying to get his attention, as if he had a hope in hell of getting it, or gaining access to the scene.

Quentin should have known Luther would follow him. He was a different breed of producer, making his subject sweat unnecessarily. And now he was a threat to the cop doing his job. The docuseries had sounded like a decent opportunity, despite his doubts, but now it was obvious that accepting the offer had been a big mistake. The situation had been heading south during their first interview, even before this bombshell.

His instinct was insisting that things were about to get much worse. The last thing he needed was Luther Gregory sticking his nose into a new spate of murders. But that's what he would do; vultures weren't known to fly away from a rotting corpse.

Quentin couldn't afford to have anyone in the department talking to the producer or to his crew. Fortunately, being deputy chief afforded him measures of control. He had worked too long and too hard for a shot at the top position. With the promotion close enough to feel like sweat on his brow, he wasn't about to let anything threaten the professional ascension he deserved.

At least the timing was right. If the promotion was already his, Quentin would have more authority but less ability to stay hands-on as this alarming situation unfolded. He had to stay on top of the investigation, and could oversee everything in his current position. At least for now, no one would question his decisions about who should stay involved, and who needed to stay the hell away from the investigation.

He couldn't officially work the case, but Quentin could

assign it to any detectives on active duty, and reprioritize their cases if necessary. And he could assist in whatever way he saw fit. No judgments or scrutiny, no second guessing or third degree. The case would be the highest of profiles, so Deputy Chief Porter would make the most appropriate calls. His earned history with both the public and the department would rest a halo above his initial decisions.

He couldn't get too close, but there was no way of staying out of it entirely. That meant managing the investigation at an arm's length, starting with who he assigned. Luck wasn't exactly on his side, but at least the situation wasn't an unmitigated disaster. Simpson had been first on the scene, and the one who called Quentin. So giving it to Reginald Simpson and his partner Desmond Merrill made sense, even if it also worked in his favor.

They were decent detectives. Not the best, but deserving of the opportunity, and no one would have any reason to be suspicious about their assignment. They took guidance well, and wouldn't ask too many of the wrong kinds of questions, assuming Quentin could effectively direct them. And of course he would, he'd been doing it for years.

Simpson and Merrill would follow orders, fall in line, and turn this investigation into the unwanted epilogue to the Magistrate Murders he needed it to be, instead of a gratuitous reexamination of the facts Deputy Chief Quentin Porter couldn't allow.

His radio crackled to life from Sergeant Jack Barnes. "Waters is here."

"Copy," Quentin said, stepping past the tarps to greet forensics specialist, Julie Waters. He updated her, feeling too many eyes on him. Not just Simpson's and Merrill's, both on the scene, along with the beat cops who'd been milling about for a while. Members of the media had already arrived, including Tabitha Keane, an annoying, pink-haired glorified gossip blogger from an appropriately named tabloid website called *GOTCHA!*

Quentin was used to the game, and none of the media made him nervous.

But he was unsettled by Luther and his crew, setting up their cameras, eager for footage for whatever the hell the next chapter of their production was about to become.

Luther had better watch himself. Quentin was already annoyed by the ambush of questions. If the man even dreamed of pushing his way onto the crime scene, Quentin would make his life a living hell.

He went back to the body, crouching down beside it as Waters started snapping photos, recording video, and noting salient details that would be needed later to determine time of death and cause of death, though that last part seemed obvious — Engle probably died being burned alive.

The body looked uncannily like the others.

The victims had been stripped naked before the murderer lit their insides on fire. Engle, lying in a husk before him now, had been the judge of that infamous trial, and now she was an echo of the very photos shown at Linus Cole's trial that had sickened everyone in attendance.

His heart was beating too hard, and yes, there was sweat on his brow. Good thing Luther and his crew were on the other side of the sawhorse and couldn't see the body, or just how shook he was.

Still crouched, Quentin was starting to feel paranoid, thinking about all the questions he wouldn't want to answer, and a few of the things no one knew. Like the note he'd never logged, and still thought about on more days than he didn't.

But mostly he had his own questions that needed answering. Who could have done this? And why?

Linus Cole was slated to be executed in just days. Was this one of his delusional groupies trying to throw doubt onto his guilt? If so, they'd gone through incredible lengths to duplicate Cole's kill scene and modus operandi. Maybe it was an acolyte, someone Cole had worked with. There had been no indications that he had a partner. And there'd been no similar crimes since his incarceration, but perhaps it was a new acolyte. Someone he met on death row? A fellow prisoner? A lover?

Quentin would need to check Cole's visitation and correspondence logs. Every visitor and correspondence was carefully screened by Coldwater Island before making their way to Cole. But the man was fiercely intelligent, and he might have found a way to communicate through some sort of code the prison officials had been too slow to decipher.

Quentin finally stood, considering what he would say to Danica after looking her in the eye and letting her know that their lives were about to get flipped upside down again. He could picture her tears, and hear her sobbing.

If Cole had an acolyte, that might very well put Danica in the crosshairs.

Yet another reason to end this before it could really get started.

One new body was already more than enough.

He sighed, walked past the tarps, looked over at Luther and pretended not to notice him, then caught Simpson's gaze and gave the detective a nod before making his way over.

As much as Quentin wanted to avoid it, he had no choice.

He would need to visit Coldwater Island, and give the inmate a visit.

It was the last place in the world Quentin wanted to go, to see the last person he ever wanted to talk to.

But first, a conversation he was looking forward to even less.

Chapter Three

DANICA

Danica didn't believe that God helped those who helped themselves, because Danica didn't believe in God. But she did believe that people were always better off after they did the difficult work of looking their problems in the eye, and ideally staring them down.

The past had a way of interfering with the present, and Danica had been trying to convince her current patient of that truth throughout the entirety of their four months of working together. Yet, every session felt like more déjà vu, and they would continue to feel that way until Cecilia was finally able to separate the way things were from the way she wanted them to be.

"That sounds like progress," Danica said, because sometimes encouragement was the only way to open doors that were otherwise locked. "Three nights in a row without any nightmares, that's a record, right?"

"Any nightmares that I can *remember,*" Cecilia corrected.

"If you can't remember them, then I think we should call that a victory."

Cecilia blinked twice, still looking like a frightened

animal. "I thought you said the stuff I can't remember is still in my head. Sitting there like 'old milk I forgot to throw out.'"

"Dreams are different."

"How so? Didn't you also say that dreams were just another way of us working things out?"

"I did." Danica smiled. "But we don't process dreams the same as we process our reality. We don't need to keep holding onto the things that happen while we're sleeping, even if they're helping us to work through our emotions."

Cecilia wasn't trying to be difficult; she desperately wanted to understand. The woman was a shell of who Danica was sure she must have been before meeting Rodney — the monster who had put her in the hospital with four broken ribs, a punctured lung, a crushed cheekbone, a damaged kidney, and enough internal bleeding to kill her. It would have, if not for the emergency surgery.

Cecilia's time was almost up, but Danica wasn't about to call it now that they were finally getting somewhere.

"Maybe I'm blocking the dreams out, because they're so terrible," Cecilia suggested.

"Maybe. Or maybe your mind knows that ruminating over a nightmare isn't helping you and has actively chosen to forget." Danica gave her a moment before adding, "What makes you think you might still be having them?"

"I'm still waking up drenched in sweat … and afraid."

"You know he can't hurt you anymore, right?"

To Danica's surprise, Cecilia didn't look away this time, instead holding her therapist's gaze and nodding as the whisper left her mouth. "*I know.*"

"He's serving six years in prison, and eligible for good behavior in four—"

"So even if I'm fine for the next few years, I could still end up dead before my fortieth birthday." That was the first time Cecilia had interrupted Danica since she had started coming to see her.

"You're safe. Rodney is more than a thousand miles away."

"So … two days driving. Or one for Rodney." Cecilia shook her head, almost violently. "You don't know him … he'll never let this go."

"I've never met Rodney, but it's my job to 'know who he is.' And I can tell you from experience — men like that are looking for a victim. Four years is plenty of time to change who you are and—"

Cecilia cut her off again, this time with a bark of laughter. "You're right. I'm sure I can become a millionaire and hire an around-the-clock security detail. That'll be easy enough, living in Allison's spare room and spending the little I make coming here so you can tell me to get over it."

Another kind smile. "I would never tell you to 'get over it,' Cecilia. This is a process and you're doing better than you're giving yourself credit for."

"Of course I am. You need me to come back next week, right?" She coughed a bitter little laugh. "I'm sorry, I know that's not fair. I just …"

At least she was talking about her feelings. *Finally*.

This was good. Cecilia had been trapped in her head for months now; she needed to let it out. Her eyes were wide and back to leaking. There was so much more she needed to say.

"Go on," Danica prompted.

"Six years, and probably out in four?" Another violent shake of her head. "I would have died if my neighbors hadn't called 911."

But then Cecilia stopped, like hitting a wall. So much to say and yet she couldn't just say it.

"Do you mind if I ask you a question?"

Cecilia looked up at her therapist. "Isn't that why I'm here?"

"Underneath all the anger, I'm sensing something else. You've said a few things that …" Danika paused, then let the rest of it out. "Are you feeling guilty at all?"

"No," Cecilia said.

But she obviously was, so Danica didn't respond.

Seconds later she corrected herself. "I guess I feel guilty for testifying against Rodney, despite what he did. He's my husband, or was. Now I've put him in jail. And for a felony instead of a misdemeanor. He'll be an ex-con forever. If I had done things differently … maybe I wouldn't have set him off like I did."

There was so much Danica wanted to say, but couldn't. Not right now. They were peeling back layers and finally getting to the heart of things. Cecilia needed her to listen more than anything else right now.

But it was a struggle to stay silent as her patient unburdened herself. Danica was a trained therapist, so it was her job to be supportive, but there were so many errant thoughts that she was dying to correct.

Cecilia didn't put her husband in jail, he put himself there.

She wasn't responsible for setting him off, Cecilia was the victim.

Rodney would be an ex-con forever because he deserved to be, for beating the shit out of his wife.

Cecilia plucked a pair of Kleenex from the box and dabbed at her eyes, finished for now.

"How does it help you to feel guilty?" Danica asked.

"What if it's my fault?"

"Can you clarify that for me?"

Cecilia needed a second, then her answer left in a stutter. "What if there's something about me that made him do that?"

"Do you think that this is all about you?"

"Well, it happened to me, didn't it?" Cecilia snapped.

"Is it possible that taking responsibility for your husband's inability to control his temper is a way of feeling like you're more in control of the situation than you actually are?"

"Oh, like I have control over any of this."

"But you want control, don't you?" Danica asked.

"Who doesn't?"

"The first step to feeling more in control is learning to notice our emotions."

"And how do I do that?" Cecilia plucked another handful of tissues from the box.

"I'd like to give you a breathing meditation. Would that be okay?"

"So yoga's gonna solve all my problems?" Another bitter laugh.

"No." Danica offered her warmest smile and a light little shake of her head. "No one thing can ever 'solve all your problems,' but a simple breathing exercise can make you more aware of what you're feeling, and help return you to center."

Cecilia looked up at her like a lost little girl. "What do I do?"

Danica both explained and demonstrated the breathing exercise, then said, "Just do that for three minutes, whenever it starts to feel like things might be too much for you."

"How long ..."

"Three minutes," Danica repeated when Cecilia couldn't finish.

"No." Another shake of her head, now more defeated

than emphatic. "I mean, how long am I going to feel this way? How long before I'm back to normal?"

"We'll be figuring out what your new normal will be together. It's hard to put a deadline on transformation, but it is why you're here." Danica glanced at the clock. They were nine minutes over, but this was her final client, and the extra time had been worth it. "I really appreciate you opening up. We've made some real progress today."

Cecilia wiped her eyes again, then looked up. For the first time since they had met, Danica saw hope.

"Thank you." Cecilia seemed to surprise herself with a tiny laugh as tears dripped down both cheeks. "I think I even feel a little bit better."

"I'm glad. Be prepared for some ups and downs. This would be a great time to finally start journaling like we talked about. Do you think you can do that?"

Cecilia nodded. "I can."

"You don't have to share what you write with me, but working out your feelings on the page will help you to get more out of our time together."

"I guess I'm ready to hear that now."

Cecilia stood, thanked her again, then left Danica alone with her thoughts.

Minutes later, she closed up, locked the office door, climbed into the back of her old Ford Ranger, and started driving to Morning Tide for what was sure to be yet another miserable visit with her mother.

Chapter Four

DANICA

"—AND THEN HE DIED," Mom finished.

"I'm sorry that happened," Danica said, dabbing her mother's chin to collect the drool.

She had no idea what Emilia was going on about, but at least her mom was talking. The most likely scenario was that she'd been telling her all about the most recent episode of whatever show happened to be streaming on Flix in the community room. She might have also been relaying an ancient story that had once been told by Miles Tate, Danica's father, murdered by the Magistrate Murderer when Danica was just a little girl.

That killer had claimed both of her parents. Dad was another burned-out corpse with *GUILTY* in blood on his forehead, and Mom was never the same. Already unsteady, her mind up and quit shortly after the murder. She had been admitted to the Morning Tide Psychiatric Care Facility a few long weeks later, and that's where she'd lived ever since.

Their visits never changed. This was what she and Danica did every week. The same babbling narratives that went nowhere and meant nothing; the same drool on the same chin, though these days that chin had a few errant whiskers; and the same sense of futility fueling it all.

Her mom had lived at Morning Tide for twenty years now, and for two decades Danica had hated the place. Despite constant maintenance, the facility could never shed its feel. The place was too dark. Its rooms all smelled faintly of urine and bleach, blanketed by tropical-scented air fresheners.

Emilia's room was a bland sort of sterile. Hallways were dark and the sitting room gloomy. Gray food in the cafeteria made Danica want to cry, but so did all the vacant stares inside it. The grounds were well cared for, but constantly in shadow, with only a few boring plants scattered about. Even the statuary was gray, and the sculptures all spattered by sky droppings, so streaked with stains that they appeared to be crying.

Danica wondered when the last time her mother even recognized the person on the other side of their conversation. Did she have any idea that it was her daughter wiping drool from her chin? Danica hated the visits, but had tried skipping them exactly fourteen times in the last decade and felt even more miserable after every one she had missed.

So here they were, same as always, her on a bench and Mom sitting beside her in a wheelchair, blanket on her lap and a tattered sweater hugging her shoulders.

That sweater had been the last gift Dad had ever bought for his wife. A birthday present, even though Emilia had been born in July. A running joke that she was always cold; all year long, even in summer. Twenty years later and Emilia still wouldn't part with what was now a ratty patch of fabric. There was less and less of the sweater over time, and these days it looked like an ancient carpet swatch, clean but ragged beyond recognition.

Yet, something about the frayed garment kept Emilia clinging to it. If she couldn't identify the daughter who still came to visit her every goddamned week, then Danica was glad she could at least remember her stupid sweater.

She took a breath; it wasn't her mother's fault.

The murder had put Emilia in Morning Tide, same as it had eventually cast Danica in her current role, listening to women like Cecilia working through their shit while she sat a few feet away, holding a tablet and doing her best to navigate her patients through the worst of it.

Danica became a behavior therapist in the hopes that she would eventually understand what had happened to Emilia, and herself to a lesser extent. Mom had suffered a psychotic break the day she buried her husband. She never really recovered, and even all these years later still suffered the occasional outburst. Loud and violent, unrelenting and lasting for twenty to thirty minutes each time before Emilia Tate could be calmed. Such emotional hurricanes were always followed by weeks or even months of total silence.

"Have you been listening to your iPod?"

No response, not that Danica expected any.

She had filled her old iPod with music she knew her mother once listened to, and asked Rebecca — her favorite of the nurses — to help Emilia use the player. But Rebecca reported that her mom had shown zero interest, even after Danica bought a base unit for her room. It was an iPod Touch, the last model Apple made before they quit making the devices altogether. The small box was filled with thousands of songs, all lovingly chosen after Danica read a study suggesting that listening to music had emotional and behavioral benefits for those suffering from Alzheimer's or other types of dementia. But even every song the Beatles ever recorded failed to put a smile on her mother's face.

"Rebecca said that you've been loving Lasagna Night …"

No response to that either. But Danica was only going through the motions, sticking to the same routine that kept her from feeling like she might be going insane herself. From guilt or shame or whatever it was that always made this all so miserable. Of course Mom wasn't going to respond about her iPod or Lasagna Night or any of the other trivialities Danica raised to pass the time. She hadn't even responded to the news that her parents had passed.

That happened a few years ago, while Danica was finishing grad school. The loss wasn't unexpected. Nana went first, then Papa lost his life to heartbreak a few months later. They had raised Danica after Emilia was admitted to Morning Tide. Her stay with them was supposed to be temporary, but instead Danica grew up feeling guilty for robbing her grandparents of the retirement they deserved. Not that either one of them had ever made her feel that way.

Regardless, after a while the guilt was like blood in her veins.

Even after all her training, Danica had never been able to help her mother, or clearly remember what had happened on the night of her father's death. Those failures felt like bullets lodged in the back of her skull.

Uncle Quent had helped her to remember key aspects when she was a child, but those fragments were more like shards of a dream than clear reality, even more frayed than the sweater warming her mother's shoulders.

And worse than not being able to help, Danica had inherited her mother's bipolar disorder. It started manifesting shortly after her thirteenth birthday and had grown increasingly severe over time. Becoming a behavioral therapist hadn't helped with that either.

At least she'd never suffered from the hallucinations. Emilia was having those even before the murders.

Mom had always refused to take any medication, until she no longer had any choice. Danica refused to make the same mistake. She resented the hell out of her pharmaceutical cocktail, but still swallowed her pills every morning and night like a good girl. If that's what she needed to stabilize herself, so be it.

But that cocktail hadn't been working as well as it used to, or should be. Thinking about it churned her stomach. Sure, Emilia was driven over the edge by her husband's death, but what if that descent into madness had only been a matter of time?

And what if Danica was already sliding down that same slippery slope?

"That's what everyone keeps telling me about yogurt," Emilia said.

"What about yogurt?" Danica asked, though her question was pointless.

But Emilia surprised her. "February 6 is National Frozen Yogurt Day."

"Oh, is that right? Anything else?"

Then Emilia surprised her again. "Genghis Khan used to eat yogurt with his armies. He founded the Mongol Empire, you know."

Danica found herself with an uncertain smile. "I did know that."

"Spread his seed everywhere. Lots of his DNA in the world.

Remarkable. This was *almost* a conversation. "So I've heard. What else are people telling you about yogurt?"

But that was it. Despite another dozen attempts, the conversation died. If Danica wanted to know anything more about yogurt today, she'd have to consult her favorite search engine.

She looked at her watch: thirty-three minutes already, so three over the minimum required to leave without taking a head full of guilt with her. She pictured her exit, wheeling Mom back into Morning Tide, or letting Rebecca do it for her, then living as more or less an orphan for yet another week.

But for some reason, Danica couldn't leave. She was feeling too anxious, and didn't understand why. Maybe she needed to go for a run, or head to the climbing gym. She wouldn't mind punching the shit out of that bag in her garage.

She looked down at the rosary sitting in Emilia's lap and thought the same thing as always: *Fuck that shit.*

It made her angry seeing the way her mother still clung to that pile of beads. Danica didn't dismiss religion out of hand. She'd been willing to give it a shot, despite how hard it had failed Emilia. She was desperate for a connection to *something*, and before deciding to become a therapist, she saw the church as worthy of exploration. But Danica stumbled into a series of dead ends and looping roads paved by lies. The rosary didn't even belong to the Catholics. Not really. They borrowed the idea of praying with beads from pagan religions who had been doing that for centuries after lifting the tradition from the Hindus.

The Magistrate Murders had left a stain on Emilia's soul, and nothing could change that. Especially not a heap of worthless beads.

She needed to center herself before leaving. So Danica started to talk, pretending the words weren't for her alone, and that Emilia could understand, or care.

"Cecilia started opening up to me today." She waited a beat, just in case, then, "I think we're finally getting somewhere. It wasn't exactly the breakthrough I've been hoping for, but it was the closest we've come so far."

Another beat, then, "At least now she's not in the same place that she's been, and I feel positive that next week's session will be even better. I'll be able to help her get through the fear and, hopefully, start putting her life back together."

Danica was only telling herself the story she wanted to hear, but she could swear that it felt like Emilia was listening.

"But the session also made me sad. I can't believe how often victims like Cecilia come into my office feeling guilty about having to defend themselves, or speaking out against the people who have hurt them."

She didn't expect an answer, and Emilia didn't offer one, but she did mumble something that sounded a little like, "Honeypots are better with giraffes."

"Why is it that bullies never take responsibility for their actions, but the people they bully do?" Danica understood the first part fine, it was the second half of that question that confounded her. "I just don't see——"

Danica stopped.

Something was wrong.

A ripple of chills tore through her body.

"What was that?" A sort of undulating motion, born in the corner of Danica's eye. Not like water rippling so much as flames dancing. As if reality itself was on fire.

She shivered again, trying to bar an onslaught of doubts piling on her psyche like an avalanche.

Was the medicine making her better or worse?

She looked at her mother and felt another heavy wave of guilt. Danica had been doing everything she could to stave off the inevitable advance of her inherited illness without taking the kind of severe meds that turned her mother into a vegetable. But in moments like this, she didn't know what was worse: the illness or the treatment.

Emilia might not be much of a companion these days, but Danica could never forget what it used to be like, back when Mom lived in a permanent state of hysteria.

"Are you cold?" asked a familiar voice.

Danica looked up, surprised to see Rebecca standing there.

"Would you like to come back inside?" She glanced down at Emilia's wheelchair in a silent invitation to help.

"No, thank you." Danica offered Rebecca a wan smile. "I just got a chill."

Emilia shuddered, like a physical echo of what Danica had just done, but much more dramatic. Then she said, "It's ash."

"What's ash?" Danica turned to Rebecca, as if the nurse might know.

"No idea?" Rebecca shrugged, shaking her head.

"Is she cold, and maybe talking about the fireplace?" Danica asked.

"Maybe, but I doubt it. The fireplace has never been lit — it's too dangerous for the patients. I'm not even sure it works for anything more than ambiance. But I do think it's cold, and—"

"Let's go ahead and get her inside." Danica stood, frustrated with her visit, same as always.

She kissed her mom on the forehead, just as her phone started ringing.

She pulled it out of her pocket and saw *Uncle Quent* on the screen. "What's up?"

"Hey Dani." A long pause, followed by a heavy sigh. "I need to ask you a favor." He cleared his throat. "And you're really going to hate it."

Chapter Five

DANICA

"THEY LOOK DIFFERENT ON TV." Danica surveyed the swarm of protestors in clusters outside the prison, demanding everything from another appeal to Cole being released.

Ever since the new governor overturned the moratorium on executions, the state seemed to be making up for lost time by lining up executions one after another. Cole's was next, and nothing short of unlikely clemency from the governor was going to save him.

"How so?" Uncle Quent asked.

Danica surveyed the crowd as his Tesla slowly approached the prison gates, trying to determine what made the crowd seem different. Its makeup was about the same as she expected, in color and social class, so far as she could tell. Las Orillas was one of those cities where it was harder to parse the one-percent from the lower ninety-nine, unless she got close enough to see the stitching on their hoodies. Even then it was a guess.

Staring out from behind the gleaming windshield, she thought it was a matter of proximity and perspective.

Being so close to all those signs made her nervous, but so did the prison. Not the looping miles of razor wire lining the fence, but the institution itself. Housed on a manmade islet just off the Las Orillas shoreline, with both San Pedro and the rolling hills of Rancho Palos Verdes looming behind it, the place felt both gothic and modern. Danica had read about the prison plenty, but until a few minutes ago when Quentin had asked her if she was sure before accelerating onto the mile-long bridge taking them from the mainland to Coldwater Island, she'd never seen the place in person.

The prison had been built in the early 30s, adjacent to a Coast Guard base, with just over six hundred prisoners. Two million in construction bought a neat trio of cell blocks. The United States Navy used the place as a receiving station during the Second World War, then later as a barracks for court-martialed prisoners, until it was ultimately turned over to the state in 1952 for use as a high-security prison, and a Southern California death row.

Coldwater Island now housed forty-seven inmates all awaiting execution, including the man who had murdered her father.

"Ignore the signs." Quentin nodded toward a group of protestors to her right.

Execute the Death Penalty!

We don't need more murder to remember the victims!

Why do we kill people who kill people to show that killing is wrong?

But those weren't the signs that bothered her. Danica was upset by the crowd on her left, the one waving placards that felt so much more personal.

Linus Cole is INNOCENT!

Linus Cole is dying for our sins!

And worst of all: *Quentin Porter is a MURDERER!*

She was intimately familiar with human irrationality, and still she had a difficult time understanding how anyone could be so stupid. The world had heard her testimony: It didn't matter how good Linus Cole might be at smiling for the cameras, he was the only suspect who had a strong personal connection to every single victim, and clearly guilty.

"People will believe whatever story makes them feel better," Quentin said into her silence. "That means they can't afford to care about the truth."

She was sick to her stomach, and still couldn't muster a response.

Cecilia hadn't visited Rodney, but Danica had spoken to several clients who had visited their abusers behind bars. She understood it could be a nerve-wracking experience, but had never been forced to stare it in the eye herself. Quentin had dropped the bomb, first by telling her about the copycat killer, then by asking her to accompany him to Coldwater, before finally overwhelming her with the many rules for what she could and couldn't wear or bring with her to the prison.

No denim, white, or anything resembling medical scrubs. No open-toed shoes, or clothing that could in any way expose her chest, back, thighs, midsection, or any other large amount of visible flesh. Nothing tight, sleeveless, or see-through. Jewelry was prohibited.

The gate rolled to a close, leaving the legions of protestors behind them.

Quentin parked, then turned to Danica. "Getting inside won't take too long, I promise."

It didn't, though every minute felt excruciating. Twenty or so before the Tesla was cleared by a guard and his canine unit, then a second search on the other side of yet another fence. Fortunately, things never got too personal, though Danica was asked to step through a scanner several times after multiple false readings.

They were finally making their way down a long corridor toward a meeting room where the guards had brought the Magistrate Murderer to meet them.

Quentin said, "The warden has arranged us to have a private place to talk, instead of the regular visitor's room."

Danica couldn't tell whether that was good or bad. "Should I be happy about that?"

"There won't be any glass partition separating us, but the room has cameras, and the guard will be stationed right outside the door."

"Will he be shackled?" Danica asked.

"Of course, and I promise that I'll never leave your side."

A small relief. Quentin meant well, and always did, but being so close to the man who murdered her father was putting Danica outside of her skin.

The long hallway might as well have been her own walk down death row. Flickers of motion lit the edges of her vision. Like a monster made of smoke peeking around every corner, before flinching back. She kept jerking her head around, working for a better glimpse of whatever it was, even though she knew that meant nothing. Even her usual breathing techniques were failing.

Quentin was talking, but his words were a din in the background.

He kept telling her what questions to ask, but she could barely hear him. She was about to meet the man who took her daddy away from her. The man responsible for her mother's breakdown. The man who had shredded her life, and robbed her of everything that actually mattered.

But he was also the man who was there when she

blacked out, and might be able to fill in some holes in her memory.

The hallway finally ended and Danica found herself standing in front of a door. Quentin was still looking at her, his brow furrowed in concern.

He gently set a hand on each of Danica's shoulders and looked into her eyes. "I'm sorry I asked you to do this, but it's not too late."

"I'm fine, really—"

"Maybe we can find a female cop whose build and coloring are similar enough to yours that we could fool—"

"You should have thought of that *before* you dragged me down here."

"You're right. And I'm sorry I asked you. But better to back out now than—"

"No." Danica shook her head. The only thing worse than having to talk to the man who murdered her father was losing the opportunity to do so. She could pull herself together. "I can do this."

Shadows at the edges of her vision were only a figment of her very angry imagination.

"So I just need to tell Cole that we can give him a stay of execution, *if* he tells us who his partner is, and how they're communicating. Then we're out of here, right?"

"Right." Quentin gave her a single, decisive nod. "Are you ready?"

Danica swallowed. "As I'm going to be."

Uncle Quent tipped his chin toward the guard.

He opened the door. Then together, they stepped inside.

Chapter Six

DANICA

They were a pair of opposites.

Danica was paralyzed, sitting on a long bench while waiting for Linus Cole. Quentin was on his feet, pacing the room and visibly sweating.

She'd never seen him so … unnerved. His fists kept clenching and unclenching, and every half minute or so he would stop as though hitting an invisible wall. He'd turn toward Danica with a slightly open mouth, then shake his head and start pacing again, his earlier attempt at whatever he wanted to say suddenly and perhaps even painfully aborted.

Seeing the new victim must have hit Uncle Quent harder than she'd realized. What a shit therapist. He deserved at least the same amount of empathy she'd give to any one of her patients, but instead she offered him less. She was always so focused on Emilia's trauma, it was easy to forget that he had lost a partner, and his best friend.

Uncle Quent was scarred by his own upheaval and distress. Danica had seen the danger of turning a blind eye to one's emotional anguish firsthand, not just with her own issues, but all the ones she was paid by the hour to hear about.

The department forced Quentin into therapy following his partner's murder, but had that been enough? The operative word was *forced.* A hostile witness made for terrible therapy. Clearing the detective for further duty wasn't the same as solving his issues. Danica could remember his bitching, even though she'd only been a little girl.

He stopped again. Opened his mouth. Really looked ready to say something this time.

"Danica—"

A clang from outside, then the door loudly swung open.

Linus Cole was escorted into the room. They had been waiting for more than ten minutes, but still she wasn't prepared in the least.

More than a flood of emotions, her head felt like it was being held underwater. She had to remember her breathing exercise, force herself to slowly pull the air through her pursed lips, then back out and over again. She tasted sweat on her lip, and could feel a belligerent itching all over her body, especially in her armpits, making her want to claw at her skin in hopes that it might go away.

Like it or not, Danica had devoted much of her life to Linus Cole. First to being terrified and hating him, then eventually trying to understand the monster and what he'd done to her family. She was a scholar on the man being led to his seat at the table across from her. She had read every article and seen every special. She'd even participated in a few of the ones where Quentin thought it would be okay.

But still, she hadn't seen him in person since the trial twenty years ago and wasn't prepared for his appearance.

He was better groomed than he'd been back then, but

Danica noted the hard edge now under his polished facade. She forced herself to stare back, unwilling to show this man any weakness by breaking her gaze, studying the Magistrate Murderer as she wondered if what she was looking at had been born of decades spent in a slaughterhouse, or innate to his diseased personality.

Quentin would say the latter, but Danica needed to see the truth for herself.

"You good in here?"

Danica wasn't sure who the guard was asking, or if she was supposed to respond.

"We're good," Quentin replied.

"We're right outside if you need anything." Another nod, then the guard turned to leave.

The rippling darkness that had been haunting Danica rolled into the room. Her thoughts turned frantic, and for a moment she could swear the acrid scent of smoke was billowing all about her. Enough to tighten her throat and threaten her breath.

She coughed, then looked away embarrassed as Cole continued to coldly stare at her.

Despite his proximity, Danica wasn't in any immediate danger. The table was large and his wrists were shackled. Still, the apparent menace in his murderous eyes chilled her to the core, and made Danica forget all that smoke and rippling darkness. The room itself seemed to shine a spotlight on this rancid stain of a man.

Cole tipped his chin toward Quentin. "He needs to leave."

"Absolutely not," Quentin said.

Cole shrugged. "Well then, let's see how this goes."

There were three seconds of pure silence, and in them Danica could feel the killer claiming control of the room.

"Fair warning ..." Cole tipped his chin toward the man

who put him in jail. "I've had a lifetime of bullshit from this bovine sphincter, so if you want a conversation, it's starting with me and you first. *He* has to be quiet."

Words died in her throat.

Danica was torn, both wanting to realize the fantasy she'd had for most of her life, about meeting this killer face-to-face and demanding to know why he'd murdered her father. Forcing him to confront what he'd done to her mother. She had always imagined herself somehow making this man feel remorse for what he'd done.

But looking at him she realized that her childhood fantasy meant nothing.

This man didn't have a single heartstring to tug on. He would probably enjoy hearing about all of the destruction he'd caused. Might even get off on it.

His face split into a sinister smile. "So, do we need theme music and a title screen to get this started, or are we good to go?"

Danica couldn't afford to look over at Uncle Quent. She had to show this human pile of shit that she was strong enough to face him without breaking. But still, Quent's overwhelming worry was hitting her in waves. She pictured him looking down at her in silence, urging her to hurry.

Danica opened her mouth, but Cole wasn't done taking things away from her.

"How did it feel, to ruin an innocent man's life?"

"You're a monster who deserves to die!" she blurted, with none of the poise she had imagined for herself. Then, since she'd already lost it, Danica added, "I can't wait for your execution. I'll be right there in the front row, eating popcorn."

Cole shrugged again, still wearing his sinister smile. "I should have known you'd still be a self-righteous little bitch." He leaned forward. "What do you think your father would have thought about you lying in court like you did?"

"I watched you murder my father!" Danica was so livid, the next line left her more like a hiccup than a thought. "You abomination!"

"*Abomination*," Cole repeated, his smile splitting into a laugh at Danica's word choice.

Quentin circled around to the other side of the table. She could finally see his face. He was honoring the killer's request to stay silent, while looking like he might tear Cole's head from his neck.

"Perjury is a crime, and a sin," Cole continued, sounding almost indifferent. Then, in a softer voice, almost admonishing: "And thou shalt not bear false witness."

He was pushing every one of Danica's buttons, including a few she had convinced herself could no longer be pressed. "You killed my father and you might as well have murdered my mother. You deserve to die."

"Sticking to your lie?" Cole coiled his face with surprise. "I don't know why I expected better from you."

She was trembling. It took everything she had to still herself.

She had spent so many years trying to forgive this man for what he had done to her family, for her sanity, not for him. But after a minute in the same room Danica was right back to hating him. Now more than ever.

Quentin could no longer hold it. "You need to shut your mouth or I'll make sure you spend the rest of your miserable life sucking food through a straw."

He slowly turned to meet Quentin's gaze. Danica expected the killer to remind him that he wasn't supposed to be talking. Instead Cole shrugged as if he had zero shits to give. "I've no doubt you could get away with that,

Deputy Chief Porter, seeing as you're the dirtiest cop I've ever met."

Quentin glared down at him, refusing to dignify his bullshit with a response.

Cole smiled at the detective before slowly turning back to Danica. "Was your Uncle Quent nice to you after Daddy died? Did he buy you pretty things and let you sit on his lap?"

The glob of spit was sliding down his face before Danica realized it had launched from her lips.

"That all you got?" Cole laughed, wiping his cheek.

Quentin clenched his fists and Danica was sure he was about to give Cole one hell of a beating. "You need to shut the fuck up before I—"

"It's fine." Danica didn't want him saying or doing something Cole could use as a weapon against them later. "I'm okay."

In truth she was furious, but her anger needed redirection. Maybe at Cole, for taking control of this situation, for acting like she was still ten years old, like he was the grown-up who knew what was best for her instead of the inhuman beast who had obliterated her life. Irrational, perhaps, but she couldn't help but feel trivialized.

Maybe that's why the hallucinations were back.

Smoke still rippled at the edges of her vision, writhing in time with her racing pulse.

Danica wanted to blurt a string of curses at Cole, spit in his face again, climb across the table and claw at his cheeks until they were trimmed in ribbons of blood. They sat in silence instead.

Finally, once collected, Danica calmly turned to Quentin. "I'm done with him."

He circled back around to her side of the table, then still standing and looking down at Cole he said, "Here's the deal: you want a stay of execution, you'll need to tell us the name of your partner."

"I'm fond of the guards, but I wouldn't refer to any of them as *partners*," Cole said, without missing a beat or even blinking. He turned from Quentin to Danica. "Tell a lie often enough and eventually you can no longer remember the truth. Are you there yet?"

Cole was smug yet biting, baiting Danica as he stared at her.

Quentin said, "He's not interested. Let's get out of here."

Cole kept staring. "Think of what it means for your soul if you let me die in here when you know in your heart that I'm innocent."

That shouldn't have felt like the slap that it did.

"Come on." Quentin took Danica by the arm and tried to pull her up from the seat. "We need to get out of here now."

She shrugged him away, still refusing to break the killer's stare. "If you're innocent, then tell me right now: *what is your proof?*"

Quentin tugged on her again, but Danica kept on ignoring him.

He finally let go and started toward the door.

To her surprise, Cole smiled even wider, and answered with a single syllable that stole all of her breath. "*You.*"

It wasn't just the word — the way he said it made her choke.

"What do you mean by that?" Danica demanded. "*Explain.*"

Uncle Quent banged on the door and bellowed for the guard.

The door swung open and he rushed inside.

Quentin was back at the bench, now forcibly pulling Danica out of her seat.

"Stoke the flames," Cole called out, still sitting calmly on his side of the table, hands neatly folded and resting on the top. "The fire that's closest kept burns most of all. It's in their bellies, Danica Tate. Remember what you know."

Chapter Seven

QUENTIN

"*PLEASE*, Danica. Can you just wait another few minutes until we're back in the car?"

She mumbled some words of assent, clearly unhappy about it.

She had been peppering him with questions ever since leaving Cole. No variety, every query just another version of *What did he mean, that I'm the evidence that proves he's innocent?*

That was a truth she could never know, but every response Quentin could possibly conjure would ring hollow for sure. Danica dissected answers for a living, and while he had managed to avoid the most probing of her inquiries for the last twenty years, circumstances now had his head in a vice.

Things got worse on the other side of that barbed-wire gate. A small group of journalists were waiting. They were probably there to cover the protest, but any one of them would be thrilled to see the prize pairing of Deputy Chief Quentin Porter, the man who put Linus Cole behind bars, walking side-by-side with Danica Tate, the woman who was a little girl when she testified against the Magistrate for murdering her father.

"Keep your head down." Quentin led her in a straight line across the lot to his Tesla. "Maybe they won't recognize you. And if they do, just say, 'No comment' — *no matter what they ask.* Got it?"

Another murmur of assent. She had to know that was wishful thinking on his part. Of course she would be recognized. She could lose herself in a crowd of everyday folks while buying groceries, but walking next to Uncle Quent in the Coldwater Island parking lot, Danica Tate didn't stand a chance.

And sure enough, they were still a hundred yards from the car when one of the predatory reporters spotted prey and hurried over toward them. A wiry Clark Kent. Quentin walked faster, and Danica matched his stride without being asked.

But the reporter was closer. More followed. By the time Quentin and Danica were spitting distance from his Tesla, they were surrounded by a small swarm of vultures in journalists' clothing.

A voice called out, "Deputy Chief Porter, have you reconsidered your opposition on Linus Cole's stay of execution, especially in light of today's killing?"

Quentin stopped, knowing he had to answer. He wasn't a beat cop, and couldn't get away with either indifference or silence. Not here, and not in front of a huddle of professional witnesses. He was deputy chief now, and if he played his cards right, soon he'd be in the top spot.

He turned around and surveyed the crowd. Made eyes with Clark, then answered in his most vehement, authoritative voice. "Linus Cole is as guilty now as he's ever been. As for the new murder, it is an ongoing investigation and we will keep you apprised as we can without risking the investigation."

The next query came from a woman, standing next to Clark; she was ready to go as if the first reporter had been holding the door for her.

The reporter turned to Danica, as if Quentin didn't exist. She had a big face and the bouffant to match it. Her voice managed to sound both inquisitive and accusatory at once.

"Will you be recanting your testimony in light of—"

"How dare you!" Danica reeled around on her.

Quentin could feel her anger, like heat from a summer sidewalk. She looked at the big-haired reporter, then turned to Clark before casting her condemning gaze at the rest of them.

"Shame on you for promoting his lies, and planting seeds of doubt in people's minds. Linus Cole is *guilty*. That man murdered my father, and I saw it with my own eyes. He—"

"That's enough." Quentin took her by the arm again, leading Danica away before she said something they would regret.

But still, the questions held their assault until they were both in the Tesla. Quentin locked the doors and cursed under his breath as he started the car and pulled away.

He swerved around the swarm of parasites, making their butter off the back of human misery.

"What the hell was that?" Quentin barked at Danica once they were on the other side of the fence. "Didn't I just tell you not to say anything to the press?"

"Yes, but—"

"And why did you let Cole get in your head?" Quentin didn't let her answer this time either. "Jesus Christ, Danica. Why didn't you leave when I asked?"

"Because—"

"And why didn't you stay on topic? Why did you let him manipulate you?"

"I didn't let him manipulate me." She finally got a word in, though her sentence sounded like an audible pout.

He twisted the knife. "You're a trained therapist. I expected more from you."

Danica fell silent, stewing as she considered her response.

It was a low blow, but she hadn't left him with much of a choice. She already took it all so personally, blamed herself for never being able to reach Emilia. Questioning her competency as a therapist right now wasn't an effort to hurt her, he just needed to throw her a few yards off track. Buy himself some time.

Quentin needed to get Cole talking, but couldn't afford for the murderer to go poking around in Danica's head, or trigger an unfortunate memory that could conflict with the testimony he had managed to successfully coach her through all those years ago.

She was too much like her father, honor bound in all the wrong ways. She would feel the need to say something, no matter how small the discrepancy, or how much damage her "honesty" might cause.

By trying to do the right thing, she would get everything wrong, remembering and then reporting a triviality that could not only stay his execution, but thanks to serious flaws in the justice system, could ultimately free the Magistrate Murderer and put another killer back on the streets.

Cole's sentence getting overturned would cost Quentin his career, not to mention calling all of his other convictions into question. One mistake, one time, and the consequences would be catastrophic. Personally, professionally, and for all of Las Orillas.

Dozens of hardcore criminals could very well end up with grounds for appeal. Too many would be back on the streets, their revolving doors lubricated by oily lawyers who valued bottom lines above ethics. It would renew pressure on the governor to put another moratorium on executions. Bad people would continue to escape ultimate justice. And all because Quentin couldn't connect the dots on those killings two decades ago.

Any decent detective would have done the same thing. Linus Cole had killed *at least* eight people. One of those had been his partner. His best friend. Danica's father.

The man wasn't just a murderer, Cole was a cop killer. He didn't just deserve prison, he deserved to die there.

Sure, playing on Danica's insecurities was a shitty thing to do, but so much was at stake.

The Tesla was still silent, his passenger still marinating in anger in her seat beside him.

Quentin cleared his throat. "Maybe you ought to see a doctor about getting some meds … you know, to help balance you out."

He didn't turn to look, but Quentin could see her expression in his peripheral vision. He hated the sight, and himself for obvious reasons. Escaping Emilia's fate was one of her biggest life goals, and the man who should be taking care of her had raised a mirror to those deepest fears instead.

But still, he was doing the right thing by keeping her quiet. He needed to think, figure a way out of this. For both of them. Danica didn't answer. Silence was better than the questions. No noise to rouse those sleeping dogs.

He finally broke the silence once they were on the other side of the bridge, back on the 710 and headed toward his home in Little Venice. "I'm sorry for asking too much from you."

No response.

"I was wrong. This is all still too raw. You have my word, I won't ask anything else of you. Not when you're already staying so strong for the sake of your mother."

It was dirty, but it appeared to be working. She seemed quietly determined more than angry now. Same as it had been for the last twenty years, Danica wouldn't want to let her Uncle Quent down. She could do this; she *would* do this. She would follow his instructions the next time, for Emilia's sake. With her help, rather than her interference, they would catch the copycat.

They were toward the end of Ocean and turning onto Seaside when Danica finally spoke. "What did he mean? About the fire that's closest kept burns most of all?"

Quentin shrugged. "The guy's a fucking wacko. Probably just trying to get into your head, sow seeds of doubt. He can't kill anymore, so it's his only outlet to cause pain, to victimize others."

Danica shook her head, looking like the gesture was mostly to herself. "He meant something. What about the 'it's in their bellies' part — does that mean anything to you?"

Quentin sighed. "That part is the killer being literal. He used to light the bodies on fire, which not only made it harder to get DNA evidence from the murderer, it made finding a matching murder weapon next to impossible. You already know this."

Danica was mercifully silent for almost a minute.

Then she ruined everything.

"I think that particular turn of phrase *a fire in the belly* is worth picking at. What if those abdominal blazes were more than Cole scrubbing evidence? What if he was working with metaphor? If he had a fire in his—"

"You're giving the guy too much credit."

"Or you're not giving him enough," Danica argued. "You can say a lot about Linus Cole, but the man does seem to know who he is. And taken literally, 'a fire in his belly' could mean a compulsion he wasn't able to stop. So beyond the killing, what was his message?"

"More importantly, what was the acolyte's?"

"What could he not help himself from doing?" she mumbled to herself.

Quentin didn't want Danica near any of this, yet sticking close to his side was still the best place for her to be. That was the only way he could protect her, himself, and all of Las Orillas. Besides, she had the perfect skillset, history, and desire to end this thing for good.

"I need your help."

Danica looked over at him. "What do you need me to do?"

"We need to build a profile of the new acolyte. Figure out what makes him tick so—"

"Of course. Anything to make sure that Linus Cole and his partner both get what they deserve."

A relief for sure, but still Quentin couldn't help but feel like the situation was quickly slipping away from him. He pictured Luther's probing stare, the horde of reporters, and the body of Judge Engle lying in a husk on the ground.

He swallowed and squeezed Danica's shoulder. "Thank you."

But he was thinking something else entirely.

Chapter Eight

DANICA

Uncle Quent was frustrating her.

He was lost in his own world, going through a pile of notes, evidence, and copies of letters he'd gotten from the prison, and doing a shit job of answering her questions.

Danica looked out at the window, her eyes on the canal and the gorgeous Tudor across the street. Like every one of the homes in Little Venice, the house was too large for its lot, leaving only a sliver of distance on either side, and barely enough of a pathway to pass in front of it.

Las Orillas homes, like much if not most of LA County, were packed too closely together, and nowhere was that truer than in Little Venice. The small yet exclusive neighborhood was built on a trio of islands in Appian Bay. Most of the streets had Italian names.

Uncle Quent lived on *La Bella Fontana di Napoli*. His home was small, and he'd paid more than a million for it back in 2002, well before the boom, but after money was suddenly much easier for him to make. The place had always felt like an odd combination of home, and somewhere Danica didn't quite deserve to be.

But right now the place felt like solace.

She'd been shaken by the reporters, and stirred into feelings she didn't want to face. Sifting through the evidence with Quentin, poring over files and his many private notes helped to fill her with purpose. Danica was happy to assist, and doing so gave her a target for her negative emotions. Fear, anxiety, and an almost crippling sense of overwhelm at the thought of all those reporters.

They didn't care about her dad as anything more than a part of the killer's story. The press didn't even really want her story, at least not in the way she would most want to tell it. Reporters worked to capture her suffering in neatly packaged clips.

"What am I looking for?" Danica asked her same question in a different way — two prior attempts had left her without any clear answer, and she needed more than Quentin was apparently wanting to offer if he expected her to develop a profile. Everything she was looking at now was from the original Magistrate trial. But that wasn't enough to build a bridge between then and now.

Quentin looked up from his pile. "There's a crazy amount of correspondence sent between Cole and his supporters. It's all handwritten, and it all needs to be gone through, in case the copycat is someone he's in communication with right now. Just write down every name you find so we can compare it to the original case and see if anything sticks out."

"Maybe we should be talking to people he knew—"

"Our time is better spent here. Simpson and Merrill are doing the legwork. We're support here, looking for the pieces that usually fall between the cracks. Sure, there's a chance they'll find what we need, but there's an awful lot to get through. And if the killer is someone who was with Cole in the old days, then our answer is here."

He cast his gaze back across the pile.

Another somersault for her stomach. Danica didn't want to say anything, but something about all of these files was making her acutely uncomfortable. She was a psychologist, not a cop. She wasn't clear about all of the protocols and didn't want to upset her uncle, or really even ask, but it was getting increasingly difficult to ignore her unease. Looking at the mountain of paperwork, it felt like they should be working somewhere more official than his coffee table.

Danica chewed on her silence for another few minutes, until she could no longer help herself. "Are you allowed to keep all of this stuff here?"

He looked up, his expression almost comically dismissive. "Most of this is just copies of what's at the precinct."

"*Most of it?* And the rest?" Danica dared.

Quentin offered her an awkward smile. "The rest is stuff your father had at his house that I brought over here after—"

"So it's evidence? Could keeping it here jeopardize the Cole case?"

"Linus Cole is about to be executed. There *is* no Cole case. If we were to present this evidence now, *that* could be grounds for a mistrial. And I'm sure that's not what you want." Something bitter entered his tone. "It sure as hell wouldn't be what Miles would have wanted. Maybe your dad shouldn't have had the evidence at his place, but he did, and now it's too late for us to do anything about it."

The answer rang hollow, the way Quentin blamed his old partner.

But Danica wasn't always able to see reason when it came to her father, and this was likely one of those times.

An anxious strain of silence settled between them. Danica could hear the sounds of papers tossed onto the table, and a loudly ticking clock filling the living room with the same metronomic beat that used to help her sleep on the occasional Saturday or Sunday afternoon.

A boat passed by outside, probably full of drinking teens judging by the raucous laughter and thumping bass lines.

Again Danica eyed the evidence. And again felt unsettled.

She closed her eyes to a memory. Her parents discussing the Magistrate case. Mom was freaking out, same as always, while Dad did his usual dance of trying to calm her. She remembered him looking far away. Mom was agitated because he wouldn't answer, or even meet her eyes. He was in his own world, mumbling something about ash while she kept yelling at him to stop ignoring her.

The memory opened her eyes.

She thought of the murderer's words as they left him. *Ash and fire.*

There had to be a connection, beyond the words and their natural link.

Danica had agreed to build the new profile, and was even looking forward to it. But she had imagined a different experience. She should be able to ask Quentin questions and get answers to help her assemble a picture.

Instead he kept staring into space, and giving her a glimpse into what Mom must have felt while Dad was dealing with a different version of this same case so many years ago.

She was on her own, at least for now.

Again Danica looked down at the pile.

The acolyte was intimately familiar with the original case. He had probably consumed every nugget of available information. The Magistrate Murders had made every Top 10 Serial Killer list Danica had given a curiosity click to, so there was no shortage of articles, books, movies, and TV shows about the killings.

Whoever was doing this was either someone Cole had known, or someone who was trying to get his attention, maybe earn his approval. Impress him.

Probably someone with a malleable personality, eager for someone or something greater than him to identify with. Someone ridiculed by others his whole life, finally thriving under the attention of a larger-than-life figure who became not only a mentor, but his personal hero.

But did they know each other?

Was it possible to shake the acolyte's faith in his God, to show him that Cole didn't care about him? That this poor sap was being cruelly used by Cole?

There was too much she didn't know, too much missing for her to build a decent profile. "This isn't everything related to the case."

"What do you mean?"

"I need to see my father's file," Danica said, intentionally phrasing her sentence as a statement instead of a question.

"Absolutely not."

"I'm an adult now. I don't need you to protect me."

He wouldn't even look at her. "You don't understand the impact that's going to have on you and—"

"It's my choice to see it and—"

"You won't be able to *unsee* it. So, no."

"You can't ask me for help and then refuse to—"

"I'm trying to protect you, Danica. There isn't anything in there you need to see, I promise. The answers are—"

"No way, Uncle Quent." Danica shook her head. "That isn't fair. You asked me to help, and I'm trying. But how am I supposed to build a profile without having all the information? Would you hold anything back from someone else trying to do the same work? No, you wouldn't. So why—"

"Because Miles was your father, and my best friend." Quentin let his response sit between them, like it was actually an answer. When the moment felt like it couldn't gain any more weight, he drew a breath and continued, shaking his head and looking like he might cry. "Losing Miles was the worst thing that ever happened to me. It was *my fault.* I should have seen it coming."

And this silence Danica felt to her marrow.

Quentin didn't really answer, because even if her father's murder was all his fault, that had nothing to do with the evidence he was withholding today.

But Danica did understand his pain, and what irrational emotional agony could do to a person. She felt guilty if anything. Only now did Danica realize that she'd never really even see him grieving. Uncle Quent had always stayed strong, to protect her. She had been too selfish or perhaps oblivious to realize that they were both victims of trauma.

"I'm sorry about all of this. Maybe I shouldn't have asked you to—"

"No," Danica said. "*I want to help.* And I have enough to get started."

"I just want to keep you safe. I'll help with whatever you need, of course, but once the profile is built you should really stay out of this, honey. The media will be all over this like stink on a skunk. Don't talk to reporters — I promise, they're never on your side. Same for the documentary crew. There's no need for you to relive any of this. It isn't healthy, and I can handle it all for you."

"What if he strikes again? Who else might he target? We should compile a list of everybody involved in the original case, all the prosecutors, maybe even his defense. Anybody else he feels is responsible for him being locked up."

"My detectives are already on that."

"We probably don't have much time. If Cole is executed, the killer may change their MO and become harder to track." Danica picked up a binder, then opened it up and stared down at the list; a catalog of items found in Cole's home after his arrest. Most included photos of the items.

She found what she was looking for. "There's a photo of an engagement ring here. Was Cole involved with someone back then?"

Quentin shook his head. "He had lots of trophies. Always ransacked the places he burned. Look at the rest of that list — it's all mementos. A couple of lockets, plenty of pictures, a mess of knickknacks. The fucker even had a house number. Apparently, he liked taking shit."

"Was the engagement ring ever specifically reported as missing?"

"You mean by the people he murdered? No." Again he shook his head. "But that doesn't mean anything. His juvie record includes joyriding, shoplifting, graffiti, arson — all the usual hits. Even as a kid, Cole was a born criminal. Even if it didn't come from one of the vics, he could have easily stole it from his foster mom, Maggie."

"Where's the ring now? In an evidence locker?"

"Yes."

Danica looked closer at the photo. The ring was almost plain. Gold with a tiny diamond. Might even be a fake diamond and fake gold, given how cheap the ring looked.

"Do you think that—"

The doorbell rang, cutting Danica off.

Quentin launched himself up from the couch and was

halfway to the door before she decided to take a chance. Knowing it was wrong, she grabbed her father's file and stuffed it into her bag.

Just in time. Quentin looked through the peephole, then turned back to Danica. "It's the documentary crew. I'm sure they want to get my reaction to the copycat killing while it's 'still fresh.' Maybe try and persuade me to share a few details, despite that being a dereliction of my duty."

The doorbell rang again, this time followed by a knock.

Her anxiety was on fire.

"Don't worry, you don't have to talk. They don't even need to know you're here." Uncle Quent nodded toward the stairs. "Wait for me up there and I'll get rid of them as soon as I can."

Danica nodded, then turned around and trudged up the stairs without a word, surprised by the weight of her guilt. He had always taken the brunt of the publicity. Even now as an adult — and a skilled trauma therapist — she was still allowing him to shield her.

Would it be so awful to tell her story one last time?

Wouldn't she be doing the world a favor by reminding everyone of what that monster had done?

No one in the world could bring more emotional weight to the argument. Her father had been murdered by Linus Cole. No one else could undercut the movement to support his appeal.

If she could find the courage.

Chapter Nine

QUENTIN

THE DOORBELL RANG AGAIN, and the knocking turned more insistent.

It was already the third one, so he really needed to hurry.

Quentin couldn't afford to be concerned with something as trivial as neatness with Luther outside, so he opened the box of evidence Danica had been rifling through and swept most of the table into it — everything that would fit. Then he gathered any other remainders he wouldn't want the cameras to catch, set the miniature mountain on top of the box, carried the entire mess into his kitchen, opened the cabinet underneath his sink, and shoved it all inside.

He rushed back to the door and opened it to Luther's penetrating gaze.

"Is it a bad time?" the producer asked without preamble.

"I was working, but I guess this is life letting me know that I could use the interruption." Quentin smiled and opened his door all the way to let Luther and his crew inside.

It was important to project the image of a busy cop who had everything under control. He glanced down at the files still scattered across his coffee table, then looked back at Luther. "After this morning's homicide, we pulled some of the old stuff out of evidence. I've been looking for threads that can connect Cole's case to the copycat we're dealing with now."

"Find anything you'd like to share?"

"Not yet," Quentin said, giving Luther his thinnest smile.

"Mind if we set up and ask you a few questions?"

"It's not a good time."

"We'll keep the interview short. We can circle back for another round later, but it's best that we get you right now while the events are still fresh."

"Best for who?"

Now Luther was starting to piss him off. Quentin wasn't just a detective, he was deputy chief of the precinct. There had been a murder this morning, and one that would not only make the front page in Las Orillas, it would be national news by tomorrow. He needed to be doing his job, not playing with Luther and his crew. A professional interviewer should know how to listen.

Quentin didn't wait for his answer. "I'm sorry, but the demands of this case have unfortunately overridden my earlier agreement to conduct this interview today. I'm going to insist that we reschedule." He didn't think it was unfortunate in the least. "The good news is, you'll ultimately have a much better story by giving me the space to do my job and catch the copycat."

"And what do you have so far?" Luther asked, undaunted.

"I'm sorry, but I can't talk about an ongoing investigation. And I really do need to get back—"

"Of course. It must be vexing so early in a new case, with all these loose threads. Other officers in your department were sharing some of the same frustrations with—"

"Who did you talk to?" Was Luther *trying* to piss him off?

"Do you mean at the precinct or the prison?" Luther asked.

Quentin could swear he saw a smile lighting his interrogator's eyes. The question must have been rhetorical, because he only waited a beat before answering himself.

"I spoke to Detectives Simpson and Merrill, plus a few officers—"

"They shouldn't have been talking to you."

"—on the scene this morning, before heading to Coldwater for a conversation with Cole."

"That must have been a waste of your time."

"Not at all." Luther shook his head. "Cole claims that the new killings prove you tampered with evidence to get your conviction."

Quentin stared at him, glad that the crew and its cameras were still waiting outside.

"Any response to that?" Luther asked.

"Not right now. Not while I'm trying to do my job."

The producer and his crew were sticking their noses where they didn't belong. Angry as that made him, Quentin understood that they were only doing their jobs. But he hadn't expected Cole to have fresh ammo for his claims of innocence, and looking at Luther now it was obvious that he would be making it a point to speak with the murderer again, and soon.

Luther was still looking at him, as if Quentin might change his answer.

He didn't. "Linus Cole is at the very least taking advantage of a copycat killer, and possibly directing his actions from prison. Be careful, anything you do now could be construed as helping him to communicate with a potential accomplice. Intentionally or not, that would make you and your crew complicit in any subsequent killings."

"What are you saying?" Luther asked.

"That you should stay away from Coldwater, and Cole, at least until this is all over."

"Is that a threat, Deputy Chief Porter?"

"Not at all." Quentin shook his head. "I appreciate that you have a job to do, but so do I. And right now I'd prefer to do my job without you in the way."

"The investigation, you mean. You'd prefer it if I weren't in the way of your investigation."

"Right. Are we done here?"

Luther nodded. "Should we schedule a time for later?"

"I'm sure you'll understand if I need to get back with you on that." He started toward the door. "I'm on my way into the station."

"Then I'll look forward to your email or text, and I'll make sure to touch base just in case you forget." Despite leaving in defeat, Luther's words still somehow chimed with victory.

Quentin waited for the crew to leave, then retrieved his evidence from under the kitchen sink and returned it to the coffee table, thereby keeping Danica from asking the kind of question he wouldn't want to answer on their way out.

And there she was, creeping down the stairs with perfect timing. "Why not just talk to them?" She hit the bottom stair and looked cautiously into the living room. "Wouldn't you rather just be done with it?"

"No." Quentin shook his head. "Not only do we have more important things to do, acquiescing to a guy like that makes him think he can do whatever he wants, whenever he wants to do it. Come on, I'll drop you home on my way into the office."

The ride was silent. Quentin could practically hear Danica thinking, but didn't want to ask what was on her mind. He was curious, of course, just not enough to initiate a conversation that would surely include an informational tax he wouldn't want to pay.

He dropped Danica at her tidy two-bedroom with a friendly wave and a promise to "talk soon." Then the passenger door slammed and left Quentin mercifully alone with his thoughts. He turned the evidence in his mind, knowing he must be missing something obvious, or just out of sight.

He parked in his usual spot, then got out and walked fast toward the precinct, glad that Merrill and Simpson were on the case. Quentin answered only to the chief, and the chief was out of the country at his youngest daughter's wedding. So that gave him some much-needed breathing room.

While he focused on stitching the evidence together, his detectives could handle the grunt work, canvassing for witnesses and gathering the various elements of proof to silence Cole's absurd claims of innocence, once and for all.

But it was also best for Simpson and Merrill to be slightly removed, seeing as Quentin wanted them both as far away from anything that might expose him as possible.

He wanted them out of his business, not gone from the picture. But neither detective was at the station. They could be chasing a lead on a late lunch. Quentin didn't want to call and inadvertently trigger any internal alarms. With no way of controlling the narrative without knowing what his detectives had found, he would be uneasy until they talked.

Simpson and Merrill might be out in the field instead of at the station like Quentin had hoped, but he could go over the notes from the investigation which waited for him on his computer.

The official autopsy wouldn't be for another day, minimum. But early indications showed at least one key difference between this and the prior murders. The fingers on Engle's hands had been burned.

He leaned back in his chair, telling himself to stop worrying so much. So long as he could keep Luther and his crew away from digging too deep or finding anything he didn't want found, everything should be fine. The important thing was to control the situation and protect Danica.

Quentin would catch this copycat, and fast. Then it would all be over.

He stared at the report for several long seconds, then dropped it onto his desk.

Maybe he should head back to Coldwater and talk to Cole about the discrepancy. Once the media started calling him the Magistrate Murderer, an already healthy ego spiraled out of control.

Quentin could maybe use that as a weapon against him.

Cole was clearly proud of his work, only refusing credit to salvage his life. Floating the idea that the copycat was "improving on his old MO" might be enough to anger Cole into turning him in.

He pulled out his phone and tapped his contacts to bring up Coldwater, but it rang in his hand before he could hit the number.

"Deputy chief," said the voice before Quentin could utter hello.

It was Merrill. "We have another body."

Chapter Ten

QUENTIN

QUENTIN LOOKED DOWN, trying his best not to vomit.

It wasn't the body's condition, grisly as it looked. He'd worked homicide for years, and had seen worse. His brewing ulcer was born from what the corpse represented. Not just *what* was happening, but how fast shit was going down.

Two bodies in one day.

Looking down at Engle's burnt husk that morning, Quentin was sure that things would go from bad to worse in a hurry, but still hadn't anticipated exactly how quickly. A few hours in and things were already falling to pieces and burning to ash.

Detective Reginald Simpson shook his head, shoulders slumping. "Looks just like the last one."

Detective Desmond Merrill reached into his pocket and took out a Snickers bar. Tore right into it.

Simpson looked at the shorter cop. "You really can't wait a half hour to eat, you fat bastard?"

"I didn't eat breakfast."

Simpson laughed, looking at Quentin. "He didn't eat

his second breakfast. I saw the fucker swallowing the rest of a breakfast burrito in his car as he pulled up to work. Looked downright barbaric."

"Fuck you. You're just jealous."

"*Jealous?*" Simpson said, laughing. "Now that is truly some delusional shit. You might wanna drug test him, Quent." Even though Simpson was older than his fifty-six-year-old rotund partner by five years, he was in fair shape and looked at least five years Merrill's junior.

Quentin felt wobbly in his knees.

"You okay? You want a Snickers?" Merrill reached into his coat pocket and pulled out another bar.

"How many fucking candy bars you got in there?" Simpson asked.

Quentin managed to laugh as he found his legs. "No, I'm good. Thanks."

He kneeled beside the body and looked closer, ignoring his stomach. No surprises, the on-duty officer told him what to expect during the call, then Merrill played echo. Still, hearing and seeing were two different senses, and the latter felt more like assault.

Gary Stevenson's body was just as charred at the edges as Engle's had been. Same for all of Cole's original victims. But it had one thing in common with the judge's body that the Magistrate's targets didn't share. The fingers, carbonized beyond recognition, like a handful of forgotten fries left in a fire.

Even without the autopsy report, Quentin felt certain: they had been burned while Stevenson was still alive. It made him want to hurl even more than he already did. Hard not to picture the man screaming his lawyer's lungs out as the acolyte watched, laughing while the flames slowly swallowed his victim's body.

Any doubts that these murders were linked to Cole and

the Magistrate case were impossible to ignore or deny once the press got hold of the name of the deceased. Quentin felt a clock on him, ticking to get this shit solved before his chief lost all faith in him, before the attention of the press became a national story.

The 2001 murders had at first seemed random, until the investigation uncovered the truth. This time the link was obvious immediately. Same now as then, every victim was a person who had somehow wronged Linus Cole.

But the link was obvious with the copycat's first killing, and indisputable now that Quentin was staring down at the second one.

Eleanor Engle was the judge who presided over Linus Cole's trial, and had been plastered across every kind of media throughout the entirety of the Magistrate coverage. Same for Gary Stevenson, Cole's attorney.

Connecting the dots was like drawing a line across two points on a piece of paper. The obvious pattern made it easy to predict what might happen next.

That forecast filled Quentin with terror. The DA was clearly at risk. Same for a dozen men and women from the jury who'd done their jobs to put the monster away. Their names had never been released to the public, but most of the jurors had been interviewed over the years, and despite many of them going unnamed, out-of-the-box facial recognition software was better than state of the art from back then. Every member of that jury was in clear and present danger.

But so was he. Quentin had zero doubt that he was holding an honored spot on the copycat's kill list. Peril came with the badge, and he'd always lived knowing any day could be his last.

Still, it was different when he could feel the bullseye warming his back.

That wasn't what scared him, or gave him pause. The most horrifying part of this mess was realizing that Danica was now in the line of fire, and there was nothing he could do about it. Despite her being a child at the time, and never having to appear at the trial in person, she did have to show herself to the court. She testified on video, and the jury asked to see her testimony a second time, incendiary as it was. Quentin managed to keep her name out of the paper for the first few days, but then it was everywhere.

The copycat would be coming for her, too.

He couldn't imagine a more devastating thought. Sure, there were a couple of truths that he would rather Danica didn't know. But those obfuscations were necessary, to keep her safe. Same as he always had, and always would.

Quentin loved her like a daughter.

In a way, she would have been, if Emilia had left Miles like she always threatened to.

But now, the idea of Danica dying, or worse, dying because of him, was the most powerful motivator he could ever have for solving this case.

Not that he needed more fuel.

His next best move was slightly more appealing than chewing on a mouthful of nuts and bolts, but another trip to Coldwater was in the cards.

Simpson tried to approach him on his way out.

"Later," Quentin said, having dialed and lifted the phone to his ear.

He was already out of the lot by the time someone came on the line.

Quentin requested another visit, was told that Linus Cole had been expecting his call and had preemptively refused to meet with the deputy chief unless his specific stipulation was met.

Quentin heard the details of Cole's condition, then requested a chat with the warden.

HE WAS 3.1 miles closer to Coldwater when the warden came on the line.

After a heavy sigh, he said the same thing. "Sorry, Port. But even if I can put you two in the room, we both know Cole is only going to talk if he wants to."

"So, no ideas?" Quentin asked, hoping for a miracle.

"Cole says it's Danica or no dice."

"What did he say, *exactly*?"

"His exact words were, 'I'd be happy to have a conversation with the daughter of Detective Miles Tate, but as to the man responsible for his murder: Deputy Chief Quentin Porter can fuck himself.'"

"Thanks, Abrams. I'll see what I can do."

Quentin hung up and dropped his phone on the passenger seat.

But still he kept driving. Thinking. Wondering what he should do.

Back in the day he'd drag that piece of shit into an interrogation room, kill the cameras and lock the door, then beat the holy hell out of Linus Cole until the asshole was pissing and shitting blood while begging to start singing the truth.

Now, with so many eyes on him, he had to be careful. With all this scrutiny — Cole's appeal and his little army of supporters, the documentary and its crew who apparently couldn't wait to catch Quentin doing something wrong, plus all the attention on the copycat killings, which would only get worse over time — there just wasn't any way to justify the risk.

He reached over and picked up his phone. Swallowed hard as he dialed.

There was no other choice: as much as Quentin hated it, he'd have to pull Danica back into the worst of this, and put her back in a room with the monster who murdered her father.

Chapter Eleven

DANICA

DANICA HAD BEEN STARING at the folder on her dining room table for a while now.

But still, she couldn't bring herself to open the file, or even pick the thing up.

She pushed herself away from the table again. And just like the last few times, she left the dining room to pace her living room while stealing glances outside, each time hoping she'd see something in need of her attention.

Anything to keep her from the folder. The one she stole from Uncle Quent, because she had been dying to see what was inside, even though the contents would kill her.

Danica went back into the dining room, but this time she walked past the table and over to her tiny liquor cart in the corner. She was never much of a drinker, and the cart was mostly decorative. It was from the 40s, and she had picked it up when her neighbor across the street was having an estate sale a few years ago, then stocked it with a cluster of bottles. A Deep Eddy, a Patron, a Captain Morgan, and her father's favorite, Artemis Tull.

She got a glass, poured herself a finger of whiskey,

drained the liquid in a furious swallow, ambled back into the living room for a final look out the window, then over to the cart again for a second finger and swig, before finally falling back into her chair at the dining room table, staring again at the folder, knowing she was out of excuses.

Danica drew another deep breath, then exhaled and picked up the folder.

Her heart was beating uncomfortably fast, so much harder than she wanted it to. She wasn't in any danger, but her brain kept insisting otherwise. Her fight or flight was feeling schizophrenic. She wanted to flee the house, pound the pavement until she collapsed. But she also wanted to sit right here and confront all those demons awaiting her stare.

Danica dropped the folder back onto the table, but this time she reached down and opened it. As expected, her father's autopsy report was on top. Another inhale and exhale, then she picked it up and flipped it over to the picture on the back.

Despite her anticipation and lack of surprise, the sight was still a bolt of lightning to her throat. She looked down at the photo, wanting to see Linus Cole dead for what he had done.

Her father's body was mutilated and burned, his body charred beyond recognition. Danica would never know it was a photo of her father without the label: *Miles Tate* adjacent to the date of his murder. The word *GUILTY*, written in what looked like crusted blood on his forehead.

Danica might have been able to handle it if not for the whiskey. But after a few seconds of staring down at the photo she lost it, shoving herself back from the table and sprinting into the kitchen.

She gripped either side of the sink and painted the porcelain with her puke.

The acrid aroma hit her hard and triggered a second round, this one closer to retching.

She finally stopped, but despite the reek Danica couldn't leave the kitchen.

The edges of her vision were swimming again. Rippling with a vision she didn't understand, and making her feel like the universe was burning. Her world curled up at its edges, teasing Danica with the horrors lying in wait to haunt her behind the folds.

She ignored them, breathing just like she'd encourage one of her patients to do, still gripping the sink, but now slowly inhaling and exhaling her way back to normal.

Once she could finally stand straight, Danica rinsed the sink and went to her bedroom.

Still following her own doctor's orders, she was determined to change her state.

So she changed into her running gear, then went outside and ran without thinking.

Whenever an unwelcome image returned, she ran faster. Her runner's high was almost immediate, but it wasn't a pleasant intoxication so much as an emptying of her mind to settle the exhaustion in her body.

She made it home an hour later, bone tired, the intensity of her exercise enough to dull the hallucinations creeping in at the edges of her vision.

But they didn't do anything to dull the image of her father's corpse fresh in her mind.

Uncle Quent had been right, it was a mistake to look at the file.

Danica should have let him protect her.

She kicked the front door closed, locked it, walked to the table, picked up the folder, then marched over to her small secretary desk and buried the file inside it.

She wouldn't look again. The folder would stay in its

drawer until she could find a way to sneak it back in with the other evidence at Quentin's house.

She never should have taken the file.

She needed a shower, to wash all of her sweat and hopefully some of her most recent memories away.

She went to the bathroom, got undressed, and turned on the water, waiting for it to get hot. She heard her phone ringing in the bedroom. She cut the water with a curse, listened for a second ring, then went back into the bedroom, naked and self-conscious, even though she was alone.

The phone was on its fourth and final ring by the time it was in her hand. Danika looked down at the screen: *Uncle Quent.*

Her heart skipped a beat; maybe he noticed the missing file and was calling her out on it.

"Hey," she answered in a monotone.

"Hey …" Then after an uncomfortable pause, "I need another favor."

"Anything," Danica said, glad that she wasn't in trouble.

"I need to have another conversation with Cole, but he—"

"Wants to talk to me."

A sigh, then, "Right."

"When?"

"Now. If that's okay."

"I'm hopping in the shower. I'll be ready when you get here."

"Thanks." He sounded defeated despite her assent. "See you then."

Danica dropped her phone on the nightstand and returned the bathroom.

She turned on the water as hot as it would go and

stepped underneath the artificial rainfall, hoping to burn some of the anxiety out of her body.

She was grateful that Uncle Quent had called her, even though he clearly didn't want to. It was time for her to stop wallowing in her trauma, and do her part to help catch the copycat. Building a profile wasn't enough. He needed her, and she was clearly failing him.

Danica had spent most of her life wishing she could have done something to stop Cole from killing her dad, and sending her mom into the mouth of madness as a result. Yet without a time machine, that was only an empty dream.

But she could save someone else's mother or father. And avenge what happened to her parents. Help Uncle Quent with the burden he had so obviously been shouldering alone for the last twenty years. Trying to keep her strong, regardless of how much doing so might've weakened him.

This time would be different. She would stick to questions about the copycat, and refuse to let Cole distract her, or drive a wedge between them.

The water scalded Danica as she drove all that death from her mind.

Chapter Twelve

DANICA

"You okay?" Quentin asked as Danica got in the car.

"I'm fine. Why?"

"You know why." He pulled into the street.

She was afraid he knew she'd taken the autopsy report.

Instead, he said, "You look sick."

"It's been a rough day."

He turned on the radio, an old Alice in Chains song, "Angry Chair," playing.

Danica turned it off.

"Not in the mood for some nineties grunge?"

"Not even a little," Danica said.

"How about some Beck, or Britpop?"

"No, thank you."

"What if we get out of the nineties?" Quentin laughed, probably hoping to lighten the mood. "Maybe some Regina Spektor. You still like her, right?"

"She's fine." Two seconds then, "I just want to think, if you don't mind."

"You don't have to do this."

"You wouldn't have asked me to come if it wasn't important."

Silence, then, "I'm only trying to help."

"I know." Danica left the *thank you* in her head.

No more words until they were on the bridge, at which point she asked Uncle Quent if he thought the protestors would still be there.

"I think that's where they're making camp until the execution is over. These killings are just giving them fuel, more certainty that they're right."

"Great," she said.

Danica felt bad for acting like a moody teenager. Quentin was only trying to help, but an overwhelming anxiety was making her feel like a marionette on a too-taut string. She could barely control her emotions, and needed a quiet drive to center herself and prepare for what she didn't want to do.

Quentin would hate her plan, and would surely try to stop her. But Danica couldn't allow that.

They drove past the protestors and journalists, made their way through the multiple layers of security, then were led down the same long hallway, stopping in front of the room where her bespoke nightmare was waiting.

"Wait," Danica said to the guard before he opened the door. Then she turned to Quentin. "You can't go in there with me."

"Like hell I can't."

"You said that Cole wanted to have a conversation with *me*. No offense, but that means you're in the way."

"I'm *in the way*?" Now he seemed genuinely offended.

"You think I *want* to go in there alone? I'd rather have a one-on-one with Satan himself. You need leads, and I'm in a better position to get them than you are right now. Neither of us wants to play by his rules, but we both want to win the game, and this is our best chance of doing that."

Quentin looked like he was chewing his way through several arguments at once. Danika turned to the guard before he could get even one of them out.

"Is there another room where Deputy Chief Porter can watch what's happening in there?"

"Of course," said the guard, to no one's surprise.

Danica turned back to Quentin. "There you go."

He shook his head. "That's not good enough."

"Why not?"

"Because you can't trust him."

"Of course I can't trust him! But I don't have to trust him to know that my going in there alone is more likely to lower his guard. Isn't that what we want?" Then, before he could answer her, "You two have history."

"So do you."

"It's not the same. You put Cole behind bars."

"He's a manipulator."

"And I'm a behavioral therapist. That makes me more qualified to handle this situation than you."

"Is that your version of pulling rank?" Quentin asked. "And bullshit. I'm a—"

"I'm not pulling rank, I'm drawing a line, much as I hate to do it. In my professional opinion, I need to go in there alone. And right now I'm here as a professional."

Quentin used an irritated second to stare at her, then stepped away from the door and waited for the guard to open it. She nodded at them both and entered the room.

Cole was already sitting on his side of the table and staring.

She met his gaze as the door closed behind her. Then she took a seat and held his stare.

"Welcome back." The Magistrate smiled.

"Who are you working with?"

He tucked a long strand of dark hair behind his ear with a widening smile. "Getting right to it, then."

Danica didn't respond.

"If we claim to be free from sin, we lead ourselves astray and the truth has no place in our hearts."

"I'm sorry?" Danica said, already unseated.

"Oh, no need to apologize." Cole smiled again.

Danica repeated her question. "Who are you working with?"

"Right now I'm working with Levar in the laundry." He looked down at his prison garb. "You can't see the *before*, so you have no idea how good the two of us are at getting all the stains out."

"That's not what I mean."

"I'd rather work in the kitchen. Believe it or not I'm a helluva chef, but they won't let me anywhere near the place." In a lower voice, as if telling her a secret. "It's probably because of all the knives. There are some decent opportunities around here. Just not for me. I hear some of the prisoners get to make everything from canoes to knick-knacks, but us death row inmates are restricted to the housing unit."

"Who are you working with *outside the prison*?" Danica clarified.

"Right now?"

Danica nodded.

"You." He laughed.

She pushed her chair away from the table and stood, hoping that he wouldn't call her bluff.

"Sit down." His voice was calm and commanding, like an invisible hand pushing down on her shoulder. She found her ass back in the seat. A small defeat, one she could maybe turn into a win with her next question.

"Fine then, *last time:* Who are you working with?"

"You're talking about what you're calling the copycat, right?"

Danica didn't answer.

"How do you think I'm working with anyone out there, while I'm stuck in here … about to be executed?"

"Was he there the night you killed my father?"

Cole looked thoughtful. "Two problems with your simple sentence. I feel a complication coming on." Then, into her silence he added, "Stand therefore, having your loins girt about with truth, and having the breastplate of righteousness."

"Congratulations. You can read. Was the copycat there the night you killed my father or not?"

"You should know, seeing as you were there … so, why don't you tell me?"

His words surprised her, but the arctic chill through her body surprised her even more.

"I asked you a question." It was all Danica had, and it left her throat sounding weak.

"You did." He nodded. "But then I asked you a better one."

They sat in silence until Cole unsettled her again. "Tell me what you remember. About that night."

Danica thought, swallowed, then started her story. "You broke into our house and surprised my father. You knocked him out, then—"

"You don't remember any of that."

"Like hell I don't."

"Exactly. What do you *remember*?"

"So you can just tell me that I don't? What's the point of that?"

"Thou shalt not bear false testimony against thy neighbor. You stop doing that, and maybe we can get started on something else."

"You can't tell me what I do or don't remember."

"You're half right. I can't tell you what you remember, but I can absolutely tell you some of the things that you cannot possibly recall. Like my breaking into your house."

"You were there."

"I was, huh? So you saw me break in?"

"I remember you there."

"Just like you remember me knocking your daddy out?" He leaned forward and narrowed his eyes. "Or did you see him on the floor and make an ass out of you and me after letting his best friend *tell you* what you saw?"

She pictured Uncle Quent observing in the other room, chewing through his bottom lip.

"I know what I remember." But a bitter wind was kissing her skin through a chink in her armor.

"*Think harder*," Cole commanded. "Where was I standing? What was behind me?"

Danica stared at him, thinking, unwilling to let the monster outmaneuver her.

He shook his head with what looked like pity. "Nothing hurts worse than being disappointed by the one person in the world who swore they would never hurt you."

"What's that supposed to mean?"

"That sometimes the person you'd take a bullet for is the one holding the gun."

"I'm leaving," Danica said, starting to stand.

"You don't even believe that."

"Stop telling me what I think and believe and remember!"

Still calm: "Then stop lying to yourself."

"You're trying to manipulate me."

"You're right. Anything to get you remembering the

right things, instead of all them specious stories you've been told. Your daddy, 'Uncle Quent,' all those——"

"Stop talking."

"——miserable lies."

Cole fell silent, but only for a moment.

"Think, little girl: *what really happened that night?*"

The ripples were back at the edge of her vision.

Hallucinations closing in, squeezing the world and making Danica feel like she might explode if she wasn't able to scream.

Her head darted back and forth, trying to capture an elusive truth, like the hallucinations and the shadows at the edge of her vision were obscuring some truth that they might give up if only she could see through them.

"What do you see?"

Danica didn't want to admit it. The images were sense-less, and surely only there because he had stuffed unwanted thoughts into her head. But here she was, looking at an image she couldn't agree with.

A younger Linus Cole, as if seen through a wall of smoke, his expression concerned and perhaps even sad. The moment came in a flicker and disappeared just as fast, leaving her alone with a present-day monster. Dressed in his prison garb, apparently scrubbed clean with Levar, staring back at Danica with his eyes gleaming in triumph.

"You're trying to alter my memories," she said, her fury boiling over. "You're using me to build your appeal case, but that will never work. I know what I remember, because I've never stopped going to therapy. Do you have any idea how often I've been asked to relive what——"

"You mean how often you've been asked to recite what you were once told, as an impressionable little girl?"

She swallowed, suddenly unable to finish her sentence.

She could barely cling to a thought. As much as she

wanted to ignore it, there was a grain of truth in what Cole was saying.

But Danica wasn't about to just sit there while the man who murdered her life waited for that grain to turn into a pearl.

"You're following in your mother's footsteps. Keep helping your corrupt—"

The door flew open and Uncle Quent barged into the room.

Cole finally broke his gaze with her and turned it on Quentin. "We were just talking about you."

Hallucinations still closing in, and now her tic was more like a tremor.

Quentin's arms were around her shoulders as he dragged her out of the room.

"Ask yourself what kind of frog Jeremiah *really* was," Cole called out.

"Shut the fuck up, you piece of shit!" Quentin bellowed.

But instead of falling silent, he finished his thought. "He never ever—"

The slamming door echoed like thunder through the hallway and surely into her permanent memory.

She stumbled along the concrete floor beside her Uncle Quent, shaken and crying, wondering about all those terrible, miserable lies.

Chapter Thirteen

DANICA

Danica kept telling herself that she wasn't a fool, but no matter how many times she nursed the thought, or whispered the words out loud to herself, she couldn't get herself to believe them.

She must have been out of her mind, thinking she could control the situation. The Magistrate was a master manipulator. A murderer and sociopath who had destroyed her sense of self, and done it in real time. Uncle Quent had been right to warn her away from him.

Or had he?

Because that was the other thing she kept telling herself.

There was something off about all of this, but she couldn't put her finger on it, or mention it out loud. Quentin would only dismiss her, same as every time she raised even the simplest questions about the Magistrate Murders. He had an answer for everything, but rarely the ones she was looking for.

Danica had always seen it as him trying to protect her.

But now she couldn't help but wonder if there was something he didn't want her to know.

See, she could hear Quentin in her head, knowing exactly how he'd respond without her raising the issue and awaiting his rejection, *that's why you shouldn't have gone in there alone. Linus Cole is a human infection. He feeds off your doubt, making you question yourself.*

That's why she was back at Morning Tide, visiting her mom again, well ahead of schedule. Danica was desperate for answers she couldn't get from her uncle, hoping Mom might be able to fill in some missing gaps in her memory.

But of course she was silent and drooling. Hadn't answered a single question. Danica heard only the light wind blowing through the many trees in the courtyard behind the facility, several birds tweeting, and an uncomfortably familiar tune.

"Mom ..." she tried again, this time resting a hand on her mother's knee.

To Danica's surprise, her mother looked over and for no more than a broken moment she saw a flicker of life. Then it died a horrible death and she was again looking into her mother's hollow eyes.

Mom turned to the trees, her ears perked to the birds, leaving Danica with a cold chill, wondering if there would ever be life inside her mother again.

Even at her most distant, Mom would babble at least. But today she gave Danica nothing. That hurt, more than usual. She was always looking for proof that Emilia was still somewhere inside the woman who sat on the bench beside her each week, that her mother was more than a husk with a heartbeat. Today Danica was looking for a different kind of proof, hazy and buried in shadows, but a truth only she could provide.

Danica sighed, mentally preparing herself to depart

from yet another pointless visit. She looked around for Rebecca, but didn't see the nurse.

She leaned over, kissed her mother on the forehead, and stood to stretch, hearing a sudden tune in her head. She sat back down.

"Does the song 'Joy to the World' mean anything to you?"

No response, not that her silence was in any way a surprise.

Danica tried something else. She wasn't much of a singer, despite her often belting it out when alone in either the shower or car. But several decibels above a whisper, she sang the lyrics.

Still no response, still no surprise.

Danica sighed again. Then she did something that felt like a mistake.

"I went to visit Linus Cole." She waited a beat, but nothing came. "There's a copycat killer out there, Mom. Uncle Quent is trying to catch him. We went to see him at Coldwater … twice now."

Mom continued to stare straight ahead.

"He kept asking me what happened, because I was there, and … I don't know, I feel like there's something Uncle Quent might not be telling me. I know the Magistrate's a manipulator, but I can't help but think there's *something* to what Cole is saying. He called Uncle Quent corrupt, and a liar."

She grabbed Emilia's hand, but her mother didn't respond, still clutching her rosary tight.

"Do you have any thoughts about any of that?" Danica asked without hope.

Another moment, then she stood to leave. The time was right; their conversation was fruitless and Rebecca was now rounding the corner toward them.

Danica bent down to kiss her mother on the forehead again. But this time, her mother reached up with surprising strength and grabbed Danica by the wrist.

She yanked her arm away without thinking, an involuntary action fueled by the speed of her mother's movement and the horror show lighting her eyes.

The rosary fell to the ground, beads raining on the grass as Danica looked down at her wrist, frowning at the line of blood, then turning to see her mother's trembling hands.

She considered the copycat, and the way he'd been burning fingers to eliminate DNA.

Emilia was still looking up at her, wearing an expression that bellowed, *What did I do?*

"He's burning their fingers, Mom. The copycat, I mean."

It just seemed like something she should know.

"Ash." Emilia shook her head, lowering her gaze to the grass so Danica was no longer subject to her terrified stare. "Burning and ash."

"What does that mean?" Then again, into her baffled silence, "WHAT DOES THAT MEAN, MOM?"

"Is everything okay?" Rebecca asked, looking sure that it wasn't.

Danica closed her eyes, but the hallucination only came out clearer. Emilia was still in her wheelchair, facing her wing of Morning Tide, but twenty years younger and dressed in a man's shirt. Smashing Pumpkins, from the band's *Mellon Collie and the Infinite Sadness* tour, at the Shrine. It fell to her knees like a nightgown, failing to hide her erect nipples, poking at the cotton. Her hair was a mess — between that and her inebriated eyes, Danica could practically smell the sex all over her.

But then she blinked and her mother was the same as

before. A simple but somewhat dressy blouse, the sweater, and pajama bottoms; her daily uniform for the last several years. Her eyes were no longer frightened, but a few lines of drool still dangled from lip to corrugated chin.

"Is everything okay?" Rebecca repeated.

"Fine." She tried to smile. "We were just having a moment."

"Anything I can help with?"

Danica needed a lot more help than Rebecca could possibly offer. "I promise I'm fine."

"Should I take her inside?"

"Yes, please."

She gave her mom a final goodbye, and a *Thank you* for Rebecca.

Back in her car, she wanted to punch the steering wheel. Frustration was part of the "charm" of her visits, but this little trip to her favorite psychiatric facility still felt several depressing levels below discouraging.

Danica was dispirited, unnerved, even. More than troubled, she was disoriented, without a North Star or guide to help her find the way.

Even after fifteen minutes on the 405, nine red lights and a half dozen that managed to stay green as she flew through them, Danica still had no answers and was starting to seriously doubt her sanity.

That was a downward spiral she couldn't afford.

She pulled into her driveway with one of the more dependent of her usual thoughts: *This therapist needs a therapist.*

She parked, killed the engine, and got out of the car, thinking about the swallow of whiskey she was moments away from. Maybe that would do the work the Serecyrol obviously wasn't, and help to clear her overcrowded head.

She opened her front door and saw the envelope on the

floor, slid through the mail slot in the door. Blood red and terrifying.

It's nothing, Danica told herself as she picked it up.

She turned it around in her hand and looked at the back. Same as the front — no markings, zero indications of where it might have come from.

She should probably call someone. There might be anthrax inside.

But that was idiotic, letting irrational fear get the best of her.

And besides, Uncle Quent would be the best person to call, and a little bullfrog inside Danica kept croaking to let her know that was the last thing she should do.

She opened the envelope, pulled out the card, and forced herself to breathe as she looked down at the two-word message, stamped in what appeared to be dried blood.

STAY AWAY.

So, Danica would be talking to Uncle Quent after all.

Chapter Fourteen

QUENTIN

Quentin kept slapping the coffee table, searching for his phone, determined to find the thing before it quit ringing. He found it under a pile of evidence midway through the final chime, then answered without wasting a second to check the screen and see who it was.

"Porter," said Chief Ed Wilson in his gruff yet politically polished voice.

"Yes, sir."

"There's a press conference tomorrow. I'll need you there with Albright to calm the story. I'm getting calls from the mayor and fifteen different journalists asking why the fuck I'm not there. Can't even take a two-week vacation for my own daughter's wedding. Jesus Christ. Please, calm these assholes down. Show me that you're ready for my job."

"Yes, sir."

"Thank you, Porter. I cc'd you and Albright talking points. Get with her."

"Yes, s—"

The call went dead.

Quentin felt grateful. Lucky to be in a position where he not only had the chance to control more of the conversation, he'd been issued a specific order to do so. Things could have easily gone the other way.

He looked at the coffee table, his eyes grazing the mountain of evidence. Maybe he should neaten things up, then take a walk and start digging through the mess all over again.

He bristled when the doorbell rang, imagining Luther on his front porch demanding an interview. He scoured his recent memory in search of a promise made and promptly forgotten. Nothing there, and when the next ring came in a trio of bursts that sounded almost like a song, Quentin stood from the sofa and walked toward the door, knowing exactly who it would be.

But her obvious alarm still surprised him when he opened the door.

Danica rushed in without a word, passed him and went into the living room.

"Everything okay?" Quentin asked.

She thrust out her hand. His blood curdled when he saw what she was holding.

Quentin already knew what was inside the envelope. He had seen one just like it twenty years ago. The exact shade of crimson.

A message for Miles on the day of his murder. Cole warning him off of the case.

Quentin told her to hold on, went to his car and grabbed his evidence kit and brought it inside. He set the box on the coffee table and grabbed a pair of gloves, then slipped them on so as not to contaminate what might be evidence.

He took the envelope from Danica, pretending as he opened it that something from a long dark yesterday wasn't gutting him. He withdrew the card, looked down at the *STAY AWAY* written in blood, and tried to hide the ache of memory that felt etched in his soul and likely showed on his face.

"Who do you think it's from?" Danica asked.

A good question, and one he honestly didn't know the answer to. Cole would never have been able to get the envelope out of jail. But much more unsettling: there was no way the copycat could have known about the original warning note from reading the papers, because he and Miles were too busy chasing Cole to ever formally log it.

Quentin had initially thought it was destroyed in the fire when Miles died. Turned out it wasn't. He omitted the note from the official report once he rediscovered it, lest he look any less competent, or dilute the hero parade the precinct was about to send his way.

He and Miles had made their decision together — better to prioritize pursuing their hottest lead in lieu of heading back to the station and handing it over as evidence. They could do that later, and if the detectives were lucky, they'd be bringing the bad guy in with them.

The longer Quentin went without handing it over, the less likely his submission became. The defense could very well use the note to discredit him. As proof that he'd bungled the case, ignoring the one piece of evidence that might have proven The Magistrate's innocence.

But that was ridiculous. Defense lawyers were assholes who thought the volume of their voice enhanced the value of their argument. They knew how to sound like they were right even when they weren't, and used that power to send known criminals through the revolving door of an occasionally crippled justice system and right back onto the street.

Quentin wasn't willing to let that happen. Not with Linus Cole.

But he still couldn't tell anyone about the note. Admitting that he failed to mention it would give Cole's already aggressive defense fresh ammunition to argue that other pieces of evidence — that had nothing whatsoever to do with that long-ago message — might have been mishandled as well.

Internal Affairs would come knocking next. Prompted by Cole's lawyers, IA would put Quentin under a microscope. He was too high-profile an officer to slip through the cracks.

He stared, pretending to study the note, but in reality Quentin was considering all the ways a twenty-year-old mistake might be returning to haunt him.

He looked up from the note to Danica. "Where did it come from — I mean, how did you get it?"

"It was on the floor when I got home. Someone slipped it through the mail slot, I guess."

"Did you check the front door for signs of breaking and entering? Maybe someone picked your lock? Do you have an alarm system yet?"

"No, no, and no. It was right inside the door. Seems like they just shoved it through. I think if they'd broken in, they would've left it somewhere more dramatic, like taped to my bathroom mirror or something, to let me know they got in and I wasn't safe. Who do you think it's from?"

"It might be the copycat, but I'd rather not think that." Quentin kept his answer honest, on alert for her sensitivities since leaving Coldwater that second time. "Maybe it's one of the fucker's sycophantic fans."

Her eyes were asking him if he really thought that was any better.

He slipped the note into an evidence bag and stared at it as if it might magically offer some answers.

The note looked like another anomaly. But it was also a worm, slithering into his gut and laying a litter of doubt. He couldn't allow the terror to bleed through his facade. He had promised Miles that he'd take care of his wife and daughter if anything ever happened to him. Quentin had failed with Emilia. He couldn't fail with Danica, too.

"It's a long shot," he said as he put the bag in his box.

"What do you mean?"

"I doubt we'll get prints, but maybe the techs can find something of use."

"Did Cole ever deliver a message like this before?"

"No," Quentin lied. "This looks like another break from the original MO."

"So what's next?" Danica looked frightened.

"I'm going to start interviewing former witnesses, people of interest, family and friends of his victims." He thought his answer would soothe her.

But it didn't.

"*You're* going to do that?"

"Why wouldn't I?"

"You're the deputy chief. What about the detectives on the case?"

"They're doing interviews, too, of course. I'll touch base with them, but some of the people from back then might respond more to a friendly face."

"*You're* the friendly face?"

"I'm very fucking friendly," he teased. Then, to soothe her worry, "I want you to hide in one of our safehouses for—"

"No way." She shook her head. "I want to help."

"You need to stay safe, Danica."

"Do you have any idea how nosy my neighbors are?

They would report a suspicious stranger immediately. And they're all on high alert right now. I'm safer here than—"

"There are flaws in your logic."

"Yours too."

"Fine." Quentin sighed. "I'll arrange for a protection detail to sit in an unmarked car outside your place. You can stay there instead of a safehouse, and I promise to call if there's anything you can help me with. Deal?"

Begrudgingly: "Deal."

He had never seen Danica look more like her father. Quentin could see Miles, glaring back at him from behind his daughter's eyes.

"Walk you to your car? I'm heading to the station."

"Sure." She sounded deflated, if not defeated entirely.

"How's your mom doing?"

"She's fine. I saw her earlier today. She was drooling for most of the visit. She only reacted after I finally told her about our visits to Coldwater, because—"

"You told her that we went to visit Cole?" *What the hell was she thinking?*

"Well, yeah? What was I supposed to do?"

"Not that! Did you tell her about the copycat?"

"Of course. Why wouldn't I?"

"Jesus Christ, Danica. Why would you do that? Don't you think your mother's been disturbed enough?" Quentin wished his anger wasn't so obvious.

"Sorry. I guess you forgot to send me the rules—"

"I didn't send you 'the rules' because I expect you to have common sense."

"Fuck you, Uncle Quent."

Danica had never said anything like that before, and yet she didn't even seem sorry. She walked off without looking back, then turned the corner toward her car without a goodbye.

Shit.

He called dispatch, ordered a unit to her house, and was told they would arrive in fifteen minutes. It should take Danica twenty at least, so Quentin put her safety temporarily out of his head.

He needed his mind as empty as he could get it.

He locked up, grabbed the evidence kit, got in his Tesla, and drove to the station.

About the time the unit should have been idling across the street from Danica's two-bedroom, Quentin was pulling into the precinct lot.

He went straight to his office, hoping he wouldn't be stopped on his way.

To his surprise, he might as well have been invisible.

He closed the door, sat at his desk, and studied the leads. Stevenson was too fresh to have generated anything, so he looked through the file for Engle, comparing it to original records in search of connection.

Then Quentin knew exactly what he needed to do.

Chapter Fifteen

DANICA

"Fuck me," she said as she pulled onto her street and saw the slew of cars and news vans waiting in front of her house.

She knew what they wanted, and would rather swim in a pool of her own vomit than give it to them. She parked her pickup a half block down, working up enough nerve to get out of the Ranger and make it all the way to her front door.

No one had spotted her yet, but identification was an inevitability. It was an oversight for now, surely every one of the gossip hounds knew her make and model. Better to abandon it now than wait around and get surrounded.

Danica drew a deep breath, then opened the door and started walking double time. But not running, or doing anything to draw attention. Every step swelled her anxiety, and by the time she was passing the constellation of vultures and their vans, Danica realized that her fists were clenched along with her jaw.

She relaxed them both, donning her persona of

control, and called out to the crowd — not too loud, but measured to prove her control.

"Excuse me." She nudged past the stragglers in back and made it to her porch.

"Ms. Tate!" called one of the reporters. Danica recognized her from Coldwater. Big face and bouffant hairdo. Her voice was still both inquisitive and accusatory. Only difference between then and now was a wardrobe change.

"Excuse me," the reporter repeated, now circling around to cut Danica off before she reached her front door. "Linus Cole has said that you've been to visit him at the prison twice."

"And?" Danica couldn't help herself; what was this woman trying to say?

The woman beamed, clearly not expecting Danica to answer. "Specifically, he said that 'the lying bitch has been in to visit me twice in one day.' Would you care to comment on what lies Linus Cole might be referring to?"

"You'll have to ask him."

She pushed her way past the bouffant, but only made it two steps before she was stopped by another reporter — a kid who looked like he should have been delivering the paper instead of writing for it.

"Have you considered rethinking your testimony?"

Danica didn't want to answer, and tried to step past him. But she was paralyzed. Her throat had gone dry and her surroundings had changed. The mob was still there, but the faces and clothes on all those journalists were suddenly different. Her bungalow was gone — now she was standing in front of the courthouse, a scared little girl about to testify in a murderer's trial.

She swallowed her panic and snapped back to reality. She marched another few steps toward her porch, but the army of hacks was still blocking her door.

She turned around to address the crowd. "No comment. And I want you all to leave."

For a second Danica was naive enough to think that might work. But that was before a battery of microphones were shoved in front of her face. Too many questions at once, she couldn't even tell them apart. She searched the crowd, hoping without reason that someone might save her.

A familiar-looking man made his way toward her, wading in from the edges. No camera or microphone. He had a serious face and glasses that seemed slightly too small for his dark face. And they were carwash clean, she couldn't help but notice.

He was suddenly right next to Danica, wrapping his arm around her after aggressively shoving a pair of journalists, one of them almost down to the ground.

"I've got you." There was something reassuring in his whisper.

He bulldozed the rest of his way to her front door, a shepherd for his flock of one.

Once on the porch, he turned toward the reporters, holding them at bay with his hands raised and palms out. Danica punched in her code and slipped inside the house as he blocked her partially open door.

Only after he had eased his way in behind her and she had locked the door did Danica realize the danger of what she had done.

He raised his hands again, still palms out, and spoke in a soothing voice. "Don't worry. I'm here to help you."

She looked back at him, wide-eyed and silent.

He smiled, then articulated and alleviated her fears. "I've been accused of being a cool cat, but I'm not the copycat."

Danica felt like she could finally breathe.

The man handed her a business card. She looked down and saw his name: *Luther Gregory.*

It rang a bell, but Danica wasn't sure where she had heard the notes before.

"I've been interviewing your uncle for a documentary series—"

"For Flix, right."

Luther smiled again, and this time it displayed his relief more than helping hers along. A nice couple of seconds, in between the moment when she realized who he was and the next when she felt insulted by his presence and wanted him gone in a hurry.

"So this is how you expect to get an exclusive?" Danica asked, suddenly angry.

"No." He shook his head. "Not at all. Your uncle and I have an agreement. I've—"

"He's not really my uncle," she said, without knowing why.

Luther nodded, but didn't respond.

"What kind of agreement?"

"Deputy Chief Porter has asked me not to bother you or your mother. It's the only way he would consent to the series of interviews." Luther was looking at Danica with an expression she couldn't quite read, despite being fluent in most body languages and the airs that went with them.

More than anything, Danica felt surprised. She had known about the Flix documentary, and that they wouldn't be talking to her. But Quentin had told her that was because she didn't have anything new to say about the case. Luther might be trying to manipulate her right now, but she didn't think so. Maybe it was the mob at her door, which she could still hear milling outside, and see through her gauzy curtains. Regardless of the reason, anger bubbled inside her.

Participation was her decision, not Uncle Quent's. It might have been cathartic, looking into the camera's eye and telling the world what Linus Cole had done to her family. Who was Quentin to forbid Luther from talking to her?

She drew another breath, offering her surrogate father the same benefit of the doubt she always did, and always had. He was only trying to protect her, same as he'd always protected her mother. Danica was glad that he told the production to stay away from Emilia. It was bad enough, her being reduced to a vegetable; she didn't deserve to get trotted out or put on display in an exhibit of pity.

"Then why are you here, if you're not supposed to be talking to me?"

"I'm not here for a conversation with you." Luther glanced at the window. "My crew and I are here because I wanted to see if we could get any information from the cops assigned to your detail."

"How do you know about that?"

"I was at the station when Porter requested it. We were supposed to interview him this morning, and even got started. But then the first call came in about Engle's body and we lost him. I was hoping the officers here might want to smile for the camera, and maybe give me an inkling about how the case is going." Luther shrugged. "They must have been delayed, because I didn't see them when I got here. Only that you were in trouble. And I know what it's like to deal with journalists."

"Aren't *you* a journalist?"

"Firsthand knowledge." Luther was looking at her, but Danica didn't know what to say. He cleared his throat and looked down at the business card, still in her hand. "You need anything, don't hesitate to give me a ring."

Danica met his eyes, feeling an unnecessary level of ire,

more combative than she wanted to be. Luther did seem genuine, and like he was truly trying to help, but between the agitation and the hallucinations every wire felt live.

"So, you think you can just play nice and get me to do an interview, despite his conditions?"

Not that Danica wanted to do an interview right now. Luther might be the nicest guy in the world, but that didn't mean she wanted to answer his questions.

"Not at all." Luther shook his head.

"Have you talked to Cole?"

"Of course."

"And what has he said?"

"A lot of stuff." Now Luther looked uncomfortable.

"*Like?*"

He shook his head again. "A lot of stuff that's not going to make you feel any better right now."

"Is this your way of getting me to agree—"

"Not at all, Ms. Tate. I'm a man of my word. If you're wondering if Cole told me who the copycat is or might be, I'm sorry, but he did not. If he had, that information would already be with the police and—"

They both flinched toward the ruckus outside.

Luther turned, took two steps toward the window, then spun back around to Danica. "Looks like your detail is here, and breaking up the crowd."

Danica nodded, feeling out of body.

"I guess that's my cue to leave," Luther said.

She opened the door. "Thanks for helping me."

"Stay safe." He offered her a friendly nod, then disappeared on the other side of the door.

Danica closed it behind him and pressed her back to the wood, sliding to the floor and sitting for a while, hands in her lap, both glad he was gone and depressed by the thought of being alone.

The copycat might be after her.

He was certainly after Uncle Quent.

She swallowed hard, tasting copper and acid as bile coated her throat.

One of them needed a lead.

But the answer wouldn't be coming today.

Her brain was soup. She needed to sleep.

Some quality shuteye, and Danica would be good as new.

Her stomach was too queasy for food, so one hot bath later she was ready for bed. Just moments after her back hit the mattress she felt herself falling and falling and …

A good night's sleep. That's all she needed.

Answers would be clear in the morning.

She just …

Chapter Sixteen

DANICA

Danica's head was a basket of last year's twinkle lights.

She barely slept. Crashed right away, but her solace only lasted an hour or so before the nightmares kicked in. She fought back, but didn't stand a chance and fell into hell immediately.

A finger of whiskey turned into a couple of fists. Danica kept checking the locks every quarter hour or so, knowing it was neurotic and hating herself every time. But the officers outside weren't enough to make her feel safe, and the more she considered it, the more she realized nothing could.

So, she drank. Getting plastered wasn't the point. Her goal was to forget, but that wasn't possible, so Danica was willing to settle for sleep. An hour's worth of whiskey later she crashed, grateful in her stupor. But the nightmares rained again, furious and unrelenting. A hurricane raging both in and on her soul.

She was in her safe space. At work, helping yet another victim of trauma by reminding them what it meant to hope. But this new client was Linus Cole, back before he was the monster he would one day be. A child, spilling his guts, inviting her to his campfire for chilling tales of horrific abuse and inviting them both to an onslaught of tears.

She felt dirty, sympathizing with the animal who killed her father in cold blood. Even in the wooly thick of her unrelenting nightmare, Danica knew it was wrong. It grated against her known reality, had her screaming in a dreamscape version of her office, then waking up with a whimper still on her lips.

Now, lying in bed and soaking in sweat, Danica wondered if she had read something in the case files to trigger the emotion. Perhaps her professional instincts insisting there was an avenue in Cole's distant path worthy of further exploration, perhaps even promising answers. After all, people like Cole weren't usually born that way. Monsters were made by abuse and neglect.

She took a shower to wash the sweat off her body and the nightmare out of her mind, wishing she didn't have a day full of clients. Cancelling was the wrong thing to do, but she wouldn't be much help to anyone with a muddy mind. Therapy was mostly headspace. The clearer Danica showed up for her appointments, the better off her clients would be.

She dressed for the day and called Uncle Quent. Barely waited for him to say *hello* before getting right to business. "What do you know about Cole's foster parents?"

"Good morning to you, too."

"Good morning. *What do you know about Cole's foster parents?*"

"What are you actually asking, Danica? You saw the files and—"

"There wasn't much there." Her patience was short. "Do you have a problem with me asking what you know?"

"Of course not. I just need a moment to catch my breath … you don't sound like yourself right now."

"I barely slept." Then a confession. "And I drank too much last night."

"Been there," Quentin said, with an anemic attempt at laughter. "But I'm still not sure what you're asking, there's really not much to know."

"Then tell me what you do know, or I'll look them up in the public record and make a visit on my own."

Quentin sighed. "I'm looking into some of these old threads, anyway. Why don't I pick you up and we can go together? Just don't get your hopes up."

"I'll be waiting."

Danica hung up, surprised by her own agitation. Yesterday was one thing, with Cole plus all the reporters, then Luther and tumblers of Artemis Tull. She still shouldn't be pissed at him — maybe it was the residual gunk from her lingering nightmare.

Quentin must have left right away, because he was pulling up to her house about twenty minutes later, in a department-issued Ford Explorer instead of his Tesla. He stopped by the on-duty cops across the street, just long enough to trade a few words before leaving with a friendly wave.

He approached Danica's door, but it was open before he could knock.

"Morning."

"Morning." He nodded, handing her a coffee.

"When did you have time to get this?"

"I was already out when you called." He waited for her to close and lock the door, then turned and started walking toward his car.

Danica followed him to the SUV. "Where's Tessie?"

"I'm not sure people will be as accommodating if I pull up in that thing."

It made sense when he said it, and even more so when they pulled up to Maggie Dowling's tiny residence a half hour later. The place was probably nice in the 1920s when it was built, but it was a shit hole on the decaying side of town now.

"This is the same place Cole grew up?" Danica asked.

Quentin nodded.

"How many kids did you say lived here?"

"Too many for a house this size."

It wasn't an answer, but she knew what he meant, and felt an overwhelming rush of pity for the children living there. Now or then, it didn't matter.

An early morning prostitute worked the corner, and what was clearly a crack house, or worse, loomed three gloomy domiciles down.

"Environments like this can really fuck a kid up," Danica said on their way to the door.

"Or give them the drive they need to get the hell out of the situation and do something better with their lives. That's exactly what Cole wants: to get in your head and garner sympathy. He's trying to manipulate you, Danica."

He knocked on the door.

Then he knocked again and again, until someone finally opened it. A woman with a long gray ponytail and a dark blue matronly dress that started at her neck and went all the way to her ankles. Despite the print of tiny white flowers, it still appeared painfully plain.

The woman clearly wasn't expecting to see the local semi-celebrities standing on her porch, but she clearly knew who they were.

"Detective Porter ..." It left her in a breath as she opened the door all the way and silently invited them both inside. He didn't correct her on his job title. "And you must be Danica … you've grown up so pretty."

"Thank you." She felt slightly unsettled. The woman was pleasant, but there was something odd about a person knowing the most horrible details of her life.

"Good to see you again, Mrs. Dowling." Quentin nodded at the open door. "May I?"

Maggie nodded, then they entered and she closed the door behind them.

"Is Philip home?" Quentin asked. Maggie shook her head and he added, "Mind if we ask a few questions?"

She shook her head again, this time with an awkward smile. "Of course not … Ask, and it will be given to you; seek, and you will find; knock, and it will be opened to you."

Her smile seemed forced, but that wasn't a surprise. Quentin had given Danica the rundown on their way over. Philip Dowling was Maggie's husband and Cole's former foster father. A religious zealot, twisted in his beliefs and in no way averse to beating children.

Maggie was an echo with a heartbeat, subservient to "the head of the family." Unless things had changed in the last twenty years, Maggie didn't like when her husband laid hands on their children, but never stood up to him and thanks to her excuses and obfuscation, barred the authorities from proving abuse.

Quentin looked around the house, seeming surprised by what he saw. Danica, too. He had described a pigsty on the way over. He and Miles had been shocked that CPS allowed children anywhere near it. But now the place looked like an advertisement for Marie Kondo: Ghetto Edition.

"No children?" Quentin said.

Maggie shook her head, leading them to the dining

room table and taking a seat. Another awkward smile. "We're not as young as we used to be."

Quentin and Danica both sat, then Maggie got right to it.

"I suppose you're here about Linus again." She didn't wait for a response. "Not sure what I can tell you now that I didn't tell you then. I've not seen him since, unless you count all them shows on TV, and my memory isn't—"

"It was my idea," Danica said. "I wasn't here the first time, and I'm helping Deputy Chief Porter to build a profile on—"

"Deputy Chief Porter? Isn't he like your daddy now?"

"Not exactly." She shifted in her seat, acutely uncomfortable. "I was raised by my grandparents after what happened. But Uncle Quent has always been there for me."

"Well …" Maggie leaned back in her seat and took a breath, looking down at her idle hands like they were missing a cup of coffee. "What can I tell you?"

"Are you expecting your husband any time soon?" Danica asked.

"What's he got to do with this?" She stole a glance over her shoulder, into the kitchen.

"Just another perspective." Danica offered Maggie a reassuring smile. "I understand that he and Linus had a volatile relationship."

She scowled. "A father's job is to raise a child in the discipline and instruction of the Lord."

"I remember you saying that." Quentin nodded toward Danica. "Would you mind explaining what you mean to—"

"It means that Philip always done his best. Isn't his fault when a child refuses to listen or bites the hand."

"And Linus was that kind of child?" Danica asked.

"After a while, once he started to show himself. He was a charismatic kid, at first. That's why we took him in. But then his true colors started to show."

Danica offered her the same nod she would give a client on her couch. "And what colors were those?"

"Maybe less like colors and more like mold on good bread." Maggie wrinkled her nose. "Linus was mean. Spiteful. Didn't obey the commandments."

"Any specific commandments he was prone to ignore?" Danica asked.

"Besides 'honor thy father and mother'?"

Danica didn't comment on her lack of genuine parentage. "Did Linus get along with the other children? Did he honor his siblings more than his parents?"

Maggie shrugged. "Maybe Roxanne or Matt. Hard to remember after all these years. He mostly spent time with Tuesday and Chris, but it's hard to say that Linus ever really got along with anyone, unless he wanted something from them. That boy always knew how to turn on the charm when he needed to."

Maggie looked behind her, over the shoulder and into the kitchen for the third time in two minutes. Quentin gave Danica a barely perceptible nod.

"Can you be more specific? In what ways did he 'turn on the charm'?"

Maggie looked at Danica as if that were an idiot's question. "Linus had a silver tongue, but you could never trust a thing that kid said … The heart is deceitful above all things and beyond cure."

That struck a chord.

Danica had read those same words just yesterday, after coming home from Coldwater, following that little serenade from Cole.

"That last part … was that a Bible verse?"

"Jeremiah 17:9." For the first time, Maggie smiled, appearing pleased by Danica's general awareness of the Lord.

Same as yesterday, Danica wondered if Cole was referencing a particular verse with that song. But now she wondered harder.

Quentin pulled the photo of the engagement ring out of his pocket. He showed it to Maggie, then set it on the table. "We found this among his stuff after the arrest. Does it look familiar to you?"

He didn't have to ask. The answer was clear on her face. Maggie leaned forward, snatched the ring, and narrowed her eyes on it. "This is mine. Linus stole it from me!"

Quentin gestured toward the wedding ring on her hand. "That a replacement?"

"Sure is. You know how men are. I can't exactly walk around without letting the world know I'm spoken for."

"Is it a family ring?" Quentin asked.

"Sure is."

But Danica didn't believe her, and she could tell by Uncle Quent's expression that he felt the same.

"I want it back," Maggie said.

"I'm sorry, but it's evidence."

"It's *mine*."

"I understand that, Mrs. Dowling, but we need to hang on to it until the execution. Additionally, it might be relevant to these new killings. You can go down to the precinct and file a claim, though I'm not sure it'll help."

"What does that mean?" Maggie's disappointment bordered on anger.

"Your claim will be considered once Cole is executed."

"That's a family heirloom, and you've already kept it for twenty years!"

"I'm sorry about that." But Danica knew he wasn't.

Something fell in the kitchen.

"What was that?" Quentin asked.

"Damn cat," Maggie said.

From nowhere it felt like an ice pick was stabbing the back of Danica's skull. In her peripheral vision she saw motion in the backyard. A figure that reminded her of Cole. But when she jerked her head around to look, the figure was gone.

She blinked hard, wishing her heart wasn't pounding like it was, and that the wavering edges of her vision would go away. As much as it frightened her, she wanted another, better look. But the figure refused to return.

Another crash in the kitchen, and now Maggie looked visibly startled.

"Damn cat?" Quentin repeated.

But before Maggie got the chance to lie again, a filthy kid shuffled sheepishly into the room. Seven or eight, Danica guessed. Dirty hair and a dirtier face. His clothes seemed clean enough, but they must have been too small for him a year ago.

"Miss Mama …"

"I told you to stay in your room until our guests were gone!"

"But—"

"But nothing. Go to your room. You know how to please the Lord."

"Yes, Miss Mama." The boy turned around and disappeared back into the kitchen.

"I thought you didn't have any children here?"

She glared at him. "I never said nothing like that. You assumed."

"I would argue that you implied," Quentin said.

"You can argue all you want. Now is there anything else I can help you with, Mister Porter?"

"No." He stood. "That'll be all for now. We'll be in touch if we need anything else."

"Close the door behind you!" Maggie barked, not bothering to stand, all of her pleasantries now gone.

Danica followed Quentin outside, then into the SUV.

They were a block away before either one of them spoke.

Quentin went first. "Will that help with your profile?"

"Why didn't she tell us about that little boy?" To hell with his question. "What is she hiding?"

"You mean, besides being a shit caretaker who shouldn't have children anywhere near her?"

"We have to report her."

He shook his head. "No, we don't."

"She's obviously hiding something. Please tell me that you're not okay with that, Uncle Quent."

"Of course I'm not okay with that. But at least the house was clean, and she probably only has the one. I'll look into it, make sure she doesn't have a bunch. I doubt she does, just enough for her and Philip to supplement their income. It's probably all they can handle."

"You think *that's* handling it?"

"You know what I mean."

"I'm not sure I do," Danica said, trying not to lose her shit.

"Let's say we report her and there's an investigation. Maybe nothing happens, or maybe the kid gets shuffled off to someone else. Maybe someone worse. We're not social services or CPS." Quentin shook his head, eyes on the road. "You can't let yourself get distracted by trying to save everyone. Right now we have a job to do."

Danica didn't know how to respond. She wasn't used to

seeing Quentin's cynical side, and wondered if it was new, or something she'd not noticed before. He'd always been Mr. Justice in her eyes, but maybe she had only been seeing what she wanted to. Or perhaps two decades had eroded the idealism he once shared with her father.

More silence, until he broke it. "Are you coming with me to question the other foster kids?"

"I have clients into the afternoon."

"That's too bad." But it didn't sound like he meant that.

Danica turned on the radio and got Cobain singing about being doused in mud and soaked in bleach. She thought about her day's first client, Li, an eight-year-girl who had been severely abused by her stepfather. Probably the reason for her dream about a pre-adolescent Cole. Danica's desire to help Li mixing with her reemerging feelings about the murders that turned her life inside out.

Her head was still a basket of twinkle lights, more tangled than ever.

At least she was making a difference with Cecilia. It was awfully soon to be seeing her again, but they agreed it was a good idea to capitalize on the momentum of their last session.

It wasn't just therapy for her clients.

A good session would put Danica's head back in the right place.

"Everything Zen" came on the radio and Quentin changed the station. "They sucked in the nineties. Twenty years haven't helped them."

No need to answer, so Danica didn't. Instead she kept thinking about Cecilia, and hoping that the day wouldn't destroy her.

Chapter Seventeen

QUENTIN

Quentin gave Danica a two-fingered wave, then pulled away from the curb.

He was grateful for her full morning, but didn't want her to know it. The interviews with Cole's former foster siblings would be much easier without her around. She asked terrific questions, and under normal circumstances he wouldn't feel like she was in the way. But right now her presence made him nervous. It felt like having Luther Gregory riding shotgun.

Quentin killed the radio. He wanted to run through a mental inventory of the subjects he needed to question, but was having a hard time with Smash Mouth reassuring him of his all-star status.

He wouldn't be interviewing Roxanne Shaw, who died of an overdose about ten years ago. Chris Stone would also be escaping his interrogation, having left this life for the next one during a prison stint for grand theft five years back. Not an excellent track record for graduates of the Maggie and Philip Dowling Home for Wayward Youth.

The third person on his list, but the first that could stand for an interview, was a furniture maker named Tuesday Howe. She probably didn't know much, but she might still be worth questioning to gain a bit more insight into who the Magistrate Murderer used to be. He also had Matt Varney, a shop teacher at Pike High School; Jim Mendelson, a whacked-out stoner barely scraping by as a convenience store clerk; and Lizzie Wondrush, the interview subject Quentin remembered most of all.

He had interviewed all the siblings back when he was building his original case against Cole, but Lizzie stood out in his mind. She was the eldest of them, and had not only managed to stay out of trouble, even back then it seemed like she'd never get anywhere near it. The other kids all had rotten things to say about their foster parents, but Lizzie had been deeply appreciative of Maggie showing her to Jesus.

That relationship with the Son of God helped her to find and marry a respectable man. Compared to the other kids, Lizzie seemed to have emerged from an alternate timeline, one where the Dowlings were good people.

Quentin remembered thinking she had a crush on Cole back when they lived at the Dowlings' together, same as he remembered her apparent distaste for Tuesday Howe. But Lizzie never uttered a direct word about either thing. Her Jesus-loving ways had her speaking of others elliptically.

Quentin pulled into his usual parking spot, then ducked into the precinct hoping to reach his office without being seen. Mission accomplished, Quentin asked Captain Joe Jenkins for contact info on everyone he planned to question before pouring himself a subpar cup of coffee while wondering why he hadn't stopped at Hill of Beans after dropping Danica off.

A few minutes later he was looking at the list. Jenkins

had overdelivered, presenting contact info for all five persons of interest. Quentin was looking down at a page full of everything he'd requested, plus an additional paragraph of info for each name.

No surprise, Wondrush and her insurance adjuster husband had made the family Lizzie had always wanted and grown up longing for. Two kids of their own, plus a trio of adoptions. Good for Lizzie, creating the kind of home life she never had. She seemed like the least likely one of Cole's former foster siblings to provide Quentin with any freshly relevant info, while also currently living the farthest away, having moved south from Las Orillas to the outskirts of Cielo Del Mar, about an hour away.

By contrast, Jim Mendelson managed a convenience store not too far from where Quentin had spent his morning with Danica, interviewing a reluctant Maggie Dowling.

He folded the paper, slipped it into his pocket, and returned to the Explorer, subpar coffee in hand. Three 90s songs later, ending with Alanis Morissette telling him, incorrectly, how ironic things were, he pulled up to the curb in front of the ironically named *Fresh Groceries*.

Walking into the place confirmed Quentin's suspicions. There weren't any groceries, or a single element that made it in any way fresh.

"May I help you?" The clerk eyed Quentin like an enemy. Prison tats said that he probably was.

"Jim Mendelson work here?"

"You a cop?"

Quentin nodded. "Sure am."

He tipped his chin toward a closed door in back. "He's in the back."

The clerk glanced down at a display case full of

fossilized donuts. "You want I should bag one for you while you're in there?"

Quentin walked to the rear without answering, then opened the door without knocking. The first thing he noticed was the sound of tinny thrash metal coming from a crappy stereo in the back room.

Jim was hunched over an open plastic tote, pricing cans and putting them into another tote. He looked up from his stool. A couple of pregnant seconds, then recognition lit his eyes. He set his pricing gun into one of the totes. "What do *you* want?"

Life had ridden Jim like a rented mule since the last time Quentin had seen him. Greasy hair fell in disheveled clumps past his eyes and ears. He had a patchy beard that looked like it had been applied with spirit gum. Sallow skin and dark circles haunted his eyes. His nose had definitely been broken, probably more than once. He wore a ragged-looking hoodie over an even rattier polo shirt with a faded logo: a bag of groceries, packed with produce, above the words *Fresh Groceries*.

"I'm here to ask you a couple of questions about Linus Cole."

"Of course you are," Jim said.

"Have you been in contact with him recently?"

"Does it *look like* I've been in contact with him?" Jim waved his arms around the room. "Seems like you could have just checked the visitor registry at the prison and saved yourself a trip."

"You've never written him a letter, or—"

"Do I *look like* the kind of guy who keeps a pen pal?"

"You might." Quentin closed the door and took several steps toward Jim, stopping about three feet away from his stool.

"I've got work to do. So unless you want to help me price cans of Alpo, I'd appreciate it if—"

"I'm not here to bother you, Jim. I just need—"

"Then don't." He stood, retrieved the plastic tote from the floor, and started toward the door, easing his way by Quentin without another word.

He followed Jim back into the store and watched him set the tote on the floor in front of a shelf with a loud thump. Then he knelt down and started stocking cans of dog food into an empty spot.

Quentin thought through his approach as Jim ignored him and Prison Tats kept eyeing him from up front.

"A few minutes of your time and I'll be out of here," he tried again.

"I know my rights." Jim stood up with the tote in his hands, turned and dropped it to the floor further down the aisle, then started to stock boxes of cookies. "I don't have to answer shit."

"You're right. You don't."

"I could call my lawyer."

"You absolutely could. But I don't know why you'd want to. Like I said, I'm not here to bother you or bust your balls in any way. I have a couple of questions you might be able to help me with. I'm assuming you've seen the news?"

Jim perked up. Whether he meant for Quentin to see it or not, the man had interest in his eyes.

Quentin kept going, or tried to. "There's a—"

"Hey, Jim!"

Quentin looked over to see a man dressed entirely in denim making his way toward them.

"You got any Kit Kats today?"

Jim flinched, then awkwardly pointed to the candy display at the front of the store, in front of the register.

The customer appeared crestfallen. His eyes fell on Quentin and he realized — Jim hadn't suddenly forgotten the street name for ketamine so much as the man in a tie standing a foot away from him had given the guy an unexpected case of amnesia.

Prison Tats was still watching, and now Quentin had to wonder if he was hoping that Jim would get into some trouble.

Undaunted, and clearly an idiot, the customer tried again. He looked from the candy display back to Jim. "You got any *fresher* ones in back?"

"No, asshole." It looked like Jim was chewing through his bottom lip. "I don't. Why don't you just go ahead and buy one of those."

The customer turned around and begrudgingly trudged toward the register, grabbed a Kit Kat, and waited for Prison Tats to finish ringing him up.

Quentin surprised him with a genuine roll of laughter. "Look, man. I'm not here to hassle you about your side hustle … I have much more important things to do."

"Like what?" Jim looked back at him, suspicious but clearly wanting to believe.

"Like making sure that Cole's accomplice — the copycat killer — gets caught. Ideally before anyone else is murdered."

"Fuck that guy," Jim said.

"Exactly. Fuck that guy. So is there anything you can—"

"They can't execute that asshole fast enough."

"What makes you say that?"

"I grew up hating Linus Cole, and ain't nothing in the last twenty years ever made me reevaluate my feelings. Once a fucker, always a fucker." He stole a glance at the candy rack. "I may have problems, but I ain't never killed no one."

"What is it that makes you hate him so much?"

"You don't remember any of what I told you the last time?"

"Refresh my memory. Pretend you've never told me anything. Why don't we start with some of the worst of it."

"I wasn't even ten years old yet when Linus locked me in an old trunk. Some footlocker he got from our neighbor's lawn on garbage day before the truck came and got it. He told me there was a *Playboy* in there if I wanted it, then soon as I got close enough, Linus shoved me inside and locked it up, then kicked that trunk down the basement stairs."

"How long were you locked inside?"

Jim's sallow skin seemed almost jaundiced, and the haunted circles more tormented. "It was a full day before Maggie noticed I was missing and Cole finally had to let me out."

"That must have been terrible," Quentin said.

"Well, it wasn't a trip to Six Flags."

"Did you ever try to get him back for what he did?"

"Hell, no. Linus was only a couple of years older than me, but that dickhead was already twice my size and five times as mean."

"Did the two of you have a lot of altercations?"

"We would have, if I hadn't spent half my time either hiding or trying to get away from him."

"When's the last time you saw him?"

"Ninth grade," Jim said, his answer loaded in the chamber and ready to go. "Linus set my hair on fire when Maggie wasn't looking."

"What did she do when—"

"Nothing. Maggie never did anything. Sometimes that

fucker Philip would give one of us a wallop, but that was rarely ever because we'd done something wrong so much as him needing something to hit after drinking so hard."

"Even when it was something as severe as setting you hair on fire … even then Maggie still wouldn't do anything?"

"Maybe she would have, I don't know. I was out of there after that. I lived on the streets until I landed a job. I doubt they even reported my leaving, since that would've meant them losing out on my part of their check."

"I'm sorry that living there was so rough on you."

He scoffed. "Like you give a shit."

"Believe it or not, I do. I'm sure you've followed the Magistrate Murders at least a little."

"I seen a couple a shows."

"So you know I lost people close to me. Like I said, Jim, I'm trying to figure out what Cole is up to now, and looking for help wherever I can get it."

He nodded, giving Quentin a silent cue to continue.

"Was he a bully to all the foster kids, or did Linus mostly pick on you?"

"He was smart enough to stick with the easier targets. Unfortunately, I was one of 'em."

"Was there anyone who helped him out? A sort of co-conspirator?"

"Not really." Jim shrugged. "Matt Varney was good at staying out of his way, but I wouldn't say the two of them were friends or anything. He was bigger than Linus, and you know bullies like to punch down."

"So what, Varney would watch?"

Another shrug. "Matt wasn't around much. He was a year or two older than Linus and always pretended to be working on projects for school. But really, he was spending all of his time at the park."

"And what did he do at the park?"

"I wasn't there. How should I know?" Yet another shrug. "He played basketball a lot, and sometimes he stayed with friends, at their houses. Matt was only around Casa de Dowling when he had to be."

Quentin's phone buzzed. He looked at the screen, saw it was Luther, then ignored the call and dropped the phone back into his pocket. "What about the girls? Lizzie and Tuesday."

For the first time since opening the stock room door, Quentin saw Jim with a smile. The expression seemed to surprise them both.

"Man, Lizzie was always so nice to me, better than anyone else in that place. And she had the best smile. I haven't thought of Lizzie in years."

"What was her relationship with Cole?"

He scoffed. "I don't think Cole gave two shits about Lizzie one way or the other. That's how he was, you either had his undivided, or you didn't exist. But still, Lizzie was always sort of obsessed with him. If anyone from those days knows shit about that asshole, it'd be her. And seeing that she breaks bread with the Messiah on a regular basis, I wouldn't be surprised to see her waving one of them signs saying that killing the killer is wrong."

"What about Tuesday?"

"Angry fucking bitch, pardon my expletives."

"Angry at who?" Quentin asked.

"Angry at everyone. But especially Cole."

"Any idea why?"

Jim shook his head. "No idea."

"You think she might still be in contact with Cole?"

"Yeah. I'm sure they write each other regularly."

"I'm guessing that's sarcasm."

"I'm guessing you're right."

"Make sure you don't go anywhere," Quentin said after a lull. "I might have more questions."

"Where the fuck you think I'm gonna go?"

Quentin grabbed a Kit Kat from the display, dropped two bucks on the counter, then nodded at Prison Tats before leaving the store.

Chapter Eighteen

DANICA

THE DAY WAS FAILING Danica's expectations in every way.

The meeting with Maggie had been unsettling enough. She was already slightly unseated for her appointment with Li, the eight-year-old whose trauma would be staying with Danica for the rest of her day. The two encounters had worn her down to a nub, and now she was meeting with Cecilia again. Unfortunately, she seemed to have regressed since her last visit, despite their leaving that session on such a positive note.

Danica tried again. "Can you help me to understand what's changed since our last meeting?"

Yet another shrug from Cecilia, her fifth so far. She was closed off, unwilling to talk, and actively ignoring their previous breakthrough.

"You were going to start journaling. Did you write about what happened?" Danica refused to break her stare. It took most of a minute before Cecilia finally shook her head. "Can I ask why not?"

Still no response.

"If you were writing about this moment right now, what would you say?"

"You said I didn't have to share what I wrote. That the exercise was to get my feelings on the page. So we could 'get more out of our time together.'"

"You sound resentful about our time together. Do you feel that the therapy isn't helping you?"

"It's fine."

"It should be more than fine, Cecilia. You said that you were 'finally ready to hear me' the last time we spoke. So, please, can you tell me what's happened in between then and now?"

"You keep asking me that."

Danica smiled, but it was hard not to sigh. "I promise to stop as soon as you answer."

She felt overheated, like she was dying of thirst no matter how much she sipped from her Hydro Flask. Images kept flickering at the edges of her vision and Danica kept wanting to turn and inspect them. But it would be a bad idea, inviting that much insanity into the room.

"I talked to my mom last night." Cecilia sounded defeated.

"And that's bad news?"

"She wants me to come home."

"You mean to come home and live with her."

Cecilia shook her head. "Not just that. She wants me to forgive Rodney."

"Forgive him for putting you in the hospital?"

"She wants me to help with an appeal to get him out early."

"So your own mother doesn't think you should stay away from the man who broke your ribs and punctured a lung? *The man who nearly killed you and forced you to move a thousand miles away?"*

Maybe she had said too much, but Danica couldn't help it.

Cecilia didn't answer, but now she was starting to cry.

"That guilt you've been feeling about leaving Rodney, and testifying against him … how much of that would you say comes from your mother?"

"She just wants me to make things right."

"You made things as right as they can be by standing up for yourself and testifying against the man who hurt you. Helping him now would be undoing that."

"Mom says that Father Murphy can talk to Rodney."

Danica couldn't believe the bullshit coming out of Cecilia's mouth, and needed her to get the hell out of the office so she could slam her fist into something. Calmly, she asked, "Wasn't Father Murphy going to talk to Rodney already? And didn't Rodney refuse? Am I remembering incorrectly, or isn't that what set him off on the night he nearly beat you to death?"

But still no answer from Cecilia.

"We can't get anywhere unless you start talking to me."

"My family never wanted me to press charges."

"Against the man who almost killed their daughter …"

"He didn't almost kill me."

"You were bleeding internally when you were admitted, Cecilia."

"I just want all of this to go away." She started crying harder.

"Of course you do. That's perfectly natural. But you have to hold him accountable. If you help him get out, then you are telling him in no uncertain terms that his behavior is okay, and mark my words: *he will do it again.*"

"You don't know that."

"You're right, I can't know that for sure. But in my personal and professional opinion, the odds of Rodney treating you right after behaving so terribly wrong are almost nonexistent."

Cecilia wiped both of her eyes. "My parents are ashamed about the whole thing."

Yeah, it's super embarrassing when the person who beats the shit out of their daughter has to answer for himself.

"So their solution is for you to forgive and forget?" Danica knew she sounded accusatory, and might very well be pushing her patient away, but a boiling anger was getting the best of her.

"Not exactly."

"Then what, Cecilia? It sure sounds like they're asking you to turn the other cheek."

"It isn't Christian to turn my back on him like I am. They want me to bring my husband back to God."

"It isn't Christian to beat your wife."

"Two wrongs don't make a right." The argument left Cecilia's lips with the consideration of a burp.

"What you're doing isn't wrong. Don't you remember any of the things you said the last time you were here?" Danica shook her head, growing ever more furious while peering down at her notes. "*I'm still waking up drenched in sweat.* Or how about, *I could still end up dead before my fortieth birthday.* Are either of those ringing a bell?"

"It's none of your business either way." Now Cecilia sounded angry.

"I'm sorry, but I can't agree with that statement. It is absolutely my business — that's the nature of our relationship. As long as you're seeing me—"

"Then maybe I shouldn't be seeing you. Maybe this is a mistake."

"I'm not sure that—"

"It's not like you ever have any answers for me. All you ever do is ask questions. Hell, anyone can *listen*. I can get that from the bartender."

Danica drew a deep and blindsided breath. "I understand that this is hard, but everyone's path to healing is different."

"Is that what you tell yourself?"

"Excuse me?" Then, when Cecilia kept staring at her without a response, "What do you mean?"

"I've seen how your head keeps jerking around, like you're seeing shit that isn't even there. How are you supposed to help me, if you're not normal?"

Hot tears stung her eyes, and hallucinations still assaulted her peripheral vision. But Danica couldn't help it — now she was feeling defensive.

"I have years of training helping people like you come to grips with their trauma. The first step is *always* facing your demons. Whatever they are."

"*People like you?* What's that supposed to mean?"

"It means that—"

"You know what? Never mind." Cecilia stood, yanked a handful of Kleenex from the box, grabbed her purse and aggressively turned toward the door. "Thank you for your help, but I'll no longer be needing it."

"Cecilia, please ... wait!"

The door slammed and Danica slid down into her chair, alone and full of regret.

Cecilia was right. How was she any different from her patients? She was only a behavioral therapist thanks to all her personal trauma. But what had that career actually ever done for her? She had failed to heal her mother, despite being driven to do so and always believing that she ultimately could.

Despite it being twenty years, Danica still hadn't managed to heal herself.

The hallucinations were worse than ever. She had an uninvited visitor living inside her skin. Danica had been telling herself she was fine for a while now, but she obviously wasn't. She started falling to pieces just moments after coming face-to-face with Cole for the first time.

Danica's encounter with the murderer had triggered this latest downward spiral.

Danica knew how to end it, but doing what had to be done somehow felt like a fate worse than death.

But that's what she would have to do.

Maybe after a finger of whiskey.

Chapter Nineteen

QUENTIN

DESPITE NOT GETTING ANYWHERE with Jim, Quentin was confident that his drive down to Cielo Del Mar would yield a decent lead. There was mercifully little traffic, and after only a dozen or so songs on the Lithium station, including "No Rain," which he hadn't heard in forever, Quent was making a left onto a narrow winding road heading away from the coast.

Ten minutes later he arrived at his destination to find the last thing he expected to see in this area. Despite the tidy units, Bayshore Breeze still looked an awful lot like a trailer park. Quentin didn't see a single home that looked large enough to comfortably accommodate a family of seven. But Lizzie's childhood had probably given her a waste not, want not way of seeing the world.

Quentin got out of the Explorer and approached the appropriate townhouse. The paint appeared relatively new and the lawn small but trim. He rang the doorbell, got no answer, then knocked three times for the same result.

He went next door. Rang the bell and the door opened immediately.

"Hi there, I'm—"

"I know who you are." The woman smiled at him, looking almost embarrassed. Her red hair was dyed. The high contrast with all of those deep wrinkles would have given her away if the gray roots didn't get there first. "Lizzie's not home."

"Any idea where she might be?"

"Of course," said the woman, seeming proud of herself. "She's at the rummage sale, down at the Episcopal. You know where that is?"

"I'm sorry, I don't."

"It's down on Corona." As if that were direction enough.

"Do you happen to know the address?"

"It's the Episcopal down on Corona."

"Great. Thanks for your time." He turned to go.

"Hey, Mr. Potter."

"Deputy Chief Porter," Quentin corrected her.

"Did Linus Cole *really* kill all those people?" She half-whispered her question.

"Of course he did."

"Because Lizzie gave me his book, *An Innocent Man*. He says—"

"I'm well aware of what he's said." Quentin's smile was thinner than a page from that book. "I'd probably say the same thing, if I was on death row. Not that I ever would be."

Another nod, then he turned around and started walking back toward the Explorer.

"He makes a compelling argument!"

Quentin clearly heard the woman declaring her doubt behind him, but he didn't turn to acknowledge her. He was bothered but hopeful. It wasn't criminal to think that a culprit like Cole could be innocent, but if Lizzie was still discussing the case with her neighbor all these years later, and believed in his clean hands, as ridiculous as the assertion might be, then maybe she had some idea about who might be helping him.

His GPS said the church was eight minutes away, but Quentin made the trip in six. He heard the chorus of what sounded like a hundred children all yelling at once as he opened the Explorer door and surveyed the scene.

A dozen rows of tables piled high with second-hand garbage, parents chatting in clusters, shoppers with arms piled high, most looking like they probably took a bus there, in stark contrast to the other well-coiffed and perfectly tailored women milling about. A cluster of dads were grilling hot dogs off to the side, near a huddle of condiment-ready wives.

"Pardon me," Quentin said to the nearest adult, "would you happen to know where I might find Elizabeth Wondrush?"

"Lizzie? Sure thing." She pointed toward a table that was piled high with assorted baked goods. "She's right over there, talking to Margot."

"Thank you, ma'am," Quentin said, then made his way to the woman he'd come to see after so many years. "Excuse me, Lizzie—"

"Detective Porter," she said, turning from Margot and stopping her conversation immediately.

"Deputy Chief." The correction felt unnecessary, both before and after he made it. He smiled at them both, looked at Margot in apology, then fixed his gaze on Lizzie. "Do you mind if we speak for a few minutes in private?"

"Of course." Lizzie doffed her apron, though he didn't see the need, or why she was even wearing it in the first place if she wasn't cooking anything and the offerings were sealed. They walked toward an empty patch of grass. Once out of earshot, she said, "Is this about his appeal?"

"What makes you think that?" Quentin asked.

"There are more killings and Linus is in prison, *about to be executed.* Isn't that finally proof enough that he wasn't the murderer you and the media have always made him out to be?"

Great. A hostile witness.

Or maybe just earnest. It had been too long since she'd blinked.

"We have a copycat," Quentin said.

"How do you know that?"

He shouldn't have to explain himself, but he needed answers that Lizzie might have. "Without getting into specifics, there are differences between the last two murders and those in the original spree."

Lizzie looked back at Quentin, incredulous. "I've seen his heart, you know."

"You'll have to pardon me for saying so, but that isn't much of a defense."

"I can see *your heart* too."

That bothered him more than he wanted it to. "And what does it say?"

"People don't like to be wrong. That's nothing to be embarrassed about, you not being any different."

"You knew him growing up. I understand not wanting to believe that your old friend could really do these things."

"Linus was never really my friend, even if I wanted him to be. Of course I didn't want to believe, but I would have if that was the right thing to do. But besides what I saw in his heart, your evidence was all circumstantial."

"We had eyewitness testimony."

"Your partner's daughter?" Lizzie looked at Quentin, daring to narrow her eyes. "She was only a little girl when she testified against Linus." Her point was already made, but she waited a beat, then added a codicil anyway. "Awfully young to serve as a credible witness."

"What are you suggesting?"

"I've just always wondered if she was old enough to *really* know what she saw. Young minds are so *impressionable*, you know?"

He ignored the insinuation. "Do you think that Linus Cole is innocent?"

"He has the right to appeal, same as anyone else."

"Have you had any contact with him recently?"

"I haven't heard from Linus since he moved out of Maggie's house, and barely anything before then. I'm sure he wouldn't even remember me."

"What was your relationship like?"

Lizzie flushed. "Linus never gave me the time of day, but he wasn't ever mean to me, either."

"Was he 'mean' to the other children?"

"Not really … or at least not exactly."

"What's the difference? Can you be more specific? I've heard stories."

"What? When? Who did you talk to?"

"Does any of that matter? I'm asking what *you* saw."

"He was a pain in the ass, same as any teenage boy. I have two of my own now. Believe me, it's not an easy age. But Linus was never a mean-spirited person."

"Have your sons ever locked someone in a trunk?"

"You're talking about Jim."

"So you know the story?"

"I was there," Lizzie said.

"But you don't think that sounds like the act of a mean-spirited person?"

She shook her head. "Linus was a pain, but it never

came from a place of malice. He was acting out, same as any troubled kid."

Quentin offered her a noncommittal nod. "Have you had any contact with—"

"You already asked me that, and I already said *no*."

"My apologies." He smiled. "I'm just—"

"What is it you actually want from me, Deputy Chief Porter? We were foster kids in the same house at the same time, a long time ago. I'm not sure there's anything I can help you with now."

"I'm just looking for a little insight as to what Linus might have been like as a—"

"I told you, he was troubled."

"Can you be more specific?"

"About what he did, or why he did it?" Lizzie asked.

"Either or both." Another smile.

"Linus was always hurting. His biological parents had abused him. Beat him badly, and even burned him a few times. He had suffered an ungodly amount of pain by the time he got to the Dowlings'."

"How long were you there before Cole … before Linus started living there?"

"About two years."

"And what was the first thing you noticed about him?"

"How scarred he was. Emotionally, I mean. He had the burn marks, of course. But you could just look in his eyes and see how much he was hurting. I used to fall asleep sometimes feeling like a bit of his aching made its way into my dreams and then stayed with me even after I woke up in the morning."

"What did the Dowlings do to help him cope?"

"Maggie did her best, but you can only kick a puppy so many times. There's always a point where no amount of kindness can fix the damage that's been done."

"You said *Maggie.* What about Philip?"

"He was usually working, so Maggie took care of us for the most part."

"Did you ever see Philip or Maggie hit Linus, or any of the other children?"

Lizzie shook her head, but Quentin didn't believe her.

"How did she 'do her best'?"

"She took us all to Sunday school, to start. Unfortunately, I was the only one of us who stuck with it. I'm so grateful to Maggie for that." She paused, as if wanting or needing acknowledgement. Quentin nodded, then Lizzie continued. "I prayed for the others every night. I still do."

"What do you pray for?"

"That somehow, God will reach them. That they'll be blessed like I have been."

"Jim works just a few miles from the Dowlings' home. At Fresh Groceries. Have you ever stopped in to see him?"

Lizzie shook her head. "I never really have a reason to drive up there anymore. School is down here and so is Adam's work."

"I spoke to Jim this morning. He seemed to think well of you."

Lizzie blushed. "Maybe I'll make a little drive, drop in and say *hi.*"

But he knew she wouldn't. "What about Tuesday?"

She shook her head again. "Tuesdays are hard for me. Rebecca has—"

"I'm sorry. I meant Tuesday Howe, one of the other—"

"Oh, of course." Lizzie nodded, disgust warping her expression. "What about her?"

"Jim thought there might have been something going on between her and Cole. Do you have any thoughts about that?"

"The two of them hung out sometimes, but there was never anything romantic."

"There *wasn't*, or you don't think there was?"

"Tuesday was always getting Linus in trouble, bless her heart. I just can't see them two together." It seemed like Lizzie was about to say something else, but then she suddenly stopped.

"Did Tuesday ever get *you* into trouble?"

"No." But again, Quentin thought there might be something she wasn't saying.

"Did you and Tuesday ever fight?"

Another shake of her head, no elaboration.

"So you're not close?"

Lizzie snorted: *next question.*

"Do you ever talk to Matt Varney?"

"I barely ever talked to him back then, I can't imagine having a reason to talk to him now."

"But you still pray for him, right?"

"I pray for everyone," Lizzie said.

"Is there anything you can tell me about Matt?"

She shrugged. "He was always hanging out with that cute friend of his … Derrick? Devon? I'm not sure, I don't remember, but it started with a *D.*"

"And Derrick or Devon came over to the house a lot?"

"Other way around. Matt was always leaving to hang out with him." Lizzie glanced back at the table of baked goods. "Is there anything else I can help you with? Because I should really get back and help Selma."

Quentin followed her gaze. The table had no customers and Selma was engrossed in something on her phone.

"I have enough. Thank you for your time." He handed her a card. "Please give me a call if you think of anything else, or if you hear from Linus or any of your other foster siblings."

"Of course." Her eyes implied something else.

Quentin got in the Explorer, but killed the radio as the engine roared to life. He drove down the winding road toward the coast, replaying his conversation with Lizzie in his head.

He believed that she had a thing for Cole back in the day, but wasn't in contact with him now. And it was hard to picture Lizzie as an executioner. She didn't seem to have the temperament, or the physical strength to pull it off without help.

It was either Howe or Varney next. High school would be getting out around the time Quentin could get there, so he might as well see if he could catch Varney before he left for the day.

Maybe Cole had something on the guy and was somehow coercing him into the killings.

He lowered his foot on the gas. He had to go faster. The clock was ticking, that second hand now like a scythe on its way to yet another victim.

Chapter Twenty

DANICA

Danica was at Coldwater for the third time in two days. Her hands were clammy, and even though it might have only been her imagination, she was sure she could smell her own sweat.

Past the protestors, then through the gate and heavy security, all by herself. She didn't ask for Quentin's help, or even want him to know where she was. She imagined it was only a matter of time before one of the cops on her detail called Quent and told him.

The hard part was supposed to be over.

"I'm sorry," said the guard, shaking his head yet again. "But Deputy Chief Porter is the only one I have permission to let in—"

"And anyone he's authorized," she attempted to correct him.

"Well, sure," the guard agreed. "But I don't see any authorization here."

Danica sighed. This was the third time around. "*I am authorized.* Look me up in the log. I've been here twice already. Deputy Chief Porter authorized me both times, and has sent me in for a follow-up interrogation with Cole. I'm supposed to be building a profile of Cole's possible acolyte. The deputy chief is waiting on my work. I'm sure you don't want me to—"

"Give me a minute," he finally surrendered. "I'll give the warden a call, see what he says."

Danica watched him dial, then stifled her smile when she could tell that he wasn't getting any response. He turned away from her, mumbled something into voicemail, then turned back around, eyeing Danica head to toe with a defeated-sounding sigh.

"If Cole is willing to talk, then I suppose it's okay."

She couldn't have asked for anything more.

A long fifteen minutes later, Danica was finally following the guard down that long hallway, hoping that her heart would slow down before she claimed her seat across from the murderer again.

He stopped in front of the door and turned to her. "He's cuffed and chained. Stay on your side of the table. Keep your distance the entire time, no matter what. I'll be waiting right outside — just holler if you need anything. I'm only a second away."

The guard eyed her with what appeared to be genuine concern, and for the first time she didn't feel like a nuisance. "Thanks."

The guard opened the door and she entered the room.

Cole was restrained, but clearly amused to see her. His wide smile seemed even more knowing, even thicker with menace.

Danica took her seat, trying to calm herself.

"What are you doing here without your guard dog?" Cole asked.

"Deputy Chief Porter doesn't know I'm here."

"You mean *Uncle Quent*?" He laughed to himself, tucking a strand of hair behind his ear.

"I'm here to help you."

"Oh, you are!" He slapped the table. "Well, that is just fantastic. I heard that you haven't really lived until you've done something for someone who can never repay you."

Danica worked to control her breathing. She needed to situate herself. It was unsettling, how ruffled she already was, and they hadn't even started.

"So how are you going to help? You here to recant all those lies you told?"

"I met Maggie today. I saw your childhood home. That must have been—"

"Ooh, the therapist is here to give me some therapy. Good job, Miss Tate. This is exactly what I've needed. You're right: our deepest wounds *are* often the openings into the most wonderful parts of ourselves. Too bad we don't have a couch." He winked and drummed his fingers on the table. "I guess this'll have to do. So, what would you like to talk about?"

"Let's start with your foster siblings."

"What about them?"

"Did you feel completely alone while you were living with the Dowlings? Or were you able to make friends with anyone while you were there?"

"So, we're going to reminisce. That sounds nice. We get a lot of that around here, but the stories are all mostly the same, once you ignore the broad strokes and all the details."

"Isn't that everything? What else is left?"

Cole laughed again. "*The truth.*"

"So," Danica redirected, "did you make any friends while—"

"Tell you what … why don't we trade a memory for a memory. *You first.*"

"Okay." She hoped he couldn't see into her fear, but two burning eyes said he most certainly could. "I remember my father taking me fishing when I was seven. We didn't have a boat, but he woke me up early and—"

"No." Cole shook his head. "Let's stay on topic. Tell me about that night."

She bit her lip to keep it from trembling. "What do you want to know?"

"You woke up on Uncle Quent's porch covered in ash. What happened next?"

Danica glared at her devil, determined to say nothing, destined to relive the worst night of her life to prove she had control of this exchange.

"You're wrong. Uncle Quent carried me into his house from the car. He must have called my mom while I was unconscious, because she was there when I woke up."

"Liar," Cole said with no emotion.

"I'm not lying."

"You are lying, and I know you're lying because I was there."

Danica couldn't breathe. She had to clench her fists several times before the air finally found her throat. "You followed Quentin from the murder scene?"

"Close your eyes and remember the truth."

"You're lying." She shook her head.

"And you're wasting my time. GUARD!"

"Wait. Fine." Danica closed her eyes.

"Never mind!" Cole yelled.

The door opened behind her. "You okay in here?"

"We're good," Danica said, turning around and nodding at the guard before facing Cole and closing her eyes again.

She thought back to that night, painful as it was.

She pictured herself blacked out in the smoke as her childhood home burned to ashes around her. It wasn't exactly a memory, but it did have the air of reality. She saw her little girl's body, looking up at Uncle Quent from the porch as he scooped her into his arms.

She saw her mother standing behind him.

That was new, and a visual echo of something she'd seen before … and recently.

Emilia in only a T-shirt — Smashing Pumpkins at the Shrine.

Still watching the reel in her mind, Danica heard a rustling in the bushes. But in the memory of whatever this was she was too exhausted to turn and look.

Everything tasted like smoke. She could barely breathe. She kept gasping for air, sucking what little she could through her teeth, feeling like she was drowning even without any water.

She opened her eyes in the real world and saw Cole as she should have, though his face was smudged with soot and tickling a memory from some bottomless well inside her.

She blinked and the soot disappeared.

"You're putting thoughts in my head."

Cole didn't respond. He kept staring at her, waiting for his manipulations to sink in.

None of what Danica had seen could be right. Quentin figured out that Cole was going to murder her father — too late to save him. Any later and Danica would have died, too.

Uncle Quent had rescued her. He said so under oath, and so had she.

Cole bored into her, his stare like full sun on a germinating seed. "Tell me."

Her voice trembled, then cracked when she spoke. "Uncle Quent picked me up off of the porch ..." Then realization: "Someone else must have brought me there."

Cole gave her a regal yet facetious nod. "You're welcome."

Fucker. It was his turn to tell her a memory, and while she should be prompting him to reveal something about the copycat killer, she couldn't bring herself to do it.

Danica had braved Coldwater all by herself to help save the next victim's life, but there was something she needed to know before she could throttle the thing that so often had her waking up drenched in sweat, and occasionally wanting to die.

"Tell me the story of how you murdered my father."

He shook his head. "That's not my story to tell."

"Like hell it isn't."

"I didn't kill your father."

"Then who did?"

He shook his head again. "My hands are dirty. You won't appreciate where I point my fingers."

"Try me."

"I wrote a book about it. *The New York Times* seemed to like it enough, said a few nice things. The book even has a part with you in—"

"I've read your fucking book. It's easy to insist you didn't do something when you offer no alibis or explanations. *An Innocent Man* isn't a book, it's a toddler's philosophy."

"It's not my job to do the department's work for them. The explanations are straightforward for those who look."

"So you'll just stay in here and await your execution instead of proving you're not the killer?"

He shrugged. "I shall pass from this life without blood on my hands."

Danica leaned toward him, much too close. "Look in my eyes and tell me that you didn't kill my father."

Cole leaned forward and it took everything inside her not to retreat. But she smelled his breath and longed for the moment to end. Without blinking, stuttering, or sounding anything less than sincere, he made what sounded like a solemn vow. "I never laid a finger on your father."

Danica fell back in her seat, wishing the world would stop spinning.

Linus Cole was a sociopath. Like most people with antisocial personality disorder, he was great at masking it and had thus drifted through life doing exactly that. Some monsters believed their lies. It was like an evolutionary adaptation to make them seem more honorable. Maybe Cole had been clinging to his falsehoods for so long, it was easy to hold faith in the fiction.

The alternative would kill her.

It would mean having to face an abortion of truth, it would mean knowing that Uncle Quent had been lying to Danica for most of her life.

"Fine, you didn't kill him. What were you doing while my father was dying?"

"Driving to your house, hoping I could get there before the real Magistrate murdered your father."

"Liar." Danica wanted to claw his eyes out.

"You asked for my memory, are you going to keep interrupting me with insults while I try and give it to you?"

She didn't respond.

"I got there too late. The house was already on fire. Your father was dead and the Magistrate was fleeing the scene."

"What else?" Cole made her ask.

"I heard a little girl crying inside, so I smashed through

the sliding glass door and followed the sound. I found you lying in the kitchen, so I picked you up and took you to Porter's where I knew you'd be safe."

"So you're the hero of this story?" She wanted to break each one of his fingers twice.

"Isn't everyone the hero of their own story?"

"A lie doesn't count. You still owe me a memory."

"Saving your life isn't enough?" He looked at her, almost triumphantly.

"How about you tell me—"

The door exploded open and Quentin burst into the room. "What the fuck is this?"

"Uh-oh. Daddy's here. Now you're in trouble."

"Fuck you!" Danica spat.

Quentin had his hands hooked under her armpits and was dragging Danica out of the room as Cole sat there smiling. No, *smirking* at her.

"Let's be brave enough to say goodbye now to feel the true reward of our next hello." Cole continued to taunt her, rattling his chains as the door swung shut behind the guard.

"What the hell were you thinking?" Quentin growled at her.

"I needed answers, and you were busy interviewing suspects."

"I thought you had a full day of clients?"

"People's lives are on the line. This seemed more pressing."

"SO YOU CAME ALONE?"

Danica flinched back. Even the guard seemed to be cowering.

Quentin took a breath and tried again. Softer this time. "*Never go in there by yourself.* Do you understand me?" He didn't wait to see if she did. "Linus Cole is a violent man.

Provoke him and he might hurt you. He won't give a shit that they'll put him in solitary. He's on death row. That asshole knows he's going to die in prison."

"I was getting somewhere with him. I needed more—"

"Cole is fucking with you and you're letting him. Everything that man says is a lie."

"How did you know I was here?" Better than asking him why the fuck he was such a goddamned liar, for now.

"You really thought they wouldn't call me?"

"I'm not a child. I don't need your protection or guards on me."

"Go home and let this go, whatever you think it is. I'm taking care of it."

"Fine." Danica walked out beside him in the corridor, waiting to get her Uncle Quent alone and safely out of earshot of anybody else.

Outside, but before they had to make their way past the protestors, she turned to him. "Cole said that he left me on your porch. He said *that's* where you found me. Is that true?"

Quentin scoffed. "You know that's bullshit."

But for the first time in her life, Danica felt sure he was lying.

Chapter Twenty-One

QUENTIN

QUENTIN FOLLOWED Danica to her house, waiting for the officers on her detail to arrive.

She got out of her truck, slammed the door, and went inside.

He sighed, waiting for the unmarked sedan to pull up beside him.

Officer Brady, sitting in the passenger seat, rolled down the tinted window. "Everything good?"

"Yeah, thank you."

"You got it, boss," he said before rolling his window back up before the car returned to its spot opposite Danica's house.

Quentin pulled slowly away.

He'd burned rubber from the Pike High School parking lot to Coldwater and managed to make the twenty-minute trip to the bridge in a quarter hour without hitting anything with his SUV. Brady had called to let him know what was happening just as he'd arrived at Pike for a conversation with Varney.

He got to the prison in the nick of time by the look of

things. Interrupted her ridiculous interrogation of Cole. Though pissed, he couldn't blame her. Danica was naturally inquisitive, and doing her job. This was his fault for including her.

Quentin had asked for help because he had no choice, then he allowed her to keep on contributing because it seemed therapeutic for her to sift through a few clues and build a profile of the copycat. Win-win on paper, but now it felt like they were both about to lose something big. If Danica knew the truth, she'd lose the only father figure she had left, and he'd lose the only daughter he ever had.

He had a mess to clean up. He needed to stay on top of new events as they occurred, but he also needed a way to discourage Danica's meddling. Or more specifically, he had to keep her from turning up something that might trigger wrong or dangerous memories.

He couldn't trust that Danica would keep a discrepancy to herself. And no matter how thorough his damage control, she would almost for sure want to report it. Like Miles. He never understood that good cops occasionally got their hands dirty. And to be great, you sometimes had to dip them in mud.

That's what it took to keep the bad guys off the streets. Monsters didn't play fair, so sometimes it took cops willing to play fast and loose with the rules to stop the monsters.

Linus Cole was behind bars instead of burning new bodies for families to mourn because Quentin had done the difficult but necessary work of putting him away, and making sure he stayed locked up for the rest of his life.

Justice was all that mattered.

He turned on the radio, but was in no mood for The Cranberries. So he said "Been Caught Stealing" into the empty cabin and filled it with Jane's Addiction instead. Quentin had considered seeing them tour with Nine Inch

Nails, back when he had first joined the force, and was still living the semi-life of a college-something. He and Miles were already partners, but Miles and Emilia weren't yet a thing. That would happen a month later, and Danica not long after that — before Quentin took what didn't belong to him and maybe ruined everything.

Maybe *Ritual de lo Habitual* wasn't such a good idea.

Back to the radio.

"Bittersweet Symphony," and that sounded better.

Quentin had been driving for five minutes, lost in thought. He swung a left, heading toward the shore to check in on Varney at his home since school was now out for the day. Seemed like an odd spot for a middle-aged high school teacher to live. One of the trendier and more expensive stretches in Las Orillas.

He felt an aggressive need for immediate answers. But the traffic was killing him, though, so he flipped a bitch and decided to visit Tuesday Howe instead.

Ten more minutes in the car instead of thirty or forty. Much better for his eroding mood.

Tuesday's place looked like an abandoned museum. A wooden warehouse or workshop with an apartment on top of it. Grimy windows curtained by ancient brown paper.

He parked next to an Escalade and got out.

He heard the high-pitched buzzing of a saw coming from inside the warehouse and spent several minutes knocking at the front door with no response.

He circled the building, looking for a window with an uncovered patch to peer through. He peeked in and saw one lone occupant, back to the window, using a bandsaw.

So he returned to the front door, turned the knob to find it unlocked, and dared to enter.

He watched the woman stop the saw and turn to carry two pieces of wood toward a larger piece she was working on. A sculpture or a piece of furniture, Quentin couldn't yet tell.

She was tall and big-boned, wearing a mask to keep the sawdust out of her sinuses, and a ratty flannel, jeans that might have never been washed, and work boots that looked like they might have gone through a couple of wars. Her sleeves were rolled up, but every inch of exposed skin was covered in sawdust, and sticking to her meaty limbs with the glue of her sweat.

Quentin cleared his throat. "Tuesday Howe?"

She turned around, revealing a stained tank top beneath the flannel. She met his eyes, removed her mask, and spoke with no emotion. "Detective Porter."

"Deputy Chief." He smiled and gave her a nod. "You don't seem surprised to see me."

"Soon as I heard news about the copycat I figured I'd be getting a call from the cops sooner or later, though I didn't expect a visit from an actual movie star."

It didn't sound like a compliment. "I'm hardly a movie star."

"Then what kind of star are you?"

"The kind that would like to ask you a couple of questions. Is this a good time?"

"Of course it's not a good time." Tuesday looked at the piece of furniture — Quentin still couldn't tell what it was — then back at him. "But it won't be any better later. You want a drink?"

An appreciative nod. "What do you have?"

"I've got Burpy's and root bear."

"A Burpy sounds great. Thanks."

Tuesday turned without a word, walked across the workshop to a big fridge against the far wall that looked like it might have been keeping things cold since the Carter administration, then opened it up and pulled out two brown bottles of a local soda that still boasted *twice the sugar and three times the caffeine!*

She didn't say *follow me*, but Quentin knew what to do.

He followed her out the front door and into an open yard littered with what appeared to be half-finished pieces and aborted projects. She pointed to a pair of Adirondack chairs, perfect scale and expertly crafted. Masterpieces in the middle of all the refuse. She took a seat and Quentin claimed the one next to her.

His phone buzzed, but he reached into his pocket to silence the call without looking at the screen.

Tuesday popped the top of her Burpy, then took a swallow. "So, what do you want to know about Linus that you don't already know?"

"When was the last time the two of you spoke?"

"How long's he been in prison?" Tuesday took another swig. "It's been longer than that."

"No correspondence whatsoever?"

"Why in the hell would I want to *correspond* with that pile of shit?"

"The two of you have history."

She shrugged. "So do Germans and Jews."

Quentin opened his bottle. "What was he like?"

Tuesday shook her head, then looked right at Quentin. "He was a stone-cold motherfucker, that's what he was like. Linus loved setting his little fires, even when we were kids. Can't say I'm surprised he ended up going away."

"Were you ever afraid of him?"

She laughed. "I never put up with his shit, and I think he respected that. No, I wasn't ever afraid of Linus."

"Did you keep in touch after he left Maggie's house?"

"For a while."

His phone buzzed again, and again Quentin ignored it. "Why did you stop?"

Another long swallow. "People change. Seemed like in Cole's case he got even worse."

"Do you think of him as *Linus* or *Cole*? You've referred to him as both."

"I guess he is both, depending on when I'm thinking about him. As a kid, I suppose Linus sounds about right, but as a convicted killer, I think Cole fits him better."

"So you've given it some thought?"

"I'm just answering your questions, even if they strike me as dumb."

Quentin took his first sip of the Burpy and winced. It had been a long time since he'd had that much sugar in his mouth. "Were you in touch during the time of the murders?"

She shook her head. "I wasn't even in the state, and if I was inclined to reach out and touch someone, Cole wasn't exactly at the top of my list."

"Where were you?"

"A few places, but mostly Portland back then."

"Why were you in Portland?" Quentin asked.

"That was in my wandering phase, when all I wanted in the world was to get the fuck out of here."

"Do you mind if I ask why? California is a final destination for a lot of people. The place they dream about living in. Las Orillas specifically."

Tuesday nodded. "Well, I bet those folks didn't grow up with the Dowlings."

"How long did you wander?"

"A few years. Long enough to finally grow up."

Another buzz. This time Quentin turned off his phone.

"Do you need to get that?" Tuesday asked.

"I've turned it off. Sorry. So, what brought you back here?"

"Wandering wasn't good for me." She shook her head,

and Quentin could see the regret in her eyes. "I fell in with some bad people, got into a bit of trouble, then bailed after I realized I was headed for something even worse. I'd been gone long enough by then to appreciate this little dump more than I had."

"What kind of trouble did you get into?"

Tuesday smiled and patted the arm of her rather stunning Adirondack. "The kind that makes you appreciate settling down and focusing on your art."

"Did Cole ever mention keeping in touch with any of his other foster siblings?"

"How would I know?"

"I'm not saying you do."

Tuesday shrugged and took another long swallow. "He and Varney were friends for a while, though I have no idea what he's up to now."

"I was under the impression that Varney wasn't around all that much when he and Cole were at the Dowlings' together."

"He was there enough." Another sip.

"Have *you* been in touch with any of your foster siblings?"

"You keep in touch with your old cold sores?"

"Did you know that Jim is working at a convenience store?"

"Why would I know that?" Tuesday asked.

"Did you know that Lizzie got married?"

"No surprises there. Linus wasn't ever going to fuck her, and Jesus doesn't smile on a girl who likes to get a little dick before saying *I do*."

"Varney teaches at Pike."

Tuesday laughed. "No shit. Matt a teacher?"

"That surprises you?"

"I don't know what you're hoping I can tell you. I left

this place to get away from a supremely shitty childhood. Why would I want to look up any of those losers when I'm trying to get my life back?"

He liked Tuesday's down-to-earth, no-bullshit attitude, and his gut said she was talking straight. He took one last sip of his Burpy and stood.

"Thank you for your time. Will you let me know if Cole contacts you?"

"Sure will," she said, also standing and casting a glance at her now empty seat. "If you promise to let me know if you're ever in the market for a high-quality chair you can pass down to your children."

"I don't have any, but you do have my word."

They shook hands as Quentin gave her his card, then left, checking his phone and finding that things had been even busier than he'd realized during his conversation with Tuesday.

There was a missed call from Captain Jenkins, without an accompanying voicemail, and a message from Merrill letting Quentin know that he and Simpson had yet to make any noteworthy progress. There was also a text from Luther looking to schedule another interview. A message from the warden, sent as a friend, letting Quentin know that Luther had been talking to Cole's lawyer, and there was no way to kill the interview without it looking like they were engaged in some conspiracy or trying to hide the truth. A voicemail from Chief Wilson reminding him of both the upcoming press conference, and the importance of his performance sobered Quentin immediately.

Lastly, and the one that dried his throat and made his socks feel like they were baking his feet, Danica had left three voicemails, and a text that read, *Call me.*

He slammed the door to his Explorer and started the engine, gritting his teeth.

Then he drove away from Tuesday's workshop and toward the press conference, thinking about the only voice-mails he hadn't listened to, and ignoring the text.

Danica preferred her stories straight, so Quentin couldn't return her call until he had one.

Chapter Twenty-Two

DANICA

DANICA TURNED ANOTHER CORNER, rounding Cheshire as she forced herself to jog faster now that she was closer to home. A straight run the rest of the way, except for that one last turn onto Spaulding.

Her lungs were still burning, but at least she was used to it. For some reason her arms were aching as much as her legs, all four limbs like burning spaghetti. Remaining upright felt like two-thirds of a miracle.

She was currently fueled by little more than confusion and rage.

The security detail pissed her off most of all. They drove behind Danica her entire run, making sure she was safe, and making her feel more exposed than if they weren't there at all.

Cecilia quit therapy. Danica didn't take it personally, except that she totally did. What had she missed? What could she have done better? Was this another example of Danica the Distracted? She lived in her head, would Cecilia die a little more each day thanks to her former therapist's inner disturbances?

All the smoke curling in from the edges. Ashes closing in on her life. Darkness like a sack on her head, dragging Danica back, further and further away from a light she'd never see again. Pitch black and the heavy stench of billowing smoke. A perfume of cinders she couldn't expel from her nostrils. An ugly twisted truth lurking behind it all.

Mom had suffered a series of hysterical fits, each one worse than the preceding according to Rebecca. *She was screaming so hard I thought her throat might be bleeding. Not that I mean to alarm you,* she'd added.

Of course not. Rebecca knew Danica preferred straight talk to quivering lines. But the image of Mom screaming herself raw wouldn't stop looping in her head. A broken projector shining 35mm of insanity onto the big screen inside her mind that she could never blink away.

But Danica was most pissed that Quentin hadn't returned any of her calls. She shouldn't be angry at him. Right now, he was a detective, doing his job. She had no right to stomp her foot like a petulant toddler because he couldn't get her to jump when she rang her little bell.

Or so said the practical side of Danica. The dominant one, screaming in her ear and stepping on her toes, kept insisting that Uncle Quent was hiding something.

That's why she was running herself into exhaustion. If Danica could empty herself out just a little more she might be able to forget about her conversation with Cole.

Because right now, it kept crawling through her thoughts like maggots in shit.

She was tempted to get plastered and pass out. Running was a start, but maybe she needed a few shots of something hot to temporarily die like she wanted to. She could resurrect herself a day later, and maybe then she'd be ready for the sun.

Danica was a trauma therapist. She knew better than most that memory was malleable. It's one of the things she had to be most careful about when helping patients recall traumatic events — never guess, lead, or suggest things to them. Let them remember everything on their own, even if it's a struggle. One wrong suggestion could cause a victim to remember things incorrectly. It could even lead someone to point the finger at an innocent party.

With the right triggers, twisting remembrance was like turning the sides of a Rubik's Cube. Enough turns, and in the right order — all of a sudden you have panels of color instead of a jumble. Easy to understand at a glance. Just like the brain likes it.

Maybe that's what Cole had done to her.

Danica kept searching her recall for signs that Cole had gone wayward, suggested memories that weren't true. But no matter how many replays their conversation received in her mind, he always seemed to be playing fair.

Cole had called her a liar, then told Danica to close her eyes.

That's what she did with clients all the time. It was coloring inside the lines. There had been no cheat code, or Rubik's Cube. Not from Linus Cole.

But humans *want* to believe.

Everyone was in denial about something. Self-deception was one hell of a motivator. Lying to yourself was simple: develop a false belief, then double down and use it to fuel undesirable but suddenly justifiable behavior. Need more confidence? *Believe* that shit.

People loved to agree with themselves. They looked for evidence to support their existing beliefs rather than anything that might wave a sword against it. Contradiction was the enemy, more so if it championed an undesirable idea.

Danica had every reason to give herself an artificial memory. But if she'd been remembering wrong, her testimony was at least partly a lie. A few delinquent lines of code in her recall that had put a man on death row.

What else might she be misremembering? And what did Danica's erroneous information say about her as a witness, a professional, a person?

Her lungs burned hotter and sweat dripped into her eyes. She couldn't stand the thought of being discredited. She might have been mistaken — *please, don't let me be mistaken* — but that didn't make her the liar that the world would need her to be.

Stories had heroes and villains. Twenty years in prison for a crime he didn't commit would make Linus Cole the good guy, flipping the script on the co-conspirators who had put him away with their lies. The bad guys in the sequel to an already compelling story.

Danica was already doubting everything. It didn't help that the hallucinations were back. Still curling at the edges, still smelling like campfire and overcooked steak, still sticking to her cells like they had ever since her last conversation with Cole.

The man who might not have murdered her father after all.

Danica smelled smoke. But this time it wasn't a stain in her olfactory system that she couldn't scrub away. It was something she could feel on her skin. And the air was heavier than it should have been.

She might be having a stroke.

But that didn't make sense. Danica couldn't be running if she were having a stroke. Still, symptoms included a sudden numbness or slack feeling in her face and limbs.

Check and double check. At least her stupefaction was symmetrical. She felt dead on both sides. But another sign was confusion, and Danica was baffled. She might have trouble speaking, if there was anyone around to hear her, and it was possible that she might not actually understand anything more than a Dick and Jane book right about now.

She might be suffering from blurred vision, but that could be from all the sweat in her eyes. Even trouble walking was understandable after an hour of furious running.

A block from Spaulding, she saw dark clouds, pluming and belching into what was an otherwise perfectly cerulean sky.

The first must be new, but it was burning fast. Acres of smoke billowing from nowhere.

This close to Spaulding the target of arson might be her.

It was enough to chill her blood. Cole's acolyte was copying all of his moves. Murder wasn't enough, he wanted to taste ash in the air.

Danica rounded Spaulding. Sure enough her house was on fire. And goddammit, she *knew it* — the two-bedroom bungalow she'd paid way too much for, was now, like everything else, being taken away from her.

She was flooded with adrenaline. The next half block came easily. In seconds she was darting across the street and clipping the neighbor's lawn on the way to her place.

The shadows and smoke were real this time, still clinging to the edges of her vision.

Had she really seen a figure darting around to the back of her house?

"Hey!" Danica gave chase, past her fence, down the side and into her back yard.

But the shadowy figure wasn't there, and Danica had no idea whether she had really even seen it at all. She looked at her house, wanting to cry, then jogged back to the front while retrieving her phone.

She called 911 without crying.

The tears came when she turned back around and saw her roof collapse in the fire. Then Danica remembered that the file with her father's autopsy report was inside, and she cried even harder.

Chapter Twenty-Three

QUENTIN

For the first time in Quentin's life, he looked out at the crowd of reporters, wishing the cameras would all disappear, and that all of these people staring back at him wanting and waiting to pepper him with questions would all just go the fuck away.

Nancy Albright, the department's public information officer, stood at the podium beside him. She had just updated the media, reading from the chief's draft of the press release: Someone has killed two people who were involved in putting Linus Cole away. Police were investigating all leads and had placed other people under police protection. Additionally, there was a reward for any assistance in helping to identify the suspect.

Immediately after Albright finished with her statement, she asked the question that would unleash the barrage.

"Does anybody have any questions?"

The reporters, of which there were nearly two dozen — the most since the Cole case — plus their TV crews, all shouted over one another.

Albright pointed to a man in a beige trench coat who

looked like the cartoon version of a journalist. A different decade and he would have been chomping on the end of a cigar.

Missing Cigar drew first blood. "This question is for Deputy Chief Porter. Linus Cole is scheduled for execution two days from now and yet he still maintains his innocence. He says that you framed him. Any comment?"

"We'd like to keep questions related to the case," Albright said.

"I'd say this is related to the case," argued the man.

"It's okay," Quentin whispered as he pulled the microphone toward himself. "Linus Cole will say anything to save his life."

"That's not an answer!" shouted another reporter, though Quentin couldn't see who.

"Linus Cole murdered his victims in cold blood, then burned their bodies in a ritualistic—"

He felt Albright's discomfort. It was her job to protect him from badgering, but he wasn't making it easy by engaging. Yet, he was filled with a righteous anger that these muckrakers would rather believe in the innocence of a man on death row than the police department whose job was to protect people from monsters like Cole.

"What if it's not a copycat?" asked Aimee Milano from Channel 2. "Could it be the same person? Could this second round of killings help to prove that Linus Cole is actually innocent?"

"Absolutely not." Quentin shook his head. "There are significant differences in the murders."

"Can you elaborate?" Milano asked.

"I can't get into specifics that would jeopardize an ongoing investigation."

"What is your reaction to protestors claiming that you

have a personal vendetta against Cole?" From a woman with hair so blonde it was almost white.

Jesus Christ. "No comment." Then, "That's absurd. Linus Cole is a murderer. That case was tried two decades ago. He's desperate."

Brian Gilcrest from *The Herald*: "Is anyone investigating Cole's allegations of witness tampering and manufacturing of evidence?"

"No comment."

Man in plaid: "Why did you take Danica Tate with you to multiple meetings with Linus Cole at Coldwater Prison?"

Aimee Milano from Channel 2: "And what was said in those meetings?"

"No comment, and no comment." Then one of the hardest smiles of his life.

Albright pulled the microphone toward her. "Thank you again for your time. That will be all."

Quentin turned from the podium, ignoring the crowd as Albright shot down further questions and ended the press conference.

Into the precinct for his interview with Luther, whose camera crew was outside recording the shit show. He hated how much the press was eating from the palm of Cole's hands.

On a surface level, he got it. And it had been good for him, too. Heroes needed a villain, and in that respect Cole was excellent. It was undoubtedly one of the biggest reasons for the Magistrate Murderer's enduring success as a story. Cole made people curious. But that didn't make him a believable or reliable witness. Too many of the people were conflating the roles. That was fine when it came to selling books, movies to the studios, or series to the streamers, but not when Quentin had to solve a case while living his life and doing his job under a goddamned microscope.

Only a moron would truly believe that Linus Cole was innocent. People had short memories and soft hearts. They had forgotten the horrors the monster perpetuated on innocents, and had thus fallen for his sob story. Quentin bet if the man weren't good-looking, or if Cole were a minority, nobody would be giving him the benefit of the doubt. He'd have been executed without question.

Two days couldn't come quick enough. Put this shit to bed once and for all.

Maybe Quentin could get some good out of this interview with Luther by reminding the world about the Magistrate Murderer's many atrocities.

Luther was waiting in his office. Quentin wasn't looking forward to following his press conference for what would surely be an hour of hardballs, but if it wasn't his ass in the seat, then Luther would be having an on-camera conversation with Danica instead.

A few days ago this had all been reasonable. One last round on the Linus Cole publicity train, on the brink of the killer's execution and in preparation for Quentin's certain ascension to chief.

Now the same exchange felt like a curse in waiting. Luther and the entire project was yet another thing to be managed, no different from the buzzards outside, perched and ready to turn Porter into the bad guy.

Hopefully Quentin would be able to wrap up any of Luther's less savory questions in a nice bow of *I'm sorry, but that's still under investigation.* It could also be a condition of his continued cooperation that neither Luther nor his crew leak so much as a frame of their footage until after the investigation had wrapped, and the needle had plunged into Cole.

Luther would want to know why, but Quentin could claim that stirring up pro-Cole sentiment might trigger a flurry of distracting, misleading, or entirely irrelevant tips.

If that didn't work, Judge Foster owed Quentin more than enough to issue a gag order.

He turned the corner toward his office and immediately wanted to turn back around. Instead he held his smile and kept walking. Pretended like he wasn't about to shit his pants just seconds after finally feeling like he maybe had things relatively under control.

Luther and the rest of his crew were all there, but they weren't set up in his office as planned. And it wasn't their fault. They were all milling about in the hallway, standing next to a pair of men in handsome suits that told more of the story.

Double fuck. Quentin would rather deal with the press right now than the goddamned FBI.

But no one could know it. He nodded at Luther, acutely aware that the cameras were rolling.

Luther nodded back, his expression stoic despite his wildly curious eyes.

"Deputy Chief Porter," said one of the two men in black, walking toward him with his hand extended. They shook then he turned to his partner. "This is Special Agent Rowan and I'm Special Agent Tyler."

"Good to meet you." Quentin went from Tyler to Rowan. Finished shaking his hand, kept pretending like there weren't cameras behind him. "What can I do for you gentleman?"

"Your office?" Rowan said with a nod.

Quentin nodded back and turned to Luther. "Sorry, I'm going to have to postpone."

He led the agents into his office as Luther said, "I can wait."

Quentin shook his head, closing the door and turning to the agents.

Rowan said, "We're here because the FBI is claiming jurisdiction over this case."

"What?" Quentin's chest constricted. "Why?"

"We've identified two prior murders in another state," Tyler replied. "We believe they're related."

"From when?"

"Four years ago," Rowan told him.

"What state?" Quentin felt his phone buzzing in his jacket pocket but he didn't dare answer now.

Tyler nodded. "Utah."

"About fifty miles outside of Salt Lake."

"What makes you think the murders are related?"

"Our murders share some of the same hallmarks as your vics," Rowan said.

"Like?"

"Mainly the burning of the fingertips." Tyler looked at his partner, waited to see if he had anything to add, then continued when he didn't. "Could be a coincidence, but either way, we're here."

Just burned fingertips? Jesus, that seems like a stretch.

But he couldn't be seen as resisting the Feds. "How can I help?"

"We'll need you to hand over all the relevant case files immediately," Rowan replied. "And we'll need whoever is handling the case to debrief us."

"I can brief you."

His phone buzzed again. And again he ignored it, cold sweat slicking his back.

The agents traded a look.

"Why you?" Tyler asked.

"Because I'm also working the case."

"You're the deputy chief. Is there a reason you're not trusting your detectives on the case?"

"Is there a reason you're questioning how I do my job?" Quentin snapped at Rowan before quickly resetting himself. "Sorry. It's been a hell of a couple of days."

He shook his head and continued. "Let me start over. Of course, we have two of our best detectives on it. I'm looking into some old leads, while Simpson and Merrill are following the new ones. I might not be able to offer them much on the copycat killings, but I'm more than qualified to help see if there's a bridge between what's happening now and Cole's murders twenty years ago."

The agents looked at one another again.

Quentin finished. "Simpson and Merrill will brief you, but I'll be there with them, in case there's anything I can add."

"Fine," Tyler said. "Just get us all the evidence and files as soon as you can."

Quentin nodded. "Of course."

"Your chief has allowed us to set up in his office, so we'll be there." Rowan nodded to his partner, then the agents left Quentin's office, leaving the door hanging wide open in a power move.

Luther approached before Quentin could close his door.

"So, what's that all about?" he asked, cameras rolling behind him.

Quentin sighed. "If you'll excuse me, I have some unexpected work."

He started to walk past them, needing some space to think. The walls felt like they were closing in on him.

"Will you be cooperating with the FBI?" Luther asked.

Quentin answered as he passed him, without turning

around. "We all want the same thing — justice. So, of course."

He needed fresh air, and was practically sucking it through his teeth by the time he got outside.

His phone buzzed. He pulled it out of his pocket as Luther and his crew continued to trail him.

Quentin looked at the screen and gave Luther his palm: *Back off, this is personal.* "Danica."

She was sobbing.

"Danica, honey, what is it?" Three more times, just like that before he could finally decipher her words.

Then a terrible chill the moment he understood.

"My house ... someone burned it down."

"I'll be right there," he said.

Chapter Twenty-Four

DANICA

DANICA WOKE up with a scream in her throat and smoke in her nostrils.

Her whimper died a quiet little death, but the scent of burning still lingered inside her. The dream was vivid, colored by a reality that had reduced her life to a pile of ashes and put her in Quentin's spare bedroom.

She lay in bed, still as she tried to reconstruct the upsetting dream.

Of course there was fire. Danica wondered if she would ever be able to stop seeing the flames that had swallowed her house as she rounded the corner. She'd bought a place she couldn't afford just to prove she was a grownup and no longer living a little girl's life. A woman who wasn't trapped by the misery of a childhood where the world was taken away from her. Now someone had robbed her of everything yet again. Her safety, security, and sense of place in this world were all suddenly gone.

Beyond the smoke, Danica remembered arguing. It was loud in the dream but lost in the morning light. She kept her eyes closed, but that didn't help any more than having them open, and the threat of darkness was a weight she couldn't bear to carry. So after a few minutes without any new memories and nothing to deconstruct she opened them again.

The taste of smoke still coated her tongue, still refusing to leave. That might have been real, rather than an artifact of the dream. Danica had no idea how much soot she might have swallowed while standing in front of her burning bungalow, before she finally wised up and called Uncle Quent.

Quentin got there fast. Around to rescue her like he always had been. He made her feel safe, and it wasn't just the promises that everything would be okay. He still had several boxes of her mother's stuff from before she got committed to Morning Tide. Danica could probably find something to wear. And thankfully, it was Saturday, so she could spend the morning shopping for new clothes and trying to forget.

She kicked the covers off of her body and took another moment to breathe, still feeling schizophrenic. Trapped between an incessantly desperate need to remember and a willful amnesia that would leave all of the ugliness in Danica's life deep in a hole and covered with dirt.

She stretched. Like the smell of smoke, Danica wasn't sure what was causing the aches in her body. A wretched night's sleep, cursed dreams, the trauma of losing her home, memories that might or might not really be hauntings.

She needed water and coffee, not necessarily in that order. So Danica went to the bathroom and cleared some space in her bladder, then headed toward Quentin's kitchen.

She could smell the coffee. Of course he had brewed it for her. None of that capsule shit for Deputy Chief Porter, not even drip. He was a French press man, and had taught Danica about the differences between good and bad brew at a very tender age.

She didn't care about any of those distinctions right now.

Instead, Danica sat on the sofa and pulled the box toward her.

But Uncle Quent had lived in her head for so long, whether he was talking about Linus Cole, good coffee, or something else, he was orator and echo.

"How do you know if coffee is good or bad?" she had asked sometime in middle school, maybe eighth grade, when Uncle Quent had first allowed her to drink it, so long as she didn't fink on him to her grandparents.

"Good coffee tastes good to you, and bad coffee tastes bad."

"But all coffee is gross," she'd insisted, wrinkling her nose at the sludge. No cream or sugar. Uncle Quent said she had to learn to like it black, before corrupting her tastebuds by making it "too girly." He'd told her that everyone's preferences were different, but that he mostly enjoyed African varieties brewed in a French press. Ever since then, so had she.

She ignored the rich scent still drifting in from the kitchen. Right now she wanted — *needed* — to look inside the box.

She lifted the lid, thinking about her trip to Cole's former foster home with Quentin. She'd barely gotten it out of her mind.

A person's childhood opened a door into who they were. Danica wished she'd been gone with Quentin to interview some of Cole's foster siblings. She fished out the appropriate folder and skimmed the file, not exactly knowing what she was looking for but hoping that something might jump out at her.

The file painted a picture of abuse and juvenile delinquency. None of the children living in the Dowling home at the same time as Cole had remained unscathed, though he seemed to have suffered the worst, both before and after he was taken from his birth parents. No sexual abuse, but Cole was exposed to every other kind. He had three broken bones before his tenth birthday. All reported as "sports injuries" — interesting considering he was never allowed to play on a team.

Lizzie and Jim came from abusive homes as well, though while Lizzie saw her new life as an escape, Jim saw it as more unearned punishment in a dismal life he didn't deserve. Both were arrested for petty theft, but Lizzie let it end there while Jim kept escalating and eventually ended up with a short stint in juvie. Matt wasn't a bad kid, according to his file, but he was truant a lot. There were more than a dozen cases of his getting caught red-handed having skipped school with his friends. Funny that he became a teacher. Only Tuesday seemed to have survived her childhood without getting into any trouble with the law.

Danica's heart ached for all five children. Any one of them could have easily been her client under different circumstances, but sexual abuse always hit her the worst. It obliterated a childhood, then became the cancer that often ruined the rest of a person's life.

Clients reinforced what Danica had learned on her way to becoming a behavioral therapist. Sexual abuse in childhood often led to higher levels of depression, guilt, shame, and self-blame, not to mention eating and sleeping disorders, heightened anxiety, repression and denial, dissociative patterns, and difficulty connecting with others.

Or as Danica thought of it, *the whole mess.*

Prior to her stay with the Dowlings, Tuesday had been molested, from the time she was seven until her thirteenth birthday — the day she announced the truth to everyone at her party. It was the first one she'd ever had, and Tuesday had organized it herself. Invited a bunch of her friends over, because what could her parents do once everyone was already there?

Most of her family members had known what was happening, and no one had ever done a single thing to stop it. One of her father's friends had even said she was "old enough to start growing into it."

Jim had been sexually abused as well, by both his mother and father.

Lizzie was malnourished to the point of starvation by the time CPS took the child away from her junkie mother.

Matt seemed to be the luckiest among them, if fortune was found in getting a new place to live, courtesy of the state after his parents were convicted of robbing a series of gas stations.

But still, despite all the obvious misery, Danica didn't see anything in the files that said, *I'm a serial killer.* If the copycat was one of Cole's foster siblings, then whatever tipped them over the edge had to have happened after they'd aged out of the system.

She pulled Quentin's notes out of the folder and began to read them. Full summaries of his most recent interviews with the foster siblings. He hadn't made it to Varney yet, but he had seen Jim, Lizzie, and Tuesday.

He didn't like Jim for the copycat, despite his anger issues. Lizzie apparently had a crush on Cole. And Tuesday might be the only one in the group with her head on straight.

Danica sighed, returning the notes to the folder and

then the folder to the box. She could dig deeper, but not until after a hot shower and some coffee.

While returning the folder, Danica saw the photo of the engagement ring, and studied it, feeling like there was something she was missing.

The ring didn't fit with anything else. It was hard to see Cole as a romantic … but what if he had loved someone in his own twisted way? According to Quentin, Cole was on track to manage that Nissan Dealership right across from the IKEA over in Carson. He'd even bought a three-bedroom house before he began to treat liquor like water and burned his life to the ground.

A three-bedroom was an odd purchase for a single man, especially one with no ambition. What if Cole was getting ready to ask someone to settle down with him and start a family?

What if that person's rejection was the thing that finally sent him over the edge? A stressor that pushed him to kill?

According to all the interviews and notes that she'd seen, Cole had no girlfriend, or even an ex, at the time of his arrest. Nobody who knew him knew of any significant others in his life.

What if it was Lizzie? Or Tuesday?

The more she considered it, the more Danica regretted not canceling yesterday's appointments.

She took the photo and slid it into the pocket of her borrowed shorts.

She closed the lid and slid the box a foot away from her, then stood from the sofa. She was dying for that coffee and shower, but she should probably say good morning first.

But closer to Quentin's room she could hear the water running. His being in the shower made it an excellent time for her to grab something else to wear. Another tee to make it through the morning, before she drove somewhere to buy a bunch of shit she didn't really want.

Danica went through the first few drawers, but they didn't have she was looking for at all. A lot of V-necks and white undershirts. Quentin had quite the collection of 90s concert tees. One of those would do.

She found them in the bottom drawer, and rifled through the collection. There were more than she had imagined — the drawer was practically stuffed. The bigger bands like Nirvana, Pearl Jam, and Alice In Chains were all represented, as were a few of the smaller samples of the Seattle sound, like Mudhoney and The Melvins.

But there, at the very bottom of the drawer, underneath a mountain of cotton, Danica found something she wasn't looking for, didn't mean to find, and filled her with a lightning strike of memory.

The bolt landed in the back of her skull, ripped its way through her body, and left her staring at the wadded cotton in her hand, wondering what it meant.

Smashing Pumpkins. Mellon Collie and the Infinite Sadness. A bootleg shirt, obviously bought outside the auditorium like most of Quentin's mementos. This one read, *The Shrine Auditorium, 1996.*

The image kept strobing in front of her eyes, no matter how hard she tried to blink it away. Mom in that same shirt, kissing her knees like a nightgown, failing to hide her hard nipples. Hair in a flurry, makeup running, and guilt like a pall on her body.

"Hey, hon … you need anything?"

Danica looked up, yanked out of her memory, or whatever it was. Uncle Quent was standing in the bathroom doorway with a towel around his waist.

Her heart was pounding. Her palms were sweating. Her world as she knew it was falling apart.

She held up the shirt, now bunched in her fist. "What is this?"

Quentin gave her a smile, but she would swear it seemed uneasy. "Smashing Pumpkins at the Shrine. Great show."

"I remember my mom wearing this shirt." Then, as much as it hurt, she added, "*Only this shirt.*"

Quentin looked socked in the jaw. He tightened his grip on the towel and carefully chose his next words. "Your mother was at a friend's house that night. I had to call her after rescuing you."

Danica shook her head and looked up at him in disbelief.

But she couldn't get herself to say anything.

"I'm not sure what's happening here," Quentin said, "but Cole is putting lies into your head. You need to stay away from him, and out of this investigation until it's over."

She nodded and pretended to agree.

But her Uncle Quent was a liar, and now Danica knew exactly what she had to do.

Chapter Twenty-Five

QUENTIN

Stupid bullshit goddamned fucking morning.

Quentin wanted to scream, but since that would only unsettle him further, he let Cobain take care of the howling for him. "Territorial Pissings" from *Nevermind*, the album that kicked all that crappy hair metal off the charts and into the dustbin of history where it belonged.

Just because you're paranoid, doesn't mean they're not after you.

He had to find a way, a better way. Because *FUCK*, Danica was asking him too many questions.

And Quentin couldn't even have a moment to collect himself. Instead he was on his way to the FBI briefing with a box full of evidence that he wanted to go through again at least one more time to make sure it only contained copies and nothing he'd omitted from turning over two decades ago. He was pretty sure he took out those items last night, but still one more time couldn't hurt. But Danica staying over had thrown a wrench in his plans.

And then this morning happened.

Why had he even kept that stupid tee?

Except that wasn't the right question. Quentin knew

perfectly well *why* he had done it, he just had no excuse for being so stupid. Sure, it was evidence of what really happened that night, but he never really believed that Danica would remember that particular detail, if anything. To him, it was one of the only reminders he would ever have of the woman he lost, along with his partner, who just also happened to be that woman's husband.

What a fucking mess.

And now the FBI would be picking at his scab, publicly.

He parked, grabbed the box from the passenger seat, then got out and walked toward the precinct, ignoring everything and everyone, same as he had the last several times he'd come or gone from work. Quentin had been a great detective, and took his role as deputy chief seriously.

Exactly when had everything started turning to shit?

He was two minutes early, but he might as well have been two hours late. Simpson and Merrill were already in the chief's office, waiting along with Rowan and Tyler.

"Morning gentleman," Quentin said to the room.

"Deputy Chief Porter." Everyone nodded his way, but Rowan spoke.

Then Tyler tipped his chin at the box. "That our missing evidence?"

"It wasn't missing. It's copies of shit you already have access to. Plus my most recent notes."

That answer apparently irritated Rowan. He tossed his partner a look that already felt like a splinter in Quentin's skin.

"Well then, let's get started," Tyler said.

It wasn't much of a briefing, and if Quentin had been feeling more like a deputy chief, he might have mentioned that there wasn't anything said in person that couldn't have been handled in a five-minute email.

Simpson and Merrill had little to report, and nothing of consequence. They had looked into the protestors, and all of the people Cole had been in contact with while in prison. Much ado about barely anything. The murderer was famous and had apparently developed quite an impressive following. Corresponded with a lot of people. But none of those pen pals had led to a single person of interest.

Quentin attempted to report his findings, but Rowan and Tyler agreed that he was only wasting his time.

"We'll take it from here," Rowan said.

"What do you mean, you'll 'take it from here'?" Quentin glanced at his box of evidence, which was now apparently in FBI custody. "This is my case, and I still have subjects to—"

"We can take care of the interviews," Tyler said, humiliating Quentin in front of his detectives.

"I'd like to finish what I started. Matt Varney still needs—"

"This case hasn't been handled appropriately." Rowan pounded a nail into the coffin of Quentin's thought. "Like I said, we'll take it from here."

Fine. Whatever. Quentin didn't need to stick around for this bullshit. They couldn't stop him from interviewing Varney, and he didn't need the box of evidence to do it. He'd taken photos of his most recent notes.

Quentin nodded to all four men in the room. "Just let me know if there's any way I can help."

"We'll make sure to do that," Rowan said, though it sounded suspiciously like *Fuck you.*

Quentin drew a deep breath, then left the chief's office, irritated that Simpson and Merrill were staying behind.

He tried to put it out of his head. He would be at the high school and talking to Varney before the hour was over. Maybe he'd leave with a lead that would make this all worth it.

But Luther was out in the parking lot, waiting in front of his Explorer.

Goddammit. This fucking guy.

"Deputy Chief Porter," Luther said, looking him up and down.

"Sorry, I'm just on my way out." Quentin wanted to open his driver's side door, but the producer was blocking his way. At least he wasn't with his crew this time.

"Where are you going?" Luther asked, like it was any of his goddamned business.

"Open investigation. You know I can't tell you."

"Something to do with the copycat case?"

"Of course. What else?"

"It's my understanding that the FBI is taking over, and that you're no longer working the investigation … is that true?"

That didn't feel like something Luther should know, let alone be able to rattle off like it was something he just read on Buzzfeed.

"I'm still the deputy chief of this precinct. I have plenty of work to—"

"Can I level with you?" Luther asked.

"I don't know … can you?"

The producer gave him a dry smile. "Being in prison, Linus Cole has a much more agreeable schedule than you do."

"What's that supposed to mean?"

"It means that we have plenty of footage with him, but barely any with you." Luther took a moment to let that sink in, but Quentin got his meaning fine. "Do you really want us to focus on telling Cole's side of this story, or would you like a chance to tell yours?"

Well, put that way, Quentin didn't really have much of a choice. "Where's your crew?"

Luther glanced toward the precinct. "I asked one of your men if we could borrow a spare conference room. They're all set up and waiting. It was my job to see if I could get you to agree so—"

"Fine," Quentin said, feeling coerced into giving the producer exactly what he wanted. He turned away from the Explorer and started walking back toward the precinct.

Five minutes later, Quentin was sitting on his side of a table with a bottle of water in a room full of lights, cameras, and the action of everyone staring down at him. The spare area was less personal than his office, much too similar to an interrogation room.

Luther started by asking a couple of questions that no one would ever care about and surely weren't intended to make the final cut. They were the producer trying to loosen his tongue. Things got more serious about five minutes in.

"Can you tell us the story about how you and Miles Tate caught Cole?"

"You mean *again*?" Quentin asked.

"You've told the story a lot, but I've never heard it first-hand. It would really help me out to hear you tell it now."

"Of course." Quentin smiled. For the cameras, not Luther. "We got our first big break in the case after real-izing that the three victims were all people who had known Linus Cole in some capacity."

"Were there any other links between the victims, or only their association with Cole?"

"Only their association with Cole."

"And how did you arrive at that conclusion?" Luther asked.

"Cole was an alcoholic, and his drinking caused him to

start making mistakes. We found a cigarette butt at the third murder site with his DNA on it. The sample was both scorched and wet by the time we got it, so we couldn't arrest him. But it was the best lead we had up until that point, and it gave us plenty to go on."

"How did you know that Miles was on the Magistrate's kill list?"

Luther's latest was drawn from the top spot on Quentin's list of frequently asked questions, and one of the ones he enjoyed answering most.

"It was a gut feeling, really. It just turned out to be right. I think part of it came from the instincts you get from life on the job, and seeing the atrocities people commit day after day. But I think the other part, and really the part that mattered most, was that Miles was my partner, and my best friend. That kind of bond goes beyond the evidence, you know? It's something you feel here," Quentin patted his stomach, then tapped his temple, "more than here."

"What happened after you got your 'gut feeling'?" Luther asked, both looking and sounding like he'd been sucking on a lemon rind.

"I raced to the Tates' as fast as I could. I was too late to save Miles, but I made it in time to rescue little Danica from what would have otherwise been a certain death."

"That was very fortunate," Luther said, back to deadpan.

"Damn right it was." Quentin bristled, acutely aware of his defensive-sounding voice. "Not only did we manage to save her life, she turned out to be a key witness and helped to put the murderer behind bars. Who knows how much longer Linus Cole would have been killing innocent people without Danica's testimony."

"You said *we* in reference to saving her life. But you were the only one at the scene, isn't that correct?"

"Police work is a collective effort." Quentin shook his head, irritated at Luther, this interview, and the entire situation. "This case has occupied a lot of my life, but it's never been about the fame."

"What *has* it been about?"

"Justice, of course." Quentin had offered that same answer plenty of times in the past, but it had never sounded so hollow.

"But you *did* become famous."

"Sure, but that was a result of the way this particular case unfolded, due to its nature and all of the media attention. It was never an objective."

"The Magistrate Murders were the foundation of your career, isn't that right?"

"I don't know about that," Quentin argued. "I had big cases both before and after the—"

"But nothing compared to this one, correct?"

He looked at Luther, unsure of how to respond.

"Do you think that you would have ever made deputy chief if you hadn't been so successful with such a high-profile case?"

"That's impossible to say." Then, a second later: "I'd like to think my other work speaks for itself."

"Would your other work have put you in line for the job as deputy chief?"

"How are these questions relevant?" Quentin wanted to yell.

"Would you agree that you owe your career to Linus Cole?"

"Absolutely not." He was furious, but needed to keep his temper in check. "I'm a deputy chief to the same medium-sized city I've served for decades. I didn't run off and get a job or pay bump elsewhere. I've devoted my life to keeping the citizens of Las Orillas safe, and that's what I would be doing now, regardless of my history with Linus Cole."

"What about—"

"And that's what I'll be doing right now," Quentin said, cutting Luther off as he removed the lav mic from his shirt, and terminated the interview. "In case you've forgotten, there's a murderer out there and I've got work to do."

"I'd really appreciate it if we could finish this now," Luther said. "I'd like to get your reactions to some of the things Cole has been telling us."

"Well, I'm sorry." His mic was dead, but the cameras were still rolling. "The rest of this interview will have to wait."

Then Quentin left the room without another word.

Chapter Twenty-Six

DANICA

DANICA WAS STANDING on Maria Foster's doorstep, holding a box of muffins and wondering if she should knock, ring the doorbell, or turn around and run away.

What was she hoping to accomplish by coming here? There were only two possibilities. Uncle Quent was either a liar, or he wasn't. One answer was worse than the other, but Danica would be opening the door to more misery no matter which one it turned out to be.

Maybe she should have called first. Her heart probably wouldn't be pounding so hard if she had. Doubts were falling like rain — or burning like fire — around her. Clients were calling and she was neglecting her duty, ignoring their pleas because she couldn't squeeze yet another problem into her overcrowded mind.

Her life was falling apart. And stupidly, part of Danica wanted yet another conversation with Cole. She would prefer an exchange with Mom, but heading to Morning Tide for yet another empty visit might kick her into the darkest part of the forest.

She knocked on the door, then went ahead and rang the bell a second later.

Then she waited for Maria to answer while wondering if she was doing the right thing.

Her doubt was crippling. She couldn't stop picturing her mother standing above her in that Smashing Pumpkins tee, or herself on the floor holding it and looking up at Quentin twenty years later. Everything inside her felt sure he was lying.

I remember my mom wearing this shirt ... Only this shirt.

Your mother was at a friend's house that night. I had to call her after rescuing you. Then, after Quentin accused Cole of filling her head with lies instead of accepting responsibility for doing the same thing himself, he made it worse. *Your mom was with Maria ... I'm sure I've told you that before.*

No, he hadn't.

Danica moved her muffins from one hand to the other, and was about to knock on the door again, but it swung open before she got a chance.

Maria was standing on the other side, looking back at her in wide-eyed surprise. "Danica! It's been forever. What are you doing here?" She shook her head. "I'm so sorry ... I mean, would you like to come in?"

Maria opened her door all the way. "I thought you were Jacquelyn. She brings me a fresh bouquet of garden roses every Saturday, and I pretend like she's not over-charging me."

Danica entered the house and handed Maria the box. "These are from The Muffin Man. Are zucchini still your favorite?"

"Wow," she said, taking the box. "They sure are. But I can't believe that you remember that."

"I guess I can remember some things better than others." The truth hurt as it left her lips.

"Wait until you're my age. I can remember what I had for breakfast on the day of Clinton's inauguration, but I'm not sure what I watched before bed last night without giving it fifteen minutes of serious thought."

"What did you have … the morning of Clinton's inauguration?"

Maria laughed. "I don't actually remember. But probably a bowl of Mueslix and half a grapefruit, that's what I had for breakfast most days back then." She glanced at the couch. "Why don't you take a seat and I'll make some tea?"

"Okay, thanks." Danica sat.

"How is your mother doing?"

"About the same."

"So … not good?" Maria shook her head. "I'm sorry to hear that."

"Sometimes she seems okay," Danica lied.

A shadow of sorrow hit Maria's face, but then she shook it away. "Well, thank you for visiting me. Leslie is living in Tucson, and Alex is married to some harpy who doesn't think a grandmother has any right to see her grandchildren, so I welcome every visitor I'm lucky enough to get." She smiled at Danica, then said, "I'll be right back."

Once her host was out of sight, and likely out of earshot, Danica stood from the couch, walked over to the mantle, and studied the neat row of pictures, stopping on one she'd seen many times before, but had never really, truly looked at until now.

The photo had Maria and Emilia, Quentin and Miles. They all looked so young, with smiles that seemed light years away from the people Danica knew. One of them dead and another clinically insane, leaving behind only the elder and the liar.

Now that she had her doubts, Danica couldn't help but wonder if her mother looked so happy because she was with her husband, or because she was with his partner. Emilia stood right in between them. Quentin on one side and Miles on the other, Maria slightly apart.

She remembered her parents fighting lot. Maybe *too much,* or so she had always thought while growing up, even more so after her father's murder. Only on the way to becoming a behavior therapist, followed by time with actual clients, did Danica finally realize that her parents were normal. Only the specifics offered any distinction between their arguments and the typical marital spats.

Plenty of couples fought about how much one spouse might be working, but Danica's dad was a cop. So Miles and Emilia didn't just argue about the number of hours he put in, their quarrels were more about his levels of unnecessary risk. But Quentin worked just as much as his partner, and was subject to the same peril. So maybe Danica was being ridiculous. Maybe Uncle Quent was telling the truth. Cole *had* managed to worm his way inside her mind and plant a false memory. Play on her subconscious fears and get her imagination doing enough damage to destroy everything that actually mattered.

"That was always one of my favorite pictures!" Maria said.

Danica turned toward the sound of her return and saw Maria entering the living room with a tray of tea and cups.

She set her tray onto the coffee table. It was an old-fashioned set, including a bowl of sugar and a pitcher of cream. "Come …" She pointed to the sofa. "Sit."

Danica left the mantle, took a seat, and waited for Maria to fix her tea. A splash of cream and a teaspoon of sugar, just like she wanted without even asking.

"So …" Maria started, picking up her own teacup and taking a sip. "Of course I've seen the news. I imagine you're here because of what's happening with these new killings, and not because you've been dying to give an old woman some company."

Danica offered her an awkward smile. "Sorry, I wish it was better circumstances."

Maria smiled back. "I have no idea how I could possibly help you, but of course I'm happy to do whatever I can."

Danica swallowed, then drew a shallow breath.

This shouldn't be so hard …

Then finally: "I've been thinking a lot about the night my father died. I was hoping that maybe you could shed some light on what happened …"

Maria looked sympathetic. Her mouth turned down in a frown as she shook her head. "I only know what was in the papers. Your mother took it all so terribly, we didn't even really ever get to talk after that. She was never the same … not that I can blame her."

"Uncle Quent said that Mom was with you the night he died."

Everything changed. Her expression, her voice, and even the way Maria was sitting. "Did he?" She shook her head again, but this time it was different, seeming almost forced. "I'm not sure I can recall."

"He seemed pretty sure of it."

"It was a long time ago," Maria said.

"Still, that sure seems like something you would remember."

"Either way, I can't see how it matters now."

"It matters to me."

Maria sighed. "I do understand your need to put those

pieces together, but it isn't going to help you feel better all these years later."

"I appreciate your concern, but that isn't for you to decide. Are you going to answer my question or not?"

Maria added some sugar to her tea that it surely didn't need, then sipped, saying nothing, maybe waiting for Danica to thicken her query.

"If my mother wasn't with you, then where was she?"

"How should I know?" Maria shook her head, looking like a liar. "It's not like we had apps to know where everyone was back then."

"Why wasn't she home with my dad?"

"You're assuming I know things that—"

"I think you *do* know, Maria. And I'm asking for you to please help me right now."

Maria looked at her. Took a sip. "Marriage is a complicated thing, dear."

That would have sounded patronizing enough without the *dear.* That last part made Danica want to hurl her teacup against the wall, just to hear it shatter.

"My mother was sleeping with Quentin, wasn't she?"

Maria took another sip, then she set her teacup on the coffee table. Her silence was long after that, punctuated with a deep sigh at the end. "You mustn't judge, dear."

"*Judge what?*" Danica tried to sound pleasant, but that was hard to do through gritted teeth.

"Your father was a good man, and a good father ..."

"*But?*"

"But he didn't understand your mother."

Danica thought she was prepared. When she'd decided to drive over to Maria's, when she'd knocked on her door and rang the bell, and while she was staring at the picture taken during a time she was desperately trying to understand. And she still thought she was prepared when asking Maria the question a moment ago.

But the answer was no less a punch to the gut. Danica had to collect her breath and remind herself that she didn't want to die. Only after Maria finally delivered the truth did she realize how much she had been clinging to the hope that Cole was lying. Because that would mean that Quentin could still be telling the truth.

"How long?" Danica asked.

Maria picked up her teacup and took a sip. "Your mother was getting ready to end it."

"How long?"

"Quentin wanted Emilia to leave Miles. Begged her to. And honestly, that's what part of your mother wanted. But she was never willing to put you through that."

"I'll have to remember to thank her for—"

"She's been punished enough, Danica," Maria said, sounding suddenly furious. "Don't you dare lay anything else on her!"

Danica leaned back, suddenly needing another sip of her tea. "How can you defend her, knowing the truth?"

"Because — some things are more important than the truth."

Danica shook her head. "This isn't fair. I've been looking for answers all my life, only to find out that—"

"I think we're done here. I'm sorry I couldn't help you more, but I have things to do."

"You can still help me."

"I'm sorry, but I can't. I told you everything I know, and I'm quite sure that's done nothing good." Maria stared at her, obviously wanting her to leave.

"Enjoy the muffins," Danica said, standing to go, wanting to cry, but holding back her tears.

She let them all go in the car, weeping as she turned

the engine, reeling at the reality that the adults in her life had lied to her. The people she trusted most had betrayed her.

Only Linus Cole had looked Danica in the eye and told her the truth.

Chapter Twenty-Seven

QUENTIN

"Sure thing, Deputy Chief Porter," said the officer on duty, directing Quentin into the school's visitor lot and nodding at his superior. "You have a great day."

Quentin parked, thinking about his time in high school and how different things used to be. Pike had a half-dozen cars assigned to the perimeter every day. Metal detectors at the school's only entrance, a separate visitor's lot, high fences that made the place look less like a campus than a prison, and teachers who were finding it harder and harder to care.

Thirty years ago, teachers taught and students generally had a clue what was going on. Instructors took the time to make sure their kids understood the materials, instead of simply teaching to the test. Smartphones ruined education, along with the unions and general apathy that lay like a blanket on the nation. Before Google, Forage, and every other search engine, kids used encyclopedias and their brains.

It was hard to know if today's students were actually

dumber, or just lazier. Graduation rates in Las Orillas were at an all-time low, especially in this part of the city, where pregnancy or gang initiation kept too much of the student body away from their caps and gowns. The link between crime and education was constantly discussed, even if few leaders seemed to be doing much about it.

But Las Orillas high schools still had one thing that many other of the country's campuses were missing, and that Quentin appreciated for the nuts and bolts instruction: shop class.

Home economics and shop had been two of his favorite classes in high school. Together they taught him sewing and cooking, woodwork and metal-craft. He'd never once sewn outside of that class, but he still loved cooking to this day. And three decades later, he still felt a sense of pride remembering his pen box, and could still imagine the sounds and smells of that class. Noisy equipment that made him feel like an artist, more than any art class ever had.

The nature of high school had changed, where skilled trades were now undervalued or eliminated entirely. Academia saw carpenters, electricians, machinists, and mechanics as lesser-than.

Craftsman like Tuesday Howe were looked down on, but Quentin had often thought that if he hadn't made his living as an officer of the law, he might have done it with his hands.

Interesting that Tuesday did what Varney taught.

Quentin checked in with the front office, then was led to Varney's classroom.

His student escort, a boy with long hair hanging in his face, stopped in front of the open door. "Lunch is half over, but Mr. Varney should be in there. Want me to go in with you?"

"Thanks, but I've got it from here."

The kid gave him a nod and then practically darted away, probably glad to have a few unaccounted minutes before returning to the office.

He quietly entered the classroom, hoping to get a look at Varney unseen. Mission accomplished: the teacher was sitting at his desk, writing something as Quentin watched from the doorway.

Even sitting, he could tell that Varney was tall and muscular. He clearly worked out, and was also impeccably groomed. Quentin would have cast him as an English teacher, or maybe an art teacher. Shop might have been last on a long list and entirely absent on a short one.

Varney stopped writing and looked over toward the door. He saw Quentin standing in the threshold and appeared almost startled. He dropped his pen and stood.

"May I help you?"

"Matt Varney?"

He nodded. "And you are?"

But Quentin could tell by his eyes that he knew. Or remembered.

"I'm Deputy Chief Porter, with the Las Orillas Police Department. We talked about twenty years ago. I just have a few questions."

Varney rounded his desk and started walking toward Quentin. "I know my rights. I'm not obligated to talk without a lawyer."

"Technically, yes, that's true," Quentin said, surprised by how immediately Varney was on the defensive. "But you are obligated to submit to formal questioning if I insist, and I thought it would be simpler if you gave me a few minutes of your time right now, then I can get out of your hair and leave you to go about the rest of your day."

"What do you want to know?" Matt crossed his arms.

"I'm not trying to bother you, Mr. Varney. I'm just hoping to get a few answers, and hopefully save some lives." Quentin walked past the shop teacher, over toward a shelf full of finished projects. He picked up what looked like a small shoe rack.

"Please put that down."

Quentin gave the shoe rack an admiring glance, then set it back on the shelf. "When was the last time you had any contact with Linus Cole?"

"I don't remember." Varney snorted. "I suppose it was the last day I was living with the Dowlings."

"And what year was that?"

Varney seemed to think, but apparently the math was difficult enough that he couldn't deliver an approximate date. "I moved in with a buddy junior year."

"Your file says that the Dowlings received checks for you until you turned eighteen. Is that not correct?"

"We had an understanding," Varney said.

"And what kind of understanding was that?"

"Maggie agreed not to hassle me if I kept quiet. So for two whole years, mum was the word."

"Are you telling me there was no accountability? You just disappeared and the Dowlings kept getting their checks?"

"She had Abed's number and would call when there was something I had to show up for, but yeah, that was pretty much how things were."

"*Pretty much*," Quentin repeated, now standing in front of another shelf on the other side of the room, still trying to keep the shop teacher off balance. He picked up a small piece of polished wood, maybe some sort of holder for a smart phone.

"Can you please put that down … and leave the students' work alone?"

Quentin returned the whatever to its shelf, then ran his hands over a handsome homemade box without picking it up. "Has Cole ever tried to get in touch with you?"

"Why would he do that?" Varney asked, approaching Quentin to close the distance between them.

"You tell me."

Varney shook his head, clearly agitated. "I stayed out of his way and he stayed out of mine."

"Seems like a smart arrangement with a guy like Cole. Anything you can tell me about—"

A student came charging into the room with a giant smile, but froze two steps inside as if he had slammed into an invisible wall. He looked from Varney to Quentin, flinching and perhaps even frightened. Tall and lanky.

"If you need help with your midterm project, you can come in early tomorrow. I'll be here before school." Varney smiled at the student.

But the kid seemed too scared to smile back. He offered his teacher a timid little nod, then made an about-face and practically ran out of the room.

Varney was working to keep his face indifferent, but it was flushed for sure.

"What's the project?" Quentin asked.

"I'm sorry?"

"The midterm project. I'm glad to hear that you're here to help your students. The world needs more teachers like you. So what's the project?"

"A step-stool. Now I need to get back to prepping today's lesson. Are we finished here?"

Quentin picked up a birdhouse, then set it down almost immediately, before Varney had a chance to correct him. "Jim said you did everything you could to stay out of Cole's way. Why?"

"He turned out to be a serial killer, didn't he?"

"Indeed." Quentin nodded. "But you didn't know that then, did you? Had you seen any signs that Cole was violent when he was younger?"

"Like I said, I stayed out of his way, and he stayed out of mine."

"So where did you go?"

"I stayed with friends."

"Friends like Abed?" Quentin asked.

"Sure. And Rick and Matt and Doug and Moe and Lisa. You need a list?"

"I might," Quentin said, though it wasn't a serious question. "Any of those friends know Cole?"

"No. That was the point." Varney glanced at the clock. "You planning to take my entire lunchtime?"

"Are you aware that there's a copycat killer on the loose?"

"I've seen the news."

"You're just not interested in helping the police?"

"I'm happy to help," Varney said. "But I'm not too sure that's what's happening here."

"What about your foster siblings?"

"What about them?"

"Do you think one of them might be working with Cole?"

Varney laughed.

"I take that as a *no*?"

"Seems like the right way to take it," Varney said.

"And why not?"

"Well, Jim couldn't fight his way out of a paper bag, let alone kill someone. Lizzie might be smarter than a bag of hammers, but not by much. And Tuesday's a selfish fucking bitch."

"Strong language," Quentin said. "Care to clarify?"

"She used to make Lizzie hand over her lunch like the second we got on the bus."

"So, when you say *selfish*, you mean *bully*."

"How about, *Tuesday Howe was a selfish bully*. Does that work?"

"So, just to be clear, you haven't kept in touch with any of them?"

"And again, *why would I do that*?"

"You say you've been watching the news?"

Varney nodded. "Enough to know what this is about, sure."

"So you know that there have been two new murders."

Another nod, but now more suspicious.

"Do you happen to have an alibi for either or both of those nights?"

Varney looked back at him, stone-faced. "Lawyer."

The bell rang before Quentin could draw his next breath.

And Varney had his words loaded and ready to go. "My next class is about to start, so unless you have questions about how to use a miter saw, this conversation is over."

"Don't leave town. We might need to have a follow-up soon."

"You know where to find me."

The two men traded a nod, then Quentin gave a final appreciative glance at the shelf full of finished projects and left the classroom.

A group of what appeared to be seniors were inspecting him as he left the room. He heard a chorus of *Five-Oh!* and *Get him!* as he walked down the hall.

Varney was definitely hiding *something*.

It was only a gut feeling. Nothing Quentin could use to

get a search warrant for his apartment. He was empty-handed for now, but he was inching forward, and more answers would be waiting at the precinct.

Hopefully, nothing else was.

Chapter Twenty-Eight

DANICA

"ANOTHER CUP?" Captain Jenkins asked Danica.

"Sure. Thanks. Why not?"

She paced the lobby of the precinct as her detail, two new cops she didn't know the names of, came inside. A young white guy and a slightly older black woman looked at her as they made their way to the receptionist's desk and were buzzed inside, to the offices in the back.

The woman paused at the doorway and turned to Danica. "Don't go anywhere without us."

Danica nodded, pacing.

She didn't know where Quentin was; neither did anyone else, it seemed. Furious as she was at him, Danica didn't want to get him in trouble. She wasn't about to ask either of the special agents poring over evidence in the chief's office, just in case Quentin was somewhere he shouldn't be, which seemed like a definite possibility.

She had never seethed quite like this, or been so caffeinated. Not even during the most brutal of her finals. But she had to keep drinking the coffee, it might be the only thing keeping Danica from wanting to kill her uncle.

No, he wasn't her uncle. He was just Quentin.

The man who had been lying to her for twenty years.

"Here you go," Jenkins said, handing Danica a fresh cup.

"Thanks. I know this isn't your job."

"It's fine. I promise." Then he disappeared behind a door next to the reception desk.

She took a seat on a cushioned bench, sipped, then stood and started pacing again, cursing Quentin in her head.

Maybe the precinct wasn't the best place to have their confrontation. Maybe she should head to the Svenson Skillet. The small family-owned restaurant had been home to several of their harder conversations. Talking there might feel more natural, less confrontational.

No. Danica set her coffee on a table between two benches. Talking to him there would ruin the Skillet forever. Pancakes and cinnamon roll French toast would remind her that the man she trusted most in the world was a dirty rotten liar.

"Danica ..." Quentin said as he stepped into the station and stopped in his tracks, surprised to see her.

"Can we talk?"

"Of course," he said, though the words didn't match his expression. He glanced at the receptionist's desk, then back at Danica. "Why don't we go for a walk?"

"After you." She nodded toward the door.

She was a gnarled ball of conflict. She wanted to scream her throat raw at him, but as much as she was loath to admit it, what she *really wanted* was for him to say something that would make everything okay. Same as he always had before.

If she couldn't trust him then, maybe she couldn't trust anyone.

And if she couldn't trust anyone, didn't that make her truly alone in this world?

They walked in an awkward silence in the parking lot until the precinct entrance was a hundred yards behind them.

Quentin stopped, well out of earshot of anybody. "So what's—"

"How could you lie to me?" The words left her mouth like a head-on collision.

Quentin looked like he wanted to flinch back, but instead he held his ground. "Whatever you're thinking, I'm sure there's an explanation."

"Oh, *I'm sure there is.*" She chewed on her next words, wanting to spit. "You always have a way of explaining everything, but I'm not letting you lie to me this time."

"I'm not going to lie …" He raised his hands in surrender. "Whatever this is, I'm happy to discuss it. But we're not going to get anywhere if you keep yelling at me. Why don't we start at the beginning. What is it you think—"

"I don't *think* anything. So let's start there — I'd like to talk about what I *know.*"

"And what do you know?" Quentin asked.

Danica had never seen him look more uncomfortable.

"I know you were having an affair with my mom!"

"Please," he said, looking past her as two cops got out of their cruiser across the way. "Can you keep your voice down?"

"That's how you want to respond to me right now? By asking me to—"

"I'm just asking that you keep this conversation between us. I'm happy to talk about this, but please don't forget where we are."

"Sorry if I'm embarrassing you at work!" she yelled even louder.

"It's not about embarrassing me, Danica. It's about not inviting any unwanted attention that might … Please, can you—"

"Refrain from asking you any difficult questions? Sorry, not going to happen."

Quentin sighed and managed to make her even more furious. "What makes you think your mother and I were having an affair?"

"You're still being evasive. Asking me a question when you promised me an answer."

"I'm a detective, Danica. I'm asking about your evidence."

"You already saw it this morning. You just lied when I asked you the first time."

"The T-shirt?" Quentin shook his head, looking incredulous. "I already told you, Cole is putting crap in your head and it's working. You're cracking under the strain. Perfectly understandable given the circumstances, but—"

"I talked to Maria!"

It was like God had pressed pause on Quentin's body. He didn't move and his expression appeared almost paralytic. But the windows to his soul were open, and in them Danica saw the truth.

He drew a slow and measured breath. Forever passed before he finally spoke.

"I loved your mother, and she loved me. What we had was between us."

"FUCK YOU!" Her fists were balled and she wanted to hit him.

Quentin stood there, still frozen, almost as if awaiting her strike. "You have every right to be angry, but this isn't what you think it is."

"THEN WHAT IS IT?"

"Please," again with the raised hands, "just keep your voice down. I don't think either of us wants anyone coming over right now."

"That's truer for you than me." But her voice fell from a nine to a four. "So go ahead and explain. Why were you fucking my mother behind my father's back?"

"We loved each other."

"Yeah, you said that. Get to the part about why you decided to be a lying piece of shit about it."

"We didn't—"

"Fuck you." Danica didn't let him finish his sentence. She might sock him in the jaw if he did.

He waited to see if she would yell at him any more, only opening his mouth again after several long moments of her huffing and puffing. "We didn't mean to hurt anyone. It was—"

"You always talked about how much you loved my father! How could you do that to him?"

"I did love Miles, Danica. More than anyone, except for your mother."

"Convenient."

He shook his head. "Things weren't good between your parents."

"I'm sure they were *real* terrible."

"You were too young—"

"What else was I too young to understand, *Uncle Quent*?"

"Emilia was going to leave him. She—"

"*Don't you dare.*" Danica let it sink in before she finished the thought. "You've lied to me my entire life."

"I didn't want to." He looked sincere and she hated him for it. "I always wanted to tell you the truth, even back then. But Emilia never wanted me to and I promised to respect her wishes."

"Again: *convenient.*"

"Maybe so, but it's the truth. Your mother was horrified by the thought that you might find out."

"So my mom's a liar, too." A cold blade slipping between her ribs. "Did my dad know?"

Quentin shook his head. "She was going to tell him."

"When?"

"She was going to leave him. It was—"

"You're lying!"

"I'm not."

"Maria said that she wasn't willing to do that to me."

"I don't care what Maria said. It's the truth. Sure, she went back and forth for a long time. But we were past the point of no return by the time Cole was in the picture. Stress was at an all-time high, and your parents were *always* fighting. So we were making plans, figuring out a way to break things to Miles, and take care of you."

"Thanks, Uncle Quent — *I feel so special!*"

"I understand how you're feel—"

"Do you?" Danica glared at him.

He looked down at the ground, then back into her eyes. "I think I have some idea."

"You made me a liar."

"I might have lied to you, but that doesn't mean that I made you a liar."

Wanting to yell, but growling through clenched teeth instead: "You forced me to lie under oath to keep people from finding out."

"I was trying to protect you."

Danica scoffed, shaking her head. "You've gotta be fucking kidding me."

Quentin didn't respond.

"You coached me to say that Mom came later, when you knew it wasn't true."

"Like I said, it was for your own good."

"A man went to prison because I lied under oath."

"*A murderer,* Danica. A murderer is off the streets, and you are safe. My relationship with your mother had nothing whatsoever to do with the case, or me doing my job. Linus Cole was guilty, and he needed to be put away."

"Maybe that's what you've been telling yourself, but it isn't the truth, Quent. Your relationship might not have had anything to do with the case, but it had *everything* to do with the trial. You changed my testimony."

"He murdered your father, Danica! This was—"

"How can I ever trust you?"

"I'm sorry that I didn't tell you the truth about this one thing, but it was always—"

"How much of your story was a lie?"

"I told you, your mother asked me to keep our relationship a secret. I don't understand why you feel the need to—"

"Know the truth? Maybe I deserve it. Maybe *that's* why I 'feel the need.'" Danica stared at him, her fury going nowhere. "So what else have you lied to me about?"

"I've always been honest with you, except for this one little detail. I've always tried to do the honorable thing."

"*This one little detail?*" Danica threw her hands in the air and rattled artificial laughter. "You've gotta be fucking kidding me. Is this what you call 'the honorable thing'?"

"Considering my promise to your mother, yes. I do."

"She's been in Morning Tide for twenty years. You're really sticking to that story? That in all that time you could never tell me the truth, even though I deserved to know it, because of an old promise you never should have made in the first place?"

Quentin sighed, and Danica saw what might have been honesty lighting his eyes. "I couldn't tell you, because you're too much like your father."

"What's that supposed to mean?"

"That you couldn't see the forest for the trees."

"My father wasn't a coward. He would have told the truth, no matter what it cost him."

"Exactly. And Cole would have gone free."

"So … perjury wouldn't have put him in jail?"

"*So*, he would have come after you and Emilia." Quentin shook his head, frustrated with her even though he had no right to be. "I saved you, Danica. And your—"

"Oh, right. Now I get it. You're the hero of this story. Sorry it's taken me so long to see things clearly. I'm glad that I have you to show me the way, just like always."

"Go home, Danica."

"I don't have a home."

"You know what I mean. My home is your home. Always has been and always will be. You need to stay safe. And the detail will watch you."

"I think they're inside eating donuts or whatever you all do in the back. Besides, I want to finish talking about this."

"We can talk about it later. I promise."

"You mean after you've had all day to think up another lie?"

"No, I mean after I've finished my work, and when you're feeling more rational."

"So *I'm* the problem here? *I'm* not being rational?"

"That's not what I'm saying."

"It's what you *just said*," she said, her voice higher than she'd intended, eroding her argument that she wasn't being emotional.

He took her hands, but Danica yanked them away.

She turned and walked away without looking back, feeling betrayed and wishing that she'd never started digging. She got in her car and took off, fuck her detail.

Maybe sometimes it really was better to believe the lies, miserable as they might be.

Chapter Twenty-Nine

QUENTIN

FUCK.

Quentin stood at the edge of the precinct parking lot, watching Danica's truck shrink until she disappeared, rounding the corner and out of the parking lot.

The fight was his fault, even if it wasn't.

Danica clearly didn't believe him, but every word was true.

His relationship with Emilia was a largely irrelevant detail. He had saved Danica and her mom from Cole, who would have gone free and come after them both. She did have a home with him, and always would.

And she was obviously being irrational, even if Danica didn't — or couldn't — see it.

He sighed, looked around the lot, and wondered what to do.

Why had he even come back? He should be following up on Varney. Even a first-year detective could see that the well-coiffed shop teacher was clearly up to something.

Quentin looked from the Explorer to the precinct,

decided to quickly check in before leaving again, and made it four steps toward the front entrance when his phone chirped with Simpson's ring.

"Porter."

"Hey, boss." Simpson exhaled.

"Don't tell me …" Quentin already knew. "We have another body."

"Same MO as the other two."

He swallowed, not wanting to hear what was next. "Do we know the vic?"

"Grant Eggars."

The foreman of the jury that convicted Cole.

"I thought we had people on potential vics."

"He didn't want protection."

"Fuck. Text me the address. I'm on my way."

He slammed the Explorer door and started the engine. Sugar Ray was singing about wanting to fly in the sky like a birdy, but that was a bullshit song and always had been, so Quentin killed the radio as he dipped out of the lot and stuck to the silence all eight miles to his final destination.

What a fucking day. He tried to wall off thoughts of Danica, thinking about Varney on his way to the latest crime scene instead, wondering how long the newest body had been there.

"STRANGE PLACE for a murder like this one," Simpson said without turning as Quentin approached.

He couldn't disagree. Conifer Street was once a red-light district, back when the Navy docked in Las Orillas. Back then the boulevard had been filled with brothels the authorities pretended didn't exist. Now it was lined with some of the city's pricier restaurants, and refurbished lofts in the shells of what used to be sweat shops before the big earthquake in the 30s.

"He's never been so public about it," Quentin said, looking down at the corpse in a roped-off alley between an Italian restaurant and a hair salon. "How long has the body been here?"

"That's the thing," Simpson said. "Looks like it was dumped here this morning."

"So Eggars was killed somewhere else, then—"

"Captain Porter." He recognized Rowan's voice before he turned around.

"Gentlemen," Quentin said, to both Rowan and Special Agent Tyler standing beside him.

"We'll take it from here," Tyler told him.

"I'd like to—"

"We'll take it from here," Rowan repeated, cutting Quentin off.

Simpson looked at him helplessly as Merrill came over to join them. He opened his mouth, looking ready to deliver some news, but snapped it shut when he saw the standoff happening in front of him.

"Keep me updated," Quentin said to Simpson, before turning and walking away.

Fucking FBI. This was his case, and for more than the usual reasons. They should see him as an asset instead of as someone standing in their way. He barely got a glimpse. Quentin saw Eggar's burned-out body, the *GUILTY* stamped in blood on his forehead, and even the burned fingertips. But there wasn't time to note anything else, and he had no way of applying what he saw to the rest of what he already did and didn't know. If there was a differentiator separating this murder from the others, Quentin had no idea of what that might be.

The special agents couldn't kick him out of his car, so he surveyed the scene from his driver's seat. He watched a cluster of journalists crowding around the cordoned-off area, his humiliation growing as he watched Tyler addressing them.

No one even seemed to know he was there. A few days ago that same cluster would have chased him six blocks to hang on his every goddamned word. What in the hell had happened?

Maybe it was a good thing. Something was obviously wrong with him if he actually *missed* being hounded by journalists. Though that really wasn't what bothered him. It was the warped perception. Danica had been mocking him when she said he was the hero of this story. But in truth, he had been, for twenty years. That narrative had apparently changed overnight, and Quentin was trapped in this new one.

It appeared as if people were actively looking for a reason not to believe him. And that hadn't started with the copycat. Luther had been playing hardball with him before the first new body was found.

Maybe this was his fault. Maybe Quentin had grown complacent. Maybe he was supposed to make everyone remember instead of assuming they would.

The solution was as simple as doing his job. Quentin could catch the copycat, just like he caught the original killer two decades ago. Then no one could ever doubt his proper place in this story again.

Unfortunately, staying at the front of this investigation would be difficult, if not altogether impossible now that the FBI had cut him out of the loop.

He started the engine and turned on the radio. Heard the opening notes to *Basket Case* as he went to put the SUV in drive, and nearly jumped out of his seat at the sound of a slap on his window.

He looked over and saw Tabitha Keane, waving to get his attention. She slapped the window again, as if he could have possibly missed her signal the first time.

Quentin lowered his window. "What do you want, Tabitha?"

He couldn't believe he was actually engaging this woman in conversation. The prospect would have seemed unbelievable a week ago. She wasn't a reporter, she was a bottom-feeding buzzard from *GOTCHA!*, a tabloid that didn't even make a lazy attempt at pretending to be anything else.

"A story, what else?" Tabitha looked back at all the cops and reporters, then back to Quentin sitting in his car. "The FBI told me to leave. I saw you talking to them a few minutes ago. Did they tell you the same thing?"

"I'm the deputy chief. Do you really think the FBI told me to scram?"

"I do, but I can see how that might be embarrassing. Want to give me something else to tell my readers?"

"How about linking to another website with actual news? Don't you have a celebrity wardrobe malfunction or something to cover?"

"I don't need a lot, Port. Just give me a nibble and I'll leave you alone."

"We ever share a drink or a meal or maybe talk about the weather?"

She shook her head. "Can't say you've ever invited me any—"

"Then don't call me Port."

"*Deputy Chief* Porter," Tabitha said, now sounding almost comically professional. "Can you tell me anything that I don't already know, either on or off the record?"

"I doubt it, but I guess that depends on what you know." He was buying time, still unsure of what to say, torn between telling Tabitha that he honestly didn't know shit because the FBI had cut him out, maybe rousing some support from a local fanbase who might object to — or hopefully even protest — his removal, and toeing the line by telling her that he couldn't reveal anything about the investigation that the FBI hadn't already made public.

"I'm sure you know I can't say anything about an open investigation," Quentin said.

"So will the FBI be updating us later?"

"I imagine that's the case."

"You don't know?" Tabitha raised her eyebrows.

"This is their investigation now."

"Is that a matter of … competence?"

"Of course not. It's a matter of jurisdiction."

"Does that mean there's a serial killer in another state that might be linked to this one?"

"That's not my place to comment."

"Right … it's for the FBI." Tabitha stole a glance behind her, then lowered her voice even more. "It's been a while since you've been in the field, hasn't it?"

"I'm in the field right now."

Her gaze moved from Quentin to his steering wheel. "Are you?"

"Do you have a point?"

"Deputy chief is a desk job, isn't it?"

He shook his head, unwilling to let her bait him further. "You're fishing in the wrong pond, Tabitha."

Then Quentin rolled up the window, put the SUV in drive, and slowly rolled away from her, surveying the scene as he turned back onto Conifer.

He didn't make it far. Threw the Explorer back into park when he saw Merrill approaching the SUV with what looked like bags full of evidence.

He got out of the SUV, jogged over to Merrill, and pulled the detective aside.

"Sorry about that back there, boss," Merrill said.

"Not your fault. Anything you can tell me?"

Merrill shook his head. "Nope, sorry, but I'll let you know if we find anything."

"Nothing at all?" Quentin pressed.

He shrugged. "The Feds pulled a few leads from a couple of whack-jobs who wrote Cole some fan mail during his time in prison, but none of the pen pals were local when the first murders happened and nothing's panned out so far."

"What are they saying?"

"Same as us for now. That maybe the fact that we keep coming up empty with the original case files is because the copycat is really just a distant admirer, instead of someone directly connected to Cole. Or maybe Mr. Magistrate told another prisoner some of the details that weren't in the news, and they've since become common knowledge. Problem with that is that death row inmates are kept away from gen-pop, so anyone he would've gotten to know is still in there, not free. We checked to make sure there'd been no releases."

Quentin agreed. Everything about this felt closer to the bone.

But he nodded and clapped Merrill on his shoulder anyway. "Thanks for the update. You'll tell me more when you can?"

Merrill nodded, looking ever-so-slightly uncertain. "Sure thing, boss. When I can."

Quentin turned around and walked back toward the Explorer, thinking.

No way this copycat wasn't related. Past and the

present were part of a whole, Quentin just needed to see more of the picture before he could understand how everything fit. He needed to take a deeper look into Cole's foster siblings, and knew exactly where to start.

Quentin had zero doubt: Matt Varney was hiding something.

Chapter Thirty

DANICA

DANICA KNOCKED on Lizzie's door. A soft knock, sounding almost like practice. Maybe she wasn't ready.

She knocked again. Louder, readier this time.

She glanced around at the two rows of townhomes lining either side of a little hidden street, a few miles up from the coast. A patch of dirt and lawn that looked a lot like low-income housing, if there was such a thing in, or anywhere near, Cielo Del Mar. The tiny neighborhood was an artifact from a time before Orange County was slang for *money* and would surely see a bulldozer soon. There weren't many patches around Newport Beach and Balboa Island left to develop. Someone owned a goldmine. The place was waiting for a gate, guards, and a hundred McMansions.

The door opened and she found herself looking at a woman who was already eyeing her with layers of suspicion. She had a decade or so on Danica, but those years had been hard, and the brutality appeared in her eyes and in the tight lines on either side of her mouth.

"Elizabeth Wondrush?" Danica said.

"Lizzie. And you must be Daria Tate."

"Danica," she corrected.

"Sorry. *Danica*. I saw you on the news a few nights ago."

"Oh?"

"You were getting mobbed in front of Coldwater, after you went to visit Linus."

"That was me." Danica smiled, uncomfortable and wanting to get off of the woman's porch. "Mind if I come inside and ask you a couple of questions?"

"Different questions than the ones that cop Porter already asked me?"

"Yes, we're handling different sides of the same investigation."

Lizzie opened her door all the way and let Danica enter. "Can we please make this fast? I have about a half an hour before this place is filled with kids again. They'll drive me crazy for two hours, then Jacob will be home. I'm truly blessed, but you know how it is."

Danica didn't, at least not from personal experience, but she wanted to get out of here as fast as possible, too. In and out, lickety-split. She mostly just wanted to show the photo of the engagement ring to Lizzie to gauge her reaction.

She was focused on finding answers, not thinking about all of the things that had gone wrong. That was a downward spiral she might not climb back out of. Twenty years' worth of lies. Every time she pulled at a thread, the tapestry of her life threatened to come apart like a torn ball of cotton.

"You want anything to eat or drink?" It sounded more like something Lizzie thought she should say than anything remotely close to a genuine offer.

"No, thanks." Danica shook her head, then nodded at

her dining room table. "Mind if we sit?"

"Not at all." Lizzie walked over to the table, pulled out a chair, and plopped onto the seat. "So, what do you want to know?"

"I just have a couple of questions."

"You said that already. Are you looking to make sure Linus is executed?"

"No, it's not like that," Danica said.

"I thought you weren't a cop."

"I'm not."

"Then why are you in my house asking me questions?" Lizzie sounded more suspicious now than when she opened the door.

"I'm a behavioral therapist and I've been asked to help develop a profile of the killer."

"You mean the one the cops are calling a copycat?"

"That's right," Danica said.

"How do the police know it's not the same killer, and that Linus is innocent?"

"Nothing is for sure," Danica answered, already questioning her response. She wasn't a cop and nowhere near sure of the right thing to say. "But the more we understand, the more likely we are to stop further murders."

Lizzie looked at her, eyes full of suspicion.

Danica added, "I'd like to help Linus if I can. I thought you might want to do the same thing."

"Help the man accused of killing your father?"

"I just want the truth to come out, even if that truth exonerates Linus."

"So what's your question?"

"I've been talking to Cole … to Linus … and I think he might be telling the truth about some things."

"Like what?"

"Do you happen to know where Linus was on the night my father was murdered?"

"I don't know where he was on any of the nights anyone was murdered. It's not like we were talking or anything."

"When was the last time the two of you spoke?"

"You mean before all of this?"

"Have you spoken since?" Danica asked.

"I wrote him a couple of letters in prison."

"Mind if I ask what was in those letters?"

A beat of uncertainty, but then she said, "I never really thought that Linus could do what you all said he did. So I wrote him a letter telling him how sorry I was, then I wrote him another one saying the same thing a few years later since he never wrote me back."

"Do you know of any evidence that suggests his innocence beyond what Linus has already said to the press?"

She shook her head. "No, sorry, wish I could help."

"What makes you so sure that Linus wasn't the Magistrate Murderer?"

"I'm *not* sure," Lizzie admitted. "But I knew Linus, and angry as he was, I just can't see him as a killer."

Danica knew from painful, first-hand experience: *people saw what they wanted to see.*

She reached into her pocket and retrieved the photo, holding it under the table. "Do you mind if I show you something?"

"Do whatever you're here to do. Like I said, the kids will be home soon. So—"

Danica showed Lizzie the photo.

"What's that?" Lizzie asked, staring down at it.

"I was hoping you could tell me."

Lizzie shrugged. "Looks like an engagement ring."

"You've never seen it before?"

She shook her head.

"It belonged to Linus," Danica told her.

"That doesn't change my answer. I've still never seen it before."

"The police found it in his apartment. They thought it was a trophy he stole from one of his victims."

"But you don't think so?" Lizzie raised her eyebrows.

"It could be … if Linus is actually guilty." Danica still needed to believe that he probably was, but she wanted for Lizzie to look at her with less suspicion so that maybe she could get to the truth. "But I think he meant to propose to someone."

Lizzie looked at her, waiting to see what was next.

"Could that someone have been you?" Danica asked.

Lizzie barked laughter, sudden and seeming to surprise even her. Then the mirth was gone and something that Danica could only describe as an ancient sorrow seeped in to take its place. "No, Linus never proposed to me."

"Did the two of you ever date?"

"Porter asked me the same thing. But no, we were never an item, we never dated. Linus was always nice enough to me, but he never looked at me in that way."

"But you wanted him to?"

"I admired the life he wanted to build for himself. Not that we ever talked, but I looked in on him a few times and he was always working toward something," Lizzie said.

"What do you mean?"

"Linus wanted a respectable, decent life, where he could be proud of what he had. Like the life I have now." Lizzie gave Danica one of the thinnest smiles she'd ever seen. "I have a husband who loves me, and I love my kids. I'm really so blessed."

Danica wondered about the real story behind the one that Lizzie was obviously telling herself.

"If Linus was planning on proposing to someone, do you have any idea who he might have—"

"Probably Tuesday," Lizzie said, surprising Danica with both the immediacy and certainty of her response. "They always had their thing."

"*Their thing*?" Danica repeated, her heart beating faster, feeling like she was circling the edge of an answer that no one had ever heard before.

"Linus loved her beyond all reason." Lizzie sighed, weary and sad. "God knows why."

Danica pocketed the photo of the ring and stood. "Thank you, Lizzie. You've been very helpful."

She started walking away from the table.

Lizzie made it to the door before her. "Do you think he did it?"

"I honestly don't know." Though looking into Lizzie's eyes, Danica longed to say *no*. "But I'm on my way to find out."

Lizzie opened the door and Danica nodded her goodbye.

Then she got in her truck and raced toward the answer.

Chapter Thirty-One

QUENTIN

Quentin was back in his Tesla as he pulled up in front of Pike High just as school was getting out for the day.

He parked four rows from Varney's Prius. Quentin had let his biases get the best of him; he'd expected a shop teacher to drive a pickup or oversized SUV, something to prove his masculinity — just like every wood or metal shop teacher Quentin had ever known or seen in a movie or on TV. But according to the DMV, Varney drove a six-year-old Prius, same kind of car a healthy percentage of the city's population now seemed to favor.

It was an hour before he came out. Long enough to leave Quentin exposed. Two-thirds of the cars were gone from the lot, leaving a scarcity of shadows behind. He had to pull out of his spot and park farther away — a glance from Varney would blow his cover, and this wasn't a detail he was officially supposed to be anywhere near.

He followed at a distance, staying well behind the Prius. His Tesla wasn't exactly inconspicuous, but it was still more invisible than the department's Explorer would have been with its light rack. The Tesla was a Prius for the affluent, and were multiplying all throughout Southern California almost as fast.

Varney lived all the way on the other side of the city, over near the Town Center in a block of condos that were sure to age poorly, but looked both new and nice enough for now.

Quentin parked a block away, then walked to the building, waited for a male resident to enter, and slipped in behind him with a smile. He didn't need to follow Varney too closely and risk discovery. He'd already gotten his address from the DMV database. He'd followed Varney in case he didn't head home first.

So he made himself comfortable in the emergency stairwell with the door propped open just enough that he could keep his eyes on the fourth floor hallway. Quentin had nowhere else to go. Danica was furious with him, and while he wanted to believe it would all blow over, and soon, part of him was terrified that the woman he'd always thought of as "almost like a daughter" would never, ever forgive him.

He needed answers. He needed to catch the killer and prove his value to the world. He needed to make this all up to her, and to himself.

He was cramping after an hour, and wondering if he was being an idiot and wasting his time shortly after that. His stomach started growling and he wondered why in the hell he hadn't stopped for a burrito before his stakeout.

The waiting paid off. A familiar student stepped off the elevator and walked in a hurried line directly toward 4C. Tall and lanky, like a scarecrow outfitted by H&M.

The boy knocked, the door opened, and the student stepped inside.

But not before Quentin managed to snap several shots on his phone. One of Ichabod walking down the hallway, a second of him knocking, and a money shot of a teenaged boy entering his teacher's private residence.

Quentin waited five minutes to make sure they were comfortable, then stood from his spot in the stairwell. He made it one step before the blinding pain in his leg suddenly stopped him. He stretched, rubbed the charley horse out of his limb, then knocked on Varney's door.

A long moment, then Quentin could sense him right on the other side, probably looking through the peephole.

"I don't have to talk to you."

"You're right, you don't. But I suggest that you do. Or maybe I could give your principal a call and ask him about the school's policy on teacher-student fraternization."

A long pause, then, "You can't prove anything."

"What kind of a cop do you think I am?" Not that Quentin wanted an answer. He had the first picture ready, and held it up to the peephole for a long moment. Then he skipped the second, scrolled to the third, and held the phone up again. "This one's my favorite. Maybe you should—"

The door opened. "You have this all wrong."

"I'm sure you can explain everything to me."

Varney was fully dressed. To Quentin's surprise, the teacher was even still wearing his tie. He looked around, but didn't see Young Ichabod anywhere.

"What's it going to take for you to leave me alone?" Varney asked.

"That's an easy one. Come clean about your relationship with Cole and I'm out of here."

Varney shook his head with a sigh. "I don't know what to tell you. Or what you even want to hear. I swear, my only connection to that asshole is being fostered in the same house for a few miserable years."

"You better get your alibis ready for the nights of the copycat killings, because—"

"You've gotta be kidding me," Varney said, his voice now finding notes of barely muted rage.

"I'm not. We know you're the copy—"

"You don't know shit! Because I didn't do anything!"

This was good, just what Quentin wanted.

"I'm sure your alibis will prove that." He tried looking past Varney into his apartment, but he couldn't see Ichabod or anything else. "Let's start with last night. Do you want to tell me where you were, starting at around 7:00?"

"You don't have anything," Varney spat. "I know how this works, you would have arrested me already if you did. You're just digging."

"I can see why you would wish that were true," Quentin said, perfectly calm. "But I'm stalling, not digging."

Now Varney looked seriously worried. "Stalling for what?"

"I've got a judge writing up an arrest warrant right now," he bluffed. "It's up to you how the rest of this goes."

His fists were clenched at his sides, and it looked like Varney might take a swing at him any second. That might be a best-case scenario. Then Quentin could arrest him and they could spend some alone time in the box. Maybe finally get the answers he needed to realign the rest of his life. Fuck the FBI and Linus Cole. Luther, too.

Varney took a breath to calm himself. "Well then, I guess we'll have to wait for that warrant."

"I'm his alibi!" Quentin heard a voice from somewhere in the living room. "Mr. Varney was with me!"

"Stay out of this," Varney said, turning away from

Quentin to the person now standing behind him, still obscured from view.

"I can't do that," said the student, pushing his way in front of the teacher. "My name is Angelo Davis. Mr. Varney couldn't have killed anyone last night. Because he was with me."

"Angelo, I need you to stay out of this. For your own good."

"I think Angelo is perfectly capable of speaking for himself," Quentin said, taking a look at the kid. Like Varney, he was fully dressed and visibly upset.

"He didn't do it. He *couldn't* have done it. And I'll swear to that in court. I got here around 6:30 last night, and I stayed until almost nine."

"And what were you doing here, for two and a half hours, alone with your teacher in his home?"

"You don't have to answer anything," Varney said to Angelo.

"Looks like your teacher might be going to jail either way." Quentin looked from teacher to student, eyes settling on Angelo and waiting for him to break. "I'm only trying to do my job, so why don't you help me?"

"Is your job trying to pin something on an innocent man?" Angelo asked.

Quentin shook his head. "I'm only looking for the truth."

"I'm nineteen," Angelo said.

"Were you nineteen when your teacher hit on you for the first time?"

Matt's face twisted in anger and he made a choking sound, but this time he let his student talk.

"It wasn't like that. Never has been." Angelo shook his head, several times, all emphatic. "Mr. Varney is my mentor."

Varney finally opened the door all the way. "Might as well come inside, before my neighbors hear."

It wasn't much of an invite. Varney's eyes were still furious.

Quentin walked over to the sofa, but he didn't sit.

Varney turned to Angelo. "You should go home. We can pick up where we left off tomorrow."

"No way." Another shake of his head. "I'm not going anywhere."

"What is it you're going to pick up on?" Quentin asked.

"We were having a conversation." Varney turned back to Angelo. "Please, go home. I'll take care of this."

"No way, Mr. Varney. There's no way I'm leaving."

"Fine." He sighed. "Why don't you make us a pot of coffee, then."

Angelo nodded at his teacher, then turned around and went into the kitchen.

Quentin waited until he was out of earshot, then lowered his voice. "Seems like a good kid. You shouldn't be taking advantage of him."

"Our relationship is purely platonic."

"Care to elaborate?"

"Angelo is gay, but he hasn't come out of the closet yet."

"And you're helping him along?"

"Not like *you're* insinuating, no." Varney took a breath. "I'm not an idiot. I realize the kid is infatuated with me, but that will pass. In the meantime, I've been talking to him about coming out."

"What else have you been talking about?"

"About a lot of other things a gay teenager with super conservative and deeply religious parents never will."

For the first time Quentin not only saw, but believed

the sincerity in Varney's eyes. He could hear it in his voice, and feel it in the tremor of their moment. He finally sat on the sofa as Varney pulled out a chair from the small table a few feet away and dragged it over to the couch.

He sat and said, "Angelo's dad wants to send him to military school for the rest of his senior year. To 'toughen him up.' That's the last thing the kid wants, and it might just kill him. Angelo's smart, so he figured that taking shop and learning some 'manly' skills might pacify his old man. So far it's working. He only has another couple of months until he graduates."

"So the two of you are *just* talking?"

"I'm helping him out however I can."

"For example?" Quentin pressed.

"I helped him get a part-time job. My friend owns the Red Tomato, so Angelo is delivering pizzas and saving up enough money so he can get an apartment when he graduates."

"Why are you helping him?"

Varney stared at his carpet for a few awkward seconds before raising his head and meeting Quentin's eyes. "Because no one was ever there for me when I needed it."

"Stay here." Quentin gave Varney a curt nod before standing and walking into the kitchen.

The coffee was already brewed, and Angelo was filling a trio of mugs.

The teen looked up and met his eyes.

"I need you to be straight with me," Quentin said.

"Of course, officer."

"Is your relationship with Matt Varney in any way physical?"

Another emphatic shake of his head. "Not at all. We just talk."

"And you would swear under oath that he was with you last night from—"

"Absolutely. Mr. Varney didn't do anything wrong."

As far as Quentin could prove, he technically hadn't. He handed Angelo his card. "If he ever does anything you don't like, or tries to take advantage of you in any way, call me."

Angelo took the card and slipped into his back pocket without so much as a glance at the font. "I'm not going to need it, officer. But thank you for being concerned about me." He looked down at the only empty mug. "Would you like a cup of coffee? It's from Kenya."

Quentin shook his head, thanked Angelo, then went back out into the living room feeling like an asshole. But still, just in case there really was something going on here, he looked at Varney one final time. "I find out you're taking advantage of that kid, I'll do everything I can to make sure you suffer more than the full consequence."

To his surprise, Varney nodded. "As you should."

"And if you know anything about Cole or the copycat and I find out that you withheld it, I'll make sure you go to prison as an accomplice."

"That's fair, but it doesn't make me know anything."

"And where were you after Angelo left?" Quentin didn't know the time of death so it wasn't as if he could pin anything with certainty on Varney at the moment. He'd hoped to just catch him in one lie that would unravel the rest.

"I had a Skype call with a friend until about eleven-thirty, and then I went to bed. I can provide you his name, or I'm sure you can contact my internet service provider."

Quentin left with a nod, but not another word.

He walked a block and got into his Tesla, irritated

enough that he needed a full minute before starting the car.

He was wrong about Varney, which left him with Jim, Lizzie, and Tuesday as candidates for the copycat. Otherwise, the FBI was right and Quentin was on the wrong track altogether.

Chapter Thirty-Two

QUENTIN

Quentin was back at the precinct, sitting at his desk, growing ever more pissed that the FBI was in Chief Wilson's office. And worse, he couldn't work from home because the FBI would be crawling up his ass if he took any of the case files out of the precinct.

He should've made copies of copies. What was the point of being the deputy chief if he couldn't do his job the way it needed to be done?

He looked up at the open door, got annoyed enough to stand from his chair and go over to close it, then he sat back down and started working again.

At least he wanted start working again. But it was hard to focus when he had so many errant threads cross-stitched in his mind. He kept thinking about all of Cole's lies and the ways in which he'd infected Danica. Maybe she was right to be angry with him for hiding his relationship with Emilia, but his obscuring that one lone truth to protect her sure as hell didn't give Danica the right to doubt everything he'd ever said. She was acting like *he* was the criminal here.

He looked down at his phone which contained notes on the foster siblings, photos of the notes he'd taken, scanning them yet again, not expecting any fresh revelations but not really knowing how else to spend his time. He couldn't get near to the current investigation. Not with the FBI, nor with Simpson and Merrill. Quentin had been ordered to the corner.

But he was still missing something, and if he looked through his notes enough times that absent clue he was desperate to discover might find its way to the top.

He might not have access to all the case files, but he did have access to old files that had been digitized. He went to his laptop and started with Jim's files, looking again at his criminal record. Multiple arrests for possession of small amounts of molly and weed. He was suspected of being a drug mule, but there had never been proof. Multiple unpaid parking tickets and a noise complaint from the apartment above his didn't make the guy a suspect of anything more than someone living paycheck to paycheck without enough gravy to cover what Quentin knew was the city's almost predatory street sweeping practices.

Las Orillas streets were never especially clean, but parking tickets on sweeping day were one of the city's most significant sources of revenue. An upstairs neighbor had called the cops on Jim to complain about a lot of "crashing and banging," but when officers arrived on the scene they found a hysterical ex-girlfriend smashing his stuff after discovering that he'd been cheating on her with a barista who worked two blocks from his job at the bodega. Not exactly the nicest thing for Jim to do, but hardly illegal.

Lizzie had a record, but not the kind Quentin was looking for. She was an easy target, and a semi-permanent victim. Her purse had been snatched twice and someone had broken into her car three separate times. That was enough to think she might be running some sort of insurance fraud, except that Lizzie had never filed a claim. She was just that unlucky. She'd lost her stereo and some CDs the first time, replaced what she could and then lost it all again. The third time her windows were smashed the hoodlums only managed to steal a pair of concert tickets. Fortunately, they were for a local band called Secrets of the Pentatonic and only put her out $20, according to the police report she probably felt foolish even making.

The last thing in Lizzie's file was a mugging in a neighborhood she should never have even been in, and wouldn't have been if she'd not been volunteering at a soup kitchen. Her world turned around right after that, thanks to the Good Samaritan who had stopped the attack — a man who was now father to her five children, biological and otherwise.

Tuesday had a clean record as well, both as a juvenile and as an adult, leaving him nothing to go on. So Quentin closed the laptop and returned to the notes on his phone.

Wandering wasn't good for me. I fell in with some bad people, got into a bit of trouble, then bailed after I realized I was headed for more. By then I'd been gone enough to appreciate this dump a bit more than I had.

"What kind of trouble?" Quentin had asked.

The kind that makes you appreciate settling down and focusing on your art.

Tuesday had spent some time in Portland. Quentin had exactly one person he could call, but wasn't sure if he should. Requesting favors was hard enough, but doing it out of the blue, with a person he'd not spoken to in years, on a case he wasn't even supposed to be working ... that was something else entirely.

Maybe he should pass the tip to Simpson, let him and Merrill see if there was anything there.

Quentin leaned back in his chair, considering his next move. Even though part of him — or maybe even most of him — knew he was only making excuses for himself, he still felt possessive of the case. It was his to solve, his truth to uncover.

So he took out his phone, scrolled through his contacts, and called his friend in the Portland PD.

"Captain Porter," Adam said when he answered. "To what do I owe the honor?"

"Not sure how much of an honor it is," Quentin said, already liking the attention.

"You're the only cop I know with a TV series."

"It was a docuseries. That hardly counts. Not like I have Kevin Bacon playing me."

"Maybe someday."

"Maybe."

"So what's up? I assume you're not calling to ask how long I smoke my brisket."

"How long *do* you smoke your brisket?"

"Well, there are a lot of variables," Adam answered, not exactly taking Quentin seriously, but fucking with him nonetheless. "You have the temperature of your smoker, the thickness of your meat, and the fat content."

"How about in general?"

"Oh, in general, I'd say an hour and fifteen minutes per pound."

"Great," Quentin said. "Thanks. Talk to you in a few years!"

Adam laughed. "So, what do you need?"

"I was hoping you could run a search for me."

"I'd rather talk more about brisket, but sure. What's the name?"

"Tuesday Howe."

"H-o-w-e, and Tuesday like the shittiest day of my week?"

"Yes, and yes. Why is it the shittiest day of your week?"

"Because there's this crap factory called Beefcakes that Roberta likes. Kids eat free on Tuesdays, which apparently obligates me to go a couple of times a month. I swear their burgers are made with raccoon ass."

"Brutal. And I won't ask how you know what raccoon ass tastes like."

"Ha. Give me a sec …"

After a few minutes of silence, punctuated by his typing, Adam ended the wait with a whistle.

"What is it?" Quentin asked.

"What are you hoping to find?"

"No idea. Honestly, I'm sort of grasping at straws. What do you see?"

"Your girl's been brought in and questioned a lot, but no charges that ever stuck."

"Go on …"

"Arson, burglary, assault, vandalism—"

"Shit."

"Shit is right. She was also a known associate of Posse 7."

"What's that?"

"An absolutely savage street gang here in Portland."

"No shit," Quentin said.

"On the contrary. We have a mountain of it. This have anything to do with your copycat?"

"That's made the news up there?"

"The Magistrate Murders was never a small story. It's national now, same as always."

"Tuesday Howe grew up with Cole. Same foster home."

"She wasn't a person of interest before?"

"Not at all. No reason to even look into her." Quentin glanced down at her file, shaking his head. "How does someone go from squeaky clean as a juvenile to falling in with a street gang?"

"Maybe her juvenile record is sealed."

"I'm looking at it right now," Quentin said.

"Well, shit, man. Anything else I can do?"

"I'll let you know if there is."

"I can also smoke a turkey, if that helps."

Quentin laughed, despite the gallon of acid in his stomach. "Thanks. I'll call you before Thanksgiving for sure."

"I'm already looking forward to it," Adam said, then he added, "Take care of yourself, Port," before ending the call.

Quentin didn't waste a beat. He had Simpson on the line in seconds.

"Hey, boss."

"That vic with the burned fingertips, you know, the one that brought the FBI down here — where was that?" Quentin asked.

"On the border of Washington and Oregon, on the Oregon side. A place called Longview."

"Motherfucker …"

"Everything okay?"

"Tuesday Howe spent a few years in Portland."

"Foster kid who grew up with Cole?" Simpson asked.

"Exactly. Any idea where the Feds are on all of this right now?"

"They're interrogating one of the crazies who's been sending our favorite serial killer love letters in prison. It's too early to know for sure, and the agents sure as hell aren't saying it, but we might have our guy."

"Why? What do the letters say?"

"It's not just the letters. The guy's practically camped out at Coldwater. Waving signs and yelling."

"So are a lot of other people."

"Yeah, but this guy has no alibi and he's totally batshit. He also broke Rowan's nose while resisting arrest. He and Special Agent Tyler both seemed to take it personally."

"Fuck. Thanks. I'll call back if I need anything else."

Quentin hung up without waiting for Simpson's response.

His forehead needed a mop and it felt like he might be diving right into a panic attack.

Something was very, very wrong.

He called Danica but got no answer.

Quentin was out of his seat, marching toward the door and yelling for Jenkins as it swung open and the man appeared like a magic trick.

"Who's on detail for Danica now?"

"Officers Alvarez and Henry. Why?"

He held up a finger, called Officer Laverne Henry. "Hey, you all got eyes on Danica?"

"No, she's not returned to your house yet."

"What?"

"Yeah, last we saw her she was with you in the parking lot, so we went to your house, saw neither of you were here, and figured you were still together."

"And you didn't think to call me to verify?"

"Sorry, sir," Henry said. "What's wrong?"

"Stay put. I'm not sure yet."

He hung up, turned to Jenkins. "I need you to get with whoever can track a phone and give me an address the fastest."

"Sure thing." Jenkins looked scared, probably frightened by Quentin's expression, or maybe the wide eyes he could feel wanting to bug out of his face. "Whose phone? Danica's?"

"Yes."

Jenkins nodded, visibly swallowing as Quentin gave him the number.

"Text me the address the second you have it." Then Quentin was out of there, flying through the precinct doors on his way to the Tesla.

He got inside and tossed his phone onto the passenger seat. He pulled out of the lot and onto Ocean as it buzzed.

He picked it up, looked at the screen, and wanted to shout a huzzah that his department was on the ball.

He registered the address and felt a cold blade of panic raking his spine.

Quentin floored the gas and raced to the killer's workshop, determined to fix this himself.

Chapter Thirty-Three

DANICA

DANICA STOOD outside the workshop with the sound of a whining saw coming from the other side, her knuckles hovering inches from the door.

She was tempted to look around first, but didn't want to get caught prying.

Tuesday might very well have the answers Danica had been looking for, but standing there she felt an uncomfortable yet inarguable pause. She was alone, without any backup.

And maybe she was being ridiculous. Despite acting like one right now, Danica wasn't a cop. She couldn't question Tuesday without her consent. Worse, if anything went wrong, what could she do?

But the alternative wasn't an option. She refused to call Quentin, or even tell him what she was doing. He didn't deserve to know. Not when he had forced her to live two-thirds of her life shrouded inside of his selfish lie.

Danica swallowed and finally knocked.

It wasn't loud enough to rise above the din, but it took everything inside her to knock any harder.

She did, her raps growing louder until she was banging on the door.

It swung open and Tuesday, or at least the woman she presumed was Tuesday, was standing on the other side of it, staring back at Danica.

"Hi there. My name is—"

"I know who you are."

"Oh …" Danica offered her an awkward smile. "I'm looking for Tuesday Howe. I was hoping—"

"To bother me?" She grunted. "Already done. Now what do you want?"

"I just had a few questions?"

"Oh yeah?" Tuesday's smile looked almost crooked on her face and Danica got the distinct impression that the woman might be toying with her. "What kind of questions?"

"About Linus Cole."

"Obviously. You here in an official capacity? Or just curious? Last I heard, you were a shrink, not a cop. So did you want to ask me all about my mommy? Maybe prescribe some Prozac?"

"I think Linus might be telling the truth … about what happened the night my father died."

Tuesday seemed surprised. She straightened her shoulders and took a step back from the door, though she still didn't invite Danica inside. "You mean the night he was murdered?"

"Yes," Danica said with a hard swallow. "The night he was murdered."

"So what do you think that Linus might be right about?"

"That's what I wanted to talk about … I was hoping that you might be able to corroborate a couple of the things he said."

"You want a soda?" Tuesday asked, opening her door all the way. "I've got Burpys."

"Water would be great, if you have it."

"Who doesn't have water?" Tuesday slammed the door and disappeared, presumably into the kitchen, or wherever she kept her Burpys and water.

Danica looked around. The place was a mess. Piles of raw wood and scrap metal. Power tools everywhere. But no place to sit, other than a gorgeous set of chairs that looked less like furniture than art.

Tuesday appeared a few moments later, holding a bottle in one hand and a glass of tap in the other. She handed the water to Danica, then twisted the top off her Burpy and started to sip.

"So … let's get down to that corroboration. What is it you wanted to ask?"

Danica placed the glass on a crate behind her, then turned back around. "I'm thinking about recanting my testimony."

"Bullshit." Tuesday took a sip from her bottle. "Why would you do that?"

Nervous as she was, Danica pulled the photo of the engagement ring out of her pocket, then showed it to Tuesday.

"Where did you get that?" she asked, her eyes lighting with what looked like surprised recognition.

"It belonged to Linus." Danica studied Tuesday's expression for a moment before adding, "But you already knew that, didn't you?"

Tuesday presented her palm. "Let me see it."

Danica didn't want to hand the photo, her only copy, over, but Tuesday's eyes were as insistent as the rest of her.

Hesitantly, she handed the picture to Tuesday.

She stared at the photo, inspecting the ring with its

diminutive diamond, her eyes narrowing before growing wider, curiosity and resolve fighting for space in her expression.

She finally handed it back with a shake of her head. "I never expected to see that again. Where is it?"

Softly, in her very best therapist's voice: "Would you like to talk about it?"

Tuesday looked upset, but an undeniable emotional connection ran like a current between them. Danica could feel it. This was the opportunity she had been waiting for. Not only could she find out what happened, she might also be able to help this wounded and vulnerable woman.

Tuesday blinked and wiped at her eyes as the first tear fell. "Would you mind handing me your glass? I could really use a sip of water."

Danica thought, *Gross*, but then ignored the notion and turned around to grab her glass.

She knew it was a mistake as soon as she was fully facing the other way.

But it was too late.

Something heavy crashed into her skull.

Then Danica fell to the floor and saw only black.

Chapter Thirty-Four

DANICA

Danica couldn't even open her eyes.

She tried, but each of her three attempts had been painful enough to make her shut them immediately. She was dizzy, like the world had shifted in orbit and violently altered directions. Someone had scooped out her insides like seeds from a honeydew, leaving only rotten fruit and bitter rind.

Worse than weak, she felt empty.

She rolled over. That didn't help. Pain was like lightning through her body.

Danica didn't expect to stand up and walk out of wherever she was. For now it would be enough to gather her bearings. Know where she was to come up with a plan.

Focusing, she realized that the pain was concentrated in her head.

She reached up, felt the back of her skull, and pulled two sticky fingers away.

Danica drew a breath and reminded herself that head wounds always looked and felt worse than they were. She drew another one, this time deeper. Her body was fine and her senses were slowly returning, the pain fading enough for her to start working toward a coherent thought.

Tuesday had hit her with something blunt on the back of her head.

But if Tuesday wanted her gone, then Danica would already be dead.

Was she still in Tuesday's workshop?

She tried to force her eyes open again, but the pain was still too great.

So Danica used her nose, sniffing the world for notes of familiarity. Tuesday's workshop had been rich with the aromas of wood and a light perfume of something burning. This place smelled ... cold ... and like too much concrete.

It also felt ... open. As if there was too much space ... and the space was ... *stale*.

Danica forced her eyes open to confirm her suspicions, then held them open despite the pain.

She was in an empty warehouse somewhere, probably in the industrial side of town, not too far from the docks. A place where she could probably scream her head off and there wouldn't be anyone around to hear or help her.

The next question, and another knife in her skull: *Had Tuesday brought her here to die?*

She heard a pair of voices in the distance. She could tell that one belonged to Tuesday, despite the muffled whisper, but the other one was unfamiliar and male.

She opened her eyes again, peering into the distance to see if she could make out the speakers. But that was too much, and she clutched her stomach a second too late.

The vomit was all over her body.

The stench made her throw up again, but she was already empty so that second round was mostly retching.

She needed a doctor, and soon. Concussions were serious; a blood clot could end her life if Tuesday didn't.

The muffled voices had her worried as much as the wound. Brain injuries were common, but diagnosis could be complicated. She was suffering from trauma for sure, but Danica didn't know if the distress to her body was from pain alone. Her balance might be off. The dizziness alone seemed like enough to destroy her, and she wasn't sure if she could trust her memory.

Danica was in too much pain to think straight, but that wasn't the same as amnesia. She remembered talking to Tuesday in her workshop, then the blinding agony. But everything else still came in a jumble.

She needed to think, hard as it was, and as painful as it might be. A grisly head wound had left her skull feeling cracked in half. But she wasn't helpless.

Danica closed her eyes and listened hard, but the muffled voices didn't get any clearer.

She forced them open, peering into the shadows, trying to focus on the dimly lit figures standing about fifty feet away, surely talking about her, maybe deciding on what they should do with her body, before it decomposed.

If Tuesday wanted me gone, then I'd already be dead, Danica told herself again.

Her vision cleared, just enough to see the couple more clearly. Tuesday for sure, talking to a man who was no taller than her, but still looked ten times as dangerous, dressed in a white T-shirt, baggy pants with split cuffs and a thin belt, plus a purple bandana tied around his forehead like a sweatband. Even in the grimy light, Danica could see that both of his arms were covered in tattoos.

But oddly, even from her broken pile on the floor, Danica saw something unmistakable.

Tuesday was clearly in charge. The gangbanger stood

in a way that appeared almost deferential, as if awaiting his orders.

Danica swallowed and a tear fell from her eye. She had to chomp on her bottom lip to keep a violent whimper from leaving it.

In that moment, she remembered everything.

The night her father was murdered.

The truth came rushing back all at once.

Linus Cole didn't kill Miles Tate.

Tuesday was the Magistrate Murderer.

And Linus was the one who pulled Danica out of the kitchen cabinet, then dragged her out of the house.

Chapter Thirty-Five

QUENTIN

Quentin was ten minutes from Tuesday's workshop and out of his fucking skin.

"Call Danica," he said to the Tesla.

But Danica still didn't answer.

"Call Merrill." That call went straight to voicemail, too.

"FUCK!" Quentin slammed his fist on the steering wheel. "Call Simpson."

"What's up, boss?"

"I need you and Merrill to meet me at Tuesday Howe's workshop."

"Sure. When?"

"Ten minutes ago."

"Ten minutes ago?" Simpson repeated.

"Just get there as soon as you can. It's an emergency."

"You wanna tell me what that means?"

"Will that keep you from getting there? Then, no. I'll catch you up in person, just get there right fucking now."

"We're on our way."

The line went dead and Quentin lowered his foot on the pedal.

His shoulders were knotted and the pits of his shirt were soaked through. He kept picturing the worst and having to ignore the assault on his mind. He was driving like a lunatic and hoping he'd pass a cop. Even though he'd slapped the mag mount beacon on top of his car, it wouldn't hurt to have a police escort with a functioning siren to help clear the way on his way to save Danica's life.

That's what he had to keep telling himself. That he would get there in time and everything would be fine. He wasn't going to lose Danica like he'd lost her father.

Quentin would have to kill himself if he failed again.

He swerved around a Honda, narrowly missed an Infinity, and clipped the sidewalk to avoid colliding with a Chevrolet. He ignored all the honking and held his speed, still hoping that he'd get spotted by an on-duty officer. He couldn't afford to go faster, and slowing down seemed even more expensive.

Racing like a rocket kept some of the worst images at bay.

He had to keep his eyes on the road. One wrong move might see the Tesla wrapped around a telephone pole. Or worse, he might clip a car and kill an innocent driver.

But focusing on the other side of his windshield was a godsend. Without the world flying by outside in a blur of unrelenting danger, he would be forced to stare at something much more harrowing. The incessant reminders of what had happened before. He kept seeing Danica's burned-out body, gutted and burned to ash, same as her father had been twenty years before.

Almost there.

His heart refused to stop pounding.

Another mile and he might finally be able to end this.

Still no cops on his ass. Surely someone had reported his maniacal driving by now?

Hopefully, Simpson and Merrill were en route.

Half a mile.

"Call Danica."

But still nothing.

He pulled into the empty lot adjacent to Tuesday's workshop, and opened his door before the Tesla had fully stopped, thankful that the car ran with a whisper, and was still far enough away that he had a reasonable hope of being invisible.

Danica's truck was sitting out front. His heart was on edge as he checked it to see that she wasn't inside.

He crept past all the stacks of wood, and made it to the building.

He peeked in, using the same window as the last time, but now he saw nothing.

He knocked on the door, but no one answered. So he punched it as hard as he could without breaking his fist. Still nothing, so he circled around to the back.

No response, so he tried to kick the door just beneath the knob.

But Quentin either wasn't strong enough or the door was reinforced, because it didn't budge from the frame.

Fuck this, he thought, walking back over to the wood pile.

Halfway there he found a length of walnut lying on the ground.

He picked it up, walked up to the window, shattered the glass and used the walnut to clear all the shards from the frame, then climbed inside and started screaming for Danica.

The place was entirely empty. He didn't need a thorough search, it wasn't like Quentin was missing his keys.

There was nowhere for two grown women to hide among the wood, tools, and various projects.

"DANICA!"

He was about to head upstairs to the apartment above the workshop when he spotted something on the floor that gutted him as he stooped to retrieve it.

Quentin turned what appeared to be an elaborately carved paperweight over in his hand. Its underside was covered with blood, and even though he had no proof, he still somehow felt certain that every drop belonged to Danica.

He looked around the room and saw a cellphone sitting on the floor half hidden beneath a pile of wood.

He picked it up, not sure if he felt hope or despair as he saw it was Danica's. The lock screen showed her as a kid with her parents.

He immediately headed upstairs and kicked the door of the apartment open, gun in hand.

But the apartment was empty.

He heard the squad car pull up as he searched the rooms, then descended the stairs with the phone and the paperweight in his hands, feeling as if his life was rapidly leaving his body.

"She's not here," Quentin said as the cops approached.

"Tuesday?" Simpson said.

"Danica." Quentin swallowed, noting the confusion and brewing fear on their faces. "Tuesday must have taken her somewhere else."

"Why?"

Quentin held up the paperweight and showed them the blood.

"Probably to kill her," he said.

Chapter Thirty-Six

DANICA

Danica was seconds away from death.

She would never leave this warehouse alive.

She could smell her own sweat, and that only made her perspire harder.

"You're awake." Tuesday walked over and kneeled next to her prone form.

Danica didn't respond. Maybe she couldn't. Fear gripped her by the throat, digging its fingers into her skin and turning fresh breaths into a prize. If she couldn't breathe, how was she supposed to speak? But if Danica didn't speak, she could never escape.

"Don't feel like talking?" Tuesday laughed as she stood.

Danica expected a kick that never came.

She wondered what Quentin was doing, and if he might be on his way.

But why would he be? She was on her own. She vaguely recalled dropping her phone.

"You don't have to hurt me," Danica tried.

"Oh, I don't? That's great news. What would you like to do instead?"

"We could talk."

"Really?" Tuesday touched Danica's chest. "You would talk to *me*?"

"Maybe I can help you."

"Do you really think so?" The kick finally came, landing hard in Danica's ribs. She swallowed a mouthful of vomit, trying not to choke on her tongue. She recovered enough to make words, then tried again. "I'm a trained therapist. I can—"

Another kick and all the air was gone from her body.

"I know what you are." Tuesday stood over Danica, leaving her gasping and still trying not to throw up. "You think *talking* is going to help? When has talking ever helped anyone like me?"

"All the time," Danica dared.

"Maybe I should cut out your tongue and cure you of a few false beliefs."

This situation was darker than any she had ever shared with a client, but the foundations were the same. A traumatized victim who didn't know how to sort through her feelings. From both sides of the nightmare, Danica had a lifetime of training to get her through this.

"I know what your mother's boyfriends did to you."

"You don't know shit." Tuesday kicked her again, but that time it felt like she might have been holding back. "Stop talking or I'll kill you right now."

"None of this was your fault. No little girl should ever have to go what you went through. Your mom was the monster, letting all of that happen to you."

Danica paused, expecting another kick, but it didn't come and so she might finally be able to breathe. Several breaths, in and out before she spoke again.

"You never got the chance to decide on your identity. It

was chosen for you, and by the person who was supposed to be taking care of you."

According to her file, Tuesday had been passed around from one man to another. But Danica didn't need to say that. Details were her enemy; she needed to focus on the emotions of what happened instead.

"I told you to shut up." But much of the fight had left Tuesday's voice.

She waited several seconds, until Danica could feel the pull of her wanting, same as she had with so many clients before. "Victims of childhood abuse like the kind you suffered take what happened to them into adulthood. They become aggressive or defensive—"

Tuesday's slap felt like it might knock Danica's head from her shoulders.

She was down on her knees in a flash, her palm a lightning strike to Danica's face.

Her ears were screaming and she couldn't hold it in.

Danica began to retch, reeking gobs of greenish bile dribbled from her mouth in gasping hiccups and coughs, blending in with the barf on her chest.

"I told you to shut the fuck up," Tuesday growled.

Danica did, for a while. Not that she had any choice. Coherent thoughts were hard enough, words refused her entirely. It took several minutes of labored breathing before she could finally believe she wasn't seconds from death.

Tuesday stared down at her the entire time, glaring in misplaced hate.

"I only want to help you … it's not your fault," Danica finally stuttered.

"You said that already," Tuesday snarled, but this time it wasn't followed by a kick or a slap. She stood and spit on the ground. A glob of phlegm landed next to Danica's face. "Bullshit. Nobody wants to help."

"That's not true—"

She kicked Danica again.

Danica clutched her stomach as Tuesday paced.

"You have no idea what I went through, growing up in that pretty little house, with two parents who gave you whatever you wanted, whenever you wanted it."

"You're right ..." Her words were a gurgle, but still she shoved them out of her mouth. "I can never know what you went through ... but I can understand if you'll let me."

"Fuck you." Tuesday kicked her again.

She couldn't take much more. Her internal organs were surely bleeding. Another kick might finish her off.

"You don't know shit," Tuesday said after a minute of pacing. Her words were out of the blue, and sounded to Danica like she must want to talk.

"Linus tried to give you that life, didn't he?"

"What life?" The two words left her lips like hostile witnesses.

"The life you think I had. With two parents who raised me in a pretty little house, who could give me whatever I wanted, whenever I wanted it — wasn't that what Linus wanted for you? Isn't that why he bought the ring—"

Danica stopped abruptly, bracing for another strike. But Tuesday's foot went nowhere, falling back on the floor as she resumed her pacing instead.

Danica wondered where the gangbanger had gone off to, and if any help might be coming.

"He forgot who we are," Tuesday told her. "Linus thought we could be better. But no one is ever better, they're only pretending to be."

She kneeled back down and grabbed Danica's face, squeezing her cheeks as she growled the rest or her message. "I *know* who I am, and that makes me stronger. You can't hurt me. *He* can't hurt me. No one can hurt me."

Then Tuesday stood and glared down at her. "But I can hurt you."

An ugly realization dawned on Danica, and that miserable truth felt more like a verdict.

All might be lost if she was right, and Tuesday couldn't be helped.

She had embraced her trauma and thus become the monster.

In her gentlest, most therapeutic voice, Danica tried yet again. "Linus wasn't trying to hurt you … he was trying to protect you."

Tuesday didn't respond.

"He took the fall for all the things you did. That's why your juvie record is clean, isn't it?"

Still no answer.

"And he took the fall for the murders, too … didn't he? You were always the—"

"He's a fool!" Tuesday shrieked, the sound of a woman convincing herself. "Linus thought he could be normal. He thought he could make *me* normal. But it was always more important to be strong."

"But you *are* strong," Danica told her.

"You're right." Tuesday smiled, walking back over to her prisoner and again kneeling beside her. "And it's time to show you exactly how strong I can be."

Chapter Thirty-Seven

QUENTIN

Tuesday's workshop was filled with the clamor and clatter of three cops on a safari for clues.

Simpson and Merrill were searching the entire building, while Quentin kept his focus on the workshop where he'd interviewed Tuesday his last time here. But so far, nothing. Not a single hint or indication as to where Danica might be, or what he should do next.

Both Simpson and Merrill were uneasy about not calling the situation into Special Agents Rowan and Tyler, but respected Quentin enough to follow his order. *Just a little more time.*

Quentin didn't know how long that would be, but felt sure there wasn't any good reason to let the FBI in on this just yet. Doing so wouldn't add another two sets of hands, it would eliminate Quentin from the equation. This was his case, and Danica was his responsibility.

This was his second time sifting through everything in Tuesday's workshop. Slower this time, moving from one side to other, picking up and inspecting every piece, before setting each item back down and moving onto the next one.

There was a wide array of woodcarving tools, some of which he was able to determine their purpose and many of which he didn't understand. From small to large, the workshop had ten times the number of tools that Quentin had seen in Varney's classroom. He mostly ignored those, searching for something more personal, despite having no idea what that might be. A few dozen hand-carved stamps seemed innocuous enough, until something struck him, and stopped his heart for a full beat.

He picked up one of the blocks and looked at the lettering. He didn't have Danica's *STAY AWAY* note on him, nor did he have the one left on Miles all those years ago on hand, but the single letter stamp seemed to be in the same style as what Quentin had seen on both of the Magistrate Murderer's warning notes.

But even with this new shred of whatever it was, he still had no idea where Tuesday might have taken Danica.

Quentin ran through a mental inventory of all the isolated spots in Las Orillas where a slow murder might go unabated. He might not know where she was, but he had a good idea of who she was.

Cole's acolyte would want to get this right, and that meant torture was part of their process. There had always been something performative about the crime scenes, so environment obviously mattered.

The jetty bordering Orange County had been closed for the last week, thanks to a minor leak from one of the oil islands a few miles off the coast. Tuesday could ensure that photo journalism was alive and well when pictures of Danica's burned-out body lying on the beach were smeared across the media landscape.

Maybe one of those empty warehouses out by the docks.

Or the wetlands out behind The Agora. The police had found a dozen bodies there in the last five years, though that was a place to bury and hide a corpse, not cast it under the bright lights like this copycat clearly wanted.

What Quentin was really worried about — what he could barely even bring himself to consider — was the possibility that Tuesday wasn't even in Las Orillas. She was all over the Pacific Northwest after Cole went to prison. If she'd taken Danica on a road trip, the two of them could be anywhere, maybe hooking up with old gang members.

"I found something!" Quentin yelled, managing to keep the panic mostly out of his voice.

Simpson and Merrill entered the room together moments later.

"What is it?" Merrill asked.

"More proof that Tuesday Howe is the copycat we're looking for." Quentin handed Merrill the small wooden block with that hand-carved stamp. "Danica got a warning telling her to 'stay away.' The lettering on her note was similar."

"She did?" Simpson said. "Where's the note?"

"Danica has it." He shook his head, changing the subject. "We didn't get the chance to turn it in. That doesn't matter. Tuesday has Danica, so let's focus: *where could she be?*"

Simpson looked bothered. "Las Orillas isn't a small city. Why don't we run forensics on the note?"

"There isn't time," Quentin argued.

"What if she's split?" Merrill asked. "She might not even be in the city. I know you don't want to call this in, but—"

"No FBI," Quentin said, too fast and emphatic, knowing full well that he might be making a massive mistake. "Not yet. Just a few minutes, let's see what we can come up with on our own."

"The marina, the docks, that stretch of closed beach over by Bolsa," Simpson started.

"Rainbow Lagoon, any of those warehouses over in the industrial park," Merrill added.

"Los Altos west," Simpson continued, "or maybe one of those abandoned shit holes over near Henderson … we have nothing to go on, she could have taken her anywhere."

"Tuesday had connections to Posse 7 up in Portland. Maybe there's something there."

Simpson and Merrill traded a look.

"What is it?" Quentin asked.

Simpson explained. "We arrested a minor involved in a drive-by last week. We don't like him for the job, and think he was taking the fall for a buddy. But we spent a couple of hours trying to break him. Only thing we managed to get was that there had been some newcomers to the city. Members of Posse 7 trying to claim parts of Las Orillas that don't belong to them."

"Does any of this city belong to them?"

"Not yet," Simpson said. "That's the point."

"So … is there anything more there?" Quentin asked.

Merrill nodded. "The kid said they were several members in one of the warehouses over near Crescent."

"Did you follow it up?"

Simpson shook his head. "Engle's body was found the next day. No time."

"Call it in, I'll meet you there," Quentin said, already on his way to the door.

"Meet us where?" Merrill asked. "All we got is a street."

"The place is abandoned. Look for the building with someone in it."

Quentin didn't wait for a response. Instead he got in the Tesla and hauled ass to Crescent.

Chapter Thirty-Eight

QUENTIN

QUENTIN WAS grateful for the lack of a moon, yet disquieted by the darkness.

He was hidden by the shadows, but could feel the grains in his hourglass falling fast. He was parked in a stretch of pitch-black nothing, behind an old building that made affordable clothing back in the 1920s, or so said the faded sign painted on its old brick exterior. He could barely read the thing, even after shining his light right on the wall.

He looked ahead and then behind him again before turning it back off.

Maybe this wasn't such a good idea. There were a lot of buildings if he was covering them all alone. He was here, but now what?

Fear clawed at his throat. Made him want to call Merrill and Simpson. Tell them the truth and order some backup. Send the FBI in.

But the situation was still too volatile. He needed to save Danica without losing her forever.

He took out his phone and considered calling again. That would be smarter than going from building to building and peeking in windows. Most had been emptied out by now, but a few were still occupied businesses, and surely a few had squatters inside. Cops raided the area every once in a while, but it was a hard place for the homeless to ignore with all the vacancies and sleeping nooks.

Quentin turned his light back on and aimed it at the end of Crescent — a belt of pure black in the distance. An accurate representation of what felt like his metaphorical horizon.

He was wasting time and had to find Danica.

He killed the light, dropped the phone in his pocket, swallowed his fear and started walking.

Quentin would find Tuesday and arrest the copycat. Save Danica and make this all go away.

Once they were safe, out of this situation with Danica no longer in danger, he could explain the situation again. Right now it felt like she hated him because she didn't understand.

Everything he had done was to protect her. Quentin had never acted out of cowardice. He made a choice to do the right thing. She was too young at the time to properly comprehend, or at least contextualize what had actually happened. And once she was old enough, Cole was behind bars. Danica had become quite the young woman, upright like her father. Downright virtuous.

Still, sometimes the venerable put killers on the street. They didn't mean to, they were *trying to do good*. But by following the letter of the law in lieu of its spirit, justice was barely spit on the ground.

He drew his gun, his senses on fire. It had been a long time since Quentin had felt the butt in his hand for anything more than in and out of the holster or posing. He needed Tuesday to be here. This had to end now. Three buildings down, and who knew how many to go.

He was walking in the dark, worried that his light might give him away to the wrong person. Probably not the right thing to worry about on a stretch of street that worked like the Vegas Strip — looming structures in shadows, lying about how far away they really were from each other.

It was getting harder and harder to swallow. Quentin considered the agonizing possibility that he might be too late. Danica might be dead already. He might fail her just like he failed her father.

Fuck the light. Still gripping the gun with his right hand, he pulled out his phone, turned on the light one-handed, then walked faster into the dim before him.

He got lucky three buildings later. The first was one of the enterprises still in business down in Ayer's Wharf. He had no idea what they bought or sold, but there were at least a thousand boxes on a third as many pallets, and a lot more than what Quentin could capture at a glance through the window. Posse 7 might be in an occupied building, but that was easier to track and less likely. He couldn't waste any time looking in places Tuesday probably wouldn't be.

The second building had squatters. An entire shanty town, without either the shanty or the town. Just huddles of humans with nowhere to go. A few might have been armed, from lead pipes to guns, but they weren't the breed of miscreant he was looking for.

The third building was empty. But while peering in the window Quentin saw Howe's Escalade.

He crossed the street, climbed over the chain link fence, and crept like the cop he used to be toward the car, close enough to grab the plate and call it in.

He circled around to the front of the SUV and looked around.

One building away he saw a flicker of light through a darkened window. Like sparking charcoal.

Or a torch.

He ran across the street, gun gripped and ready to fire. Slapped his back against the building's wall. Heart pounding — he was going to do this.

But do what?

It wasn't that going in there was suicide, he was putting Danica at risk without a plan.

He needed backup.

Quentin texted Merrill and Simpson with an SOS and a location. They could inform the FBI, and anyone else on duty, but hurry.

A full minute and no answer.

Another five of them was fucking ridiculous.

He'd seen the spark another three times. In each of those strobes he imagined the worse.

Danica could be dead or dying. Every second mattered and the detectives hadn't answered any of his texts. He couldn't wait any longer. He called 9-1-1 and reported a hostage situation in progress, then left the phone on, slipping it into his shirt pocket, as he circled around to the back of the building. He'd have a better chance of surprising Tuesday away from the light.

There were three locks in his way, all easy to pick. And nerve-wracking. Attempting to get it right fast while barely making a sound, with heavy chains that wanted to rattle like angry ghosts. Another five minutes spent working in and for silence, his heart the loudest thing around him, thoughts divided between his focus on popping the locks and wishing he was holding his gun.

Quentin set the final chain like a curled snake on the ground, then gripped his weapon with one hand and quietly opened the door with the other.

But Quentin hadn't been quiet enough.

Something — probably a baseball bat, though it was hard to see in the dark with the weapon descending so fast — smacked into his wrist with the force of fastball.

The gun flew from his hand onto the floor.

Quentin screamed as the first kick landed on his shin, then again as he fell to the floor and a second foot exploded between his legs.

His hand scrambled for the gun, but Quentin wasn't sure where it was and a parade of fumbles wasn't helping. A heel landed on his knuckles, then immediately ground down on them.

Quentin bellowed again and got kicked in the jaw.

There were two gangbangers, both laughing.

"Put that in your new documentary," one of them said.

Then the other spit on him.

Quentin could barely see his attackers, but he wanted them to know he was trying. That he wasn't afraid, and would still stare them down despite his beating.

In the dark he could mostly only define them as carica-tures. Mexican Laurel and Hardy, with face tattoos.

Laurel took Quentin's gun and put it in his waistband. The other took his phone and must not have realized Quentin was on a live call, as he threw it to the floor and stomped the thing to pieces of glass and plastic.

Hardy went behind Quentin, roughly grabbed him by the wrists, and started to drag him out of the room. He made it three steps before abruptly stopping. "Yo, fuck-head, you coming?"

"I was just taking a shot for the boys." Laurel finished shooting his photo, then kneeled down and picked up the gun from where he had arranged it to point at Quentin's pint of blood.

He was dragged for a while before Hardy yanked him up a foot just so he could hurl him for another few.

Quentin crashed to the floor and found himself looking at Danica, tied up and lying a few feet away, seeming just as beat to shit as he was.

Tuesday loomed beside her, a fire burning behind.

And with a smile, Hardy said, "We have a present for you."

Chapter Thirty-Nine

DANICA

This was all her fault.

Danica didn't think of herself as sexist, but the evidence was staring at her.

Quentin was responsible for some of this, but she was guilty, too. She had also failed to do her job. Profiled the wrong person because she'd made an assumption that the acolyte was a man. If Danica had been on her game, and considered the murderer to be a woman, she would have concluded that it was a jilted lover.

Knowing she was responsible for Quentin lying in a broken pile of meat, about to get tortured more than he already had been, left her dangling at the edge of insanity's cliff.

"This is all your fault," Tuesday told her, as if she needed the reminder, showing Danica the tip of her wood burner, now glowing orange. "We're here because of you."

Danica hadn't spoken a word since Quentin earned a swift kick for warning her not to, and she didn't break her silence now.

Don't take her bait, Danica!

"This is going to hurt you a lot more than it will hurt me." Tuesday kneeled next to Quentin. "But I promise to make it pretty when I'm done."

Danica couldn't stay quiet, and Tuesday knew it. She stared at her, until Danica finally broke. "You don't have to do this."

"You're right, I don't. Are you apologizing for forcing my hand?" Tuesday gave her a sickly smile, and in the campfire's flickering light it looked downright cancerous. "I'm just kidding." She laughed, still kneeling, but now with her knee on Quentin's body, looking over at Danica instead of down on him. "I should be thanking you."

Tuesday turned her back to the victim and touched the pen's burning tip to his arm. Uncle Quent made one hell of an attempt to keep his scream inside, but then he lost it anyway, practically yodeling with obvious embarrassment.

"I wasn't drawing anything yet. I only wanted to hurt him." She turned back to Danica. "I never wanted to hurt you. But I am glad you made it so easy for me to finish my work with your uncle. He was going to be a hard one for me to catch on my own. *Maybe* even not worth the effort. I was undecided. You helped to tidy things up. I knew that if he found your phone he would come here alone, because after all these years he still needs to cover his lies."

Tuesday stood and put a foot on Quentin. "Now that you're here, there's nothing I can do about your safety, but you can help me make this man suffer twice. First when I put my art on his body. Imagine seeing someone writhing through a tattoo with hellfire. An actual branding, but painstakingly slow. You can look forward to that." She looked from Danica to Quentin. "But the real torture will come when I force him to watch me slowly kill you."

Quentin screamed, but nothing intelligible.

"Quiet or I start with her," Tuesday barked.

Quentin fell silent immediately.

"We can do this two ways." Tuesday held the pen and stared down at her victim. "I can call my friends in here and they'll hold you back while I do this. You're probably not going to enjoy that one as much because Tomás really likes to shoot people in the dick. He says that's the best way to make it so a guy'll give you anything you want. And he's the sort to go straight for the right answer, first time out. Your other option, and this is the one I suggest you take if things like unimaginable agony matter to you. Take off your shirt and help me help you. Why suffer more than you need to? Especially when there's already going to be so much."

Tuesday stared at Quentin until he doffed his shirt.

Then she smiled, told him to lean back, and started her work.

Danica couldn't see what Tuesday was drawing, but her Uncle's agonized screams painted hellscapes in her head. Black horizons with monsters made of bubbling blood. A darkness that attacked her on a molecular level.

Danica would disappear from the world before this night was over, and there was nothing she could do. The woman enjoying her torture controlled her destiny.

But Danica wasn't screaming for herself. When she finally turned her throat into an abraded tunnel of blood, her anguished bellows were for Quentin alone. His agonized screams caused her to vomit again. His pain was piercing and the torturous wails made her feel it in her cells.

She turned her head, closing her eyes as she continued to throw up. This time she kept them closed, and squeezed them tight, ignoring Tuesday's order to watch her.

"I said that you will watch until I finish, and you will watch until I finish."

Tuesday sounded perfectly calm, and that somehow made her even more terrifying. She set down her pen and dragged Danica closer to Quentin, up against some metal monster of machinery.

Something clattered behind her. A sound of hope since Tuesday was too wrapped up in delivering her threat to notice it.

"Now you can hear him better, to make up for some of the seeing you missed. Close your eyes again and I'll do something worse. You got it?"

Tuesday didn't wait for an answer, because of course she didn't need one.

But after another half-minute of staring at her captor's back while she drew on Quent with a flaming hot pen, and seeing his face popping out from the side like a Jack-in-the-box in agony, Danica finally stuttered her plea.

"You don't have to do this." That was as close as she could get to begging. Another inch nearer and Tuesday would turn the pen her way. "You've proven that you can hurt Quentin, and that you can hurt me. You have all the power … you don't need to prove anything else."

"You think that's what this is about?" Tuesday scoffed, then left the smirk on her face. "You think this is about me proving something to you?" She laughed. "I don't need to prove that you're weak. That you're pathetic. That you could never survive the things that I've been through. I'm—"

"You're right. I couldn't." And then she dared: "But you couldn't either."

"I'm here, aren't I?"

"Not all of you, Tuesday."

"I told you no more of your therapy bullshit!" Then

she turned to her victim and barked, "Pull up your pant leg!"

He followed her order and got scorched for it. His scream scurried into Danica's ears and died there. Tuesday held the pen on his leg for a while, and Danica imagined it melting through his skin to the bone.

She shook the thought away and felt both hotter and colder than she ever had before. Tuesday was hunched over, focused on her art, elbow moving and Danica imagining her pivoting wrist, moving in small circles as she burned her misery into Quentin's flesh.

As his bellows turned into whimpers and mewling, Danica kept begging, getting louder and louder. More force, all she had, almost believing that if she pled hard enough, some decent part of Tuesday inside might still hear her.

Danica lost track of her words. It was mostly mumbling at the end. Incoherent petitions and prayers, a rambling list of reasons why Tuesday should prove her humanity; Danica just knew she still had it inside her.

But Tuesday kept burning and Quentin kept screaming, so Danica knew she could no longer beg.

Because begging was only feeding the beast.

So she stopped and swallowed her every instinct.

Quentin was gasping and sobbing, he'd lost the ability to make intelligible words a while ago.

It was all up to Danica. She had to find a way to distract the monster.

"I remember everything. About the night you murdered my father."

Tuesday didn't respond. Her elbow kept moving, but Quentin had finally fallen silent. Danica hoped he was unconscious, but feared he might be dead.

"I remember my father screaming. I remember all the

smoke. I remember the smell of his burning flesh, like cooking meat. Sometimes it's still in my nostrils. I remember cowering in the kitchen cabinet, so terrified that I couldn't even breathe. I was a roach on the floor, waiting to get stepped on. I never imagined a person could feel so afraid. I've spent every second since then with a part of me terrified that I would be that scared again someday. And right now, my worst nightmares are coming true."

Danica whimpered, but it was different this time.

Tuesday finally stopped, pausing her torture to listen, like an artist finally receiving the accolades she'd always deserved, and never stopped longing for.

Danica had to keep talking, now that she had a plan. She didn't know what had clattered to the floor when Tuesday moved her victim in for a better view, but she had been searching for it ever since. The tip of her middle finger finally found whatever it was, and kept working to spin it closer, a centimeter at a time.

"I remember you and Linus arguing," Danica said.

"What were we arguing about?"

Danica ignored her. She had the power in this story. "I remember you leaving. And I remember Linus dragging me out from the cabinet where I was hiding. I remember him taking me home."

Tuesday's face twisted at the memory.

"I remember Linus crying."

"Linus was a pussy!" Tuesday spat. "He wasn't an artist like me."

Danica's fingers closed around the handle of what she now knew was a chisel. "Uncle Quent was powerless." She shook her head, a show of Tuesday's power. "He was devastated when Linus left me on his doorstep." She swallowed, performance meant everything. "He realized that my dad was dead … and he had no idea when or where you would strike next."

"Your father knew exactly where I would 'strike next,' sweetheart. Daddy died because of your Uncle Quent here."

"How did he know?"

"Because I told him." Tuesday gave Danica a mean little rattle of a laugh, then turned to an unconscious Quentin and slapped him with her free hand. "You're gonna wanna wake up for this. All those lies you've been keeping from her? They're about to come out in five … four … three … two … now what were you saying?"

Danica swallowed and repeated her question. "How did he know?"

"Because I told him. I sent your father a note, same as the one I sent you. *You're next.*"

"My father never got a note."

"He got the note and he read it. So did your uncle."

"You can't know that he read it."

"Sure I can. Right, Q?" Tuesday laughed and turned to Quentin, groaning and working to keep his eyes open. Back to Danica. "I hid across the street and watched them both read it."

Something died inside Danica and the tears were already coming.

She stared at Quentin, furious that he was too out of it to face her. His lids fluttered, but were mostly closed. Each of them may as well have weighed a hundred pounds in his state.

But he deserved to see her rage, and it only made her angrier that the situation had turned him blind to it. He knew that the Magistrate Murderer was coming for her father next, and instead of being at his partner's side,

Quentin spent the evening literally fucking Danica's mother.

Again she felt truth like bile bubbling up in her throat. The truth was unfathomable. Unconscionable. Dishonest and depraved.

"How could you?" Danica blubbered. "Is it true?"

He didn't answer. Didn't even look at her.

"Answer me," she begged.

Nothing from Quentin, not even a groan.

Tuesday slapped him. "Answer her question, Q!"

His eyes fluttered open and with a puff of violent breath he sputtered, "*Yes.*"

Tuesday set the pen on the floor, far out of everyone's reach, then turned toward Danica.

"You'd think he would have been waiting for me, knowing what he knew … but he wasn't." Tuesday shook her head: *shame, shame.* "He was probably doing all kinds of nasty to your mama. Isn't that right, Q? Fucked her right into the looney bin, didn't you?"

She laughed again, and that was too much for Danica.

Her heart was about to explode. Or her head. Maybe all of her.

Stomach first: Danica started retching and retching, chunks of her liver maybe, since she couldn't imagine what else she had left.

Ever since the night of her father's murder, and her mother's eventual tumble out of reality, there were two things Danica knew as facts. Now both had been yanked out from under her.

Linus Cole wasn't the villain who destroyed her life.

Quentin wasn't the one who had saved her.

In truth it was the other way around.

And Uncle Quent was the monster she never knew he could be.

There were two demons in this room, and Danica would have to fight one of them off.

But now she had a healthy hold on her chisel, and was steadily scraping through her restraints.

One of these monsters was dead, and the other was going to prison.

Chapter Forty

DANICA

Tuesday kept laughing.

She had no idea that Danica was planning to plow her in the neck with a chisel the second she had the chance. She would only get one of them, so she'd been picturing the arc of her arm, over and over until she knew it like the memory of her father's Sunday morning face.

"The truth will set you free, isn't that what they say?" Another laugh, followed by a dramatic shake of her head. "*The truth.*"

Tuesday was right to laugh. Danica was an idiot. It was hard to believe she'd been so foolish, so unprofessional, so blind to the obvious machinations of a narcissist who loved the spotlight and couldn't stand to be wrong.

It was easy to see, now that she was staring at it. How oblivious she had been, to never question the convenience of Quentin's story. The way every piece fit so neatly together. When the picture was finished, he was the hero, ready for a coat of lacquer and gloss to keep those pieces in place.

But Quentin wasn't her hero. He wasn't anyone's hero.

And he wasn't going to save her.

Porter couldn't even save himself.

Danica had to distract Tuesday enough for her to make a move.

One shot. Again she pictured the arc.

The lull in monologuing had gone on for too long. If Tuesday didn't start talking soon, she would return to her work on Quentin. Danica had to keep her going, and yet the exchange could never turn frivolous when every word mattered.

Tuesday was living at the edge of a hinge. One wrong word might put that pen in Quentin's eye.

She needed to see herself as the monster. She *wanted* to be the villain, because that was the role that made her feel safe. So long as Tuesday was the predator, everyone else had to be prey.

And Danica could never play another predator convincingly. It would be like a father lion eating its cub. She would have to find another way to conquer the pride. Take Tuesday back to a time when she was something else.

"Linus used to take the blame for you."

Tuesday turned, filling her face with mock surprise. "Do I look like I need that motherfucker to rescue me?"

"Why did he do it?"

A beat, then, "Because he's a moron."

"Because he loved you."

Tuesday scoffed. "Love is bullshit. An excuse to bitch out loud and to yourself. It turns a person into the worst of themselves, full of self-pity and idiotic wallowing."

"Love is scary."

"Fuck you, *love is scary.*" Tuesday glared at her. Another laugh. A shake of her head, meant to show how sorry she felt for Danica's ignorance. "You know what love does to you? It gets your ticket punched for the Pity Train. But guess what, the cars always fall off the track at the cross-roads of Get the Fuck Over It and Move the Fuck On."

"It's also the reason Linus took the blame for you. Even when you framed him for murder, he still kept his mouth shut. Because Linus Cole has always loved you."

"I didn't frame him, I was trying to free him."

"Free him from what?" Danica asked.

"From the rules that everyone pretends make you safe. They don't, they make you a victim. I'm not a victim."

Danica could strike at any time. The chisel was tight in her hand. But Tuesday was still too aware. She was faster and stronger than Danica.

But the tormented still had something that the torturer did not. The element of surprise, and the ability to understand the situation in a way that Tuesday couldn't. Her captor would never see herself as a victim, because that would cast her as prey over predator, but that didn't change what she was.

"You're not a victim," Danica agreed. "You were trying to protect Linus."

Tuesday stared back at her, looking like she might be a blink from a speech. Or total silence. Or perhaps skipping the woodcraft on Quentin's stomach and getting right to the part where she tortured Danica in front of his dying eyes.

"They were trying to make him something he's not," she finally said.

"That's why you killed them. You didn't have any other choice. You loved him, too. Maybe even more than he loved you. You only hurt the people who hurt Linus, or were trying to take him away from you."

"He started talking crazy. All the time, about wanting kids and a house to raise them in. Sounded like he'd been watching one too many *Afterschool Specials* and spouting off like an idiot." She curled her lip. "I bet he's more himself in prison than he ever would've been behind a bullshit picket fence."

"He proposed and you turned him down."

"Damn right I turned him down. Bad enough that he's trying to make himself something he's not. It's horse shit for him to think I want any part of that."

"Love doesn't mean trying to turn someone into something they're not."

"You can say that shit three times and put it on a T-shirt." Tuesday shook her head as if resetting herself. "Well, enough of that. Might as well finish my work on this miserable fuck." She slapped his cheek. "Wake up, Q!"

She turned and picked up her pen from the floor.

Danica missed her chance. The odds of Tuesday exposing her neck like that again were nil. She'd lost her perfect moment. That might have cost Quentin his life. Hers would be next.

Tuesday leaned into her victim with a dramatic whisper. "I heard you love justice. I bet there are clips on YouTube of you saying that bullshit sixty-nine times in a row. *I love justice … I'm all about justice … justice is blind.* Is that right, Q? Is justice *really* blind?"

She brought the pen and it wasn't a bluff. This was Danica's only chance. Tuesday was about to burn one of Quent's eyes right out of its socket.

Danica sprung, swinging the chisel as she leapt.

And just as she'd pictured it over and over, the end her weapon buried itself in the side of Tuesday's neck.

But unlike in her imaginings, Tuesday didn't spill to the floor. Instead she screamed and threw Danica off of her so hard that she slammed back into the wall of machinery behind her. At least one of her ribs snapped when she landed.

The pain was blinding, and Tuesday was on her.

They writhed on the floor, both screaming, blood raining like a busted sprinkler around the room.

Danica managed to wrestle herself a surprise advantage, but it only lasted a second, then she was falling to her knees and tumbling forward.

Tuesday was behind her, and would surely be raining hell upon her head any second, with something blunt, and just enough force to keep her death one ugly whisper away.

She heard shouting, then the popping of guns.

Tones clashing like dueling orchestras from two separate concert halls.

"Fucking fuck," Tuesday said.

Danica couldn't see, blinded by both her pain and the dark, but she could hear Tuesday scrambling off in the other direction.

The popping stopped and voices took their place. Not the gangbangers. This sounded more like the good guys.

It was the last thing she thought. A nice enough way to go. Even if she never opened her eyes again, at least Danica would die knowing that the cavalry had arrived.

She sighed and settled into the feeling of nothing.

Chapter Forty-One

DANICA

DANICA DROVE to Coldwater Island alone.

She had already spoken to the warden, both to schedule her visit and to update him on all that had happened. She had also spoken to Simpson and Merrill when they saved the day in Tuesday's warehouse. She had spoken to the FBI, after a battery of questions following the killer's arrest. She hadn't yet spoken to the press, and barely a word to Quentin, both because he was comatose, and probably would be for a while, and because Danica couldn't stand to look at him.

Maybe that would change, and maybe it wouldn't. She didn't owe him a thing.

She hated what happened to him, and herself for thinking that maybe he deserved it.

Of course she did, but now sometimes she felt glad for his suffering, before she shoved the thoughts away and admonished herself.

Protestors swarmed outside, their narratives about to explode once news got out that the postponed execution was about to be called off.

Everything had changed, and Danica was walking proof. Reporters were all still in the dark about the details, but there were enough leaks that they knew something was brewing, and were staking a claim in or near every possible watering hole. Coldwater most of all.

This time Danica was led down the hallway by the warden himself. Her limbs filled with a different strain of chills. Her body still wanted to shudder, but everything had changed. She no longer felt scared of Linus Cole. Instead she was grateful. She hated that his lying for Tuesday kept a killer on the street all these years, costing more unfortunate misery. But gratitude was an emotion Danica couldn't have ever imagined having about the person she had grown up thinking of as the Magistrate Murderer, and the man who had obliterated her life.

"You okay?" The warden looked concerned. "You sure you don't want me to go in with you?"

"I'm sure."

"He still did an awful lot of terrible things. He allowed bad—"

"I know," Danica said.

"He isn't a hero."

She nodded. "I understand."

The warden sighed and opened the door.

Linus was sitting in his usual spot on the other side of the table, but he didn't smile at her like she expected him to. He gave Danica a light nod as the door closed behind her, then waited for her to sit.

Maybe he didn't know she was here. Quentin always made it sound like criminals knew more inside than outside half the time. She figured there would be a leak. Prisoners would know what happened before the reporters waiting on the other side of the barbed wire.

Maybe the warden would have let him know, or his lawyer, or one of the guards.

Maybe Linus didn't need to be told because he could see it like a painting on her face.

"I've changed my testimony," she said.

Another nod. "That sounds like good news."

"It is." Her smile felt awkward, but necessary.

"You remembered?"

"No." A tear ran down her cheek. "Tuesday tried to kill me."

Linus frowned. "I'm very sorry to hear that."

"It's not your fault." It kind of was, but guilt and gratitude were colliding inside her.

"What are you going to do, now that you know the truth? Besides change your testimony?"

"I don't know." Danica shook her head and reclaimed control of the conversation. "You knew Tuesday was the killer. Why did you go to prison for her?"

"Simple math," Linus said.

She looked back at him, letting her eyes ask the question for her.

"If I knew Tuesday was killing people and kept quiet, then I was an accomplice who deserved his sentence anyway. But put an innocent man behind bars for twenty years, that man is owed some sort of recompense. Wouldn't you agree?"

It was hard not to. The county would pay dearly for this.

"Besides," he added, "I did know she was killing people. And I didn't stop her. I deserved some time no matter what, and if I died inside, so be it."

"One more question."

"Feel free to ask a hundred. I'm a piñata of answers. Keep whacking me with questions if you want the candy of satisfaction." Same tone as always, but nothing Linus said sounded like a threat. She wondered how much of what she had inferred from him before was due to a lack of context or outright misinterpretation.

"I'm sorry," she said.

"You don't have to be. Your uncle does, though."

"I know." She shook her head. "And he's not my uncle."

Her tears fell faster.

"Did Tuesday kill him?" Linus asked.

"Just about. He's in a coma."

"I'm not so sorry to hear that."

Danica accidentally laughed, then hated herself.

"Don't feel guilty. I can still be the bad guy."

"You're not the bad guy."

"You had another question …"

Danica nodded. "You spent twenty years of your life locked up for the woman you loved. Was it worth it?"

"It was."

He offered no explanation, and Danica didn't know how to understand it. She did, in the most clinical sense, like reading a case study straight from a textbook. But it was hard to fathom. Linus wanted to be a good man, and Tuesday was obviously a monster.

"You can't help who you fall in love with, you know," he said when Danica didn't respond. "You're not supposed to. Because then it's something less than love. I wish I never fell for her, I wish it every day and all the time, but you can't ever lie to your body." Linus looked down with a shake of his head, then back up and right into her eyes. "Keeping quiet was the wrong thing to do, I know that. Always did. But it was the right thing for me."

Danica didn't understand, and never would. But she

didn't need to. Knowing the truth was enough to help her sleep at night.

"I think Tuesday would agree with you."

Linus smiled. "She always did, except when it came to the thing where she wouldn't. So, any more questions?"

Danica shook her head. "I don't think I can take any more answers right now."

"Fair enough."

"So are you going to write another book?" Danica asked.

Another smile, more of a smirk. Pleased with itself. "Already written."

She laughed. Surprised, though really she shouldn't have been.

"Everyone's going to want *your story*," Linus said. "Don't do what your … what Porter would have done."

"Not a chance in hell."

Danica stood, said her goodbye, then went and knocked on the door.

The warden looked at her face, gave her a nod without prying, then led her back down the hallway.

Next stop, Morning Tide for a conversation with Mom.

She would talk about the weather, or maybe her clients. Anything but what had happened. She knew the truth, and wasn't about to squeeze a drop of sour juice from a dried-out rind. She could leave the scab alone.

But there was still one final gauntlet to get through.

Before she could even climb into her car, Danica would have to make her way past the horde of reporters. Their potential questions were deafening in her head.

What did you say to Linus Cole? And what did he say to you?

Is it true that Chief Porter is in critical condition at St. Mary's Hospital?

When did you become aware that your Uncle Quent was a liar who got your father murdered and is responsible for putting an inno-cent man in jail?

She couldn't bear it.

Maybe in some far-off tomorrow, but certainly not today.

Danica looked out at the crowd and confirmed her suspicions. Three dozen reporters like vultures on a fly-ridden body. But then a sight that made her feel something surprising.

A man standing at the edge of the crowd, his glasses so clean she could see them gleaming from where she stood, temporarily paralyzed, just inches away from the barbed-wire fence.

Luther smiled and invited her over toward where he was standing beside a white van, next to his crew. She walked over, hurrying past all the reporters, ignoring everyone on her beeline.

"You look ready," Luther said.

Danica looked at the prison behind her, then turned back to the producer. "I think it's the perfect backdrop if you want to get started now."

"There will be a lot of background noise," Luther said.

"Can you clean that up later?"

"Absolutely."

"Absolutely," someone from the crew echoed.

Luther nodded. "Then let's get started."

Danica was mic'd and ready in less than a minute.

"You're just outside Coldwater Island, after having spoken to the man found guilty of murdering your father twenty years ago, on the day after his execution was post-poned. How are you feeling right now?"

Luther looked at her, and Danica wondered if she knew.

Then she realized that it absolutely did not matter.

"I'm feeling … talkative," she finally finished.

Luther smiled, clearly pleased. "And what would you like to talk about?"

"I'm here to tell you the truth about Linus Cole and Quentin Porter."

Danica drew a deep breath, then exhaled with the first fresh breath of an overdue life. "I'm not doing this for fame. I'm doing this for justice. And to end all the miserable lies."

Chapter Forty-Two

QUENTIN

QUENTIN WOKE up with his chest burning in more ways than one.

His entire body felt consumed by flames, but the heat everywhere around his heart felt like open wounds filled with smoldering coals.

Guilt was the gasoline, and all the things he should have done the flames.

He kept playing back reels of sight and clips of sound in his head. Over and over, a haunting on repeat. He'd only been awake for a few minutes and already he wanted to die. It might be better if he never felt anything ever again. Just passed on in his sleep like he deserved to.

He got caught in that loop a little too long before he managed to finally pull himself out of it.

That was the weakness talking.

And Quentin could always outsmart the weakness.

He was still the deputy chief. He could still cover this up.

Not *cover it up*. He meant *make it right*.

He could still do that. He simply had to acknowledge

the stakes and then decide what he would do to protect the little he still had.

Nothing was more important than Danica.

He had to make everything right with her.

There was more at risk here as well. Quentin remembered Simpson and Merrill arriving on the scene. The FBI and everyone else couldn't have been far behind.

He had no idea what they all knew, but he was still safe if Danica didn't blow it for them both. For a moment, the crippling agony almost felt good. Almost like a promise. It was hard to believe that she would turn on him in this condition, regardless of what he had done in the distant past to protect her.

Quentin still had time to fix things.

His career didn't have to get flushed down the toilet.

His entire arrest record wouldn't have to be called into question.

His image could stay intact, and the offers could keep on coming.

He could make it through this. The copycat killer had been taken down. He saw it with his own eyes. Linus had let it all happen. He deserved to live the rest of his life behind bars, and Danica would have to know that.

Making this right would be straightforward. He just had to tell the best possible version of the truth, and keep the poisonous stuff out of it.

He was a wounded hero. There would be more specials, more books, and more money. He could use it to buy Danica a new house, and maybe her forgiveness.

That would be more than worth her saving him from disgrace.

Unless he was lying to himself, which a part of Quentin knew was true.

That part harbored no illusions. Danica hated him, and he deserved her loathing.

He called for a nurse, then got impatient when one didn't appear before him in seconds.

His chest was burning even worse than before, now that he remembered just where the fire was coming from.

Quentin got out of the bed, ambled over to the mirror, then lifted his gown and stared at his reflection.

It took him a second to see it, two before the sight finally registered, and three to deliver his scream.

GUILTY burned into his flesh, the *Y* still half finished.

Quentin bellowed from the pain, and because he knew it was right.

Eight teams of assassins. One high-profile target. Winner takes all.

Brothers Emil and Robert are professional assassins trying to do one last high-dollar hit together before they retire and get out of the game for good.

GET THE THE TARGET TODAY

A Quick Favor

Thank you for reading *Miserable Lies*.

If you enjoyed this book would you please consider writing a review of it on your favorite bookselling site so other readers might enjoy it too. Just a couple of sentences. That would mean a lot to me.

Thank you!

Sean and Dave

About the Author

Nolon King writes fast-paced psychological thrillers set in the glitzy world of entertainment's power players with a bold, insightful voice. He's not afraid to explore the darker side of human nature through stories featuring families torn apart by secrets and lies.

Nolon loves to write about big questions and moral quandaries. How far would you go to cover up an honest mistake? Would you destroy your career to protect your family? How much of your soul would you sell to get the life of your dreams? Would you cheat on your husband to keep your children safe? Would you give in to a stalker's demands to save your marriage?

Also By Nolon King

Hidden Justice

Hidden Justice

Hidden Honor

Hidden Shame

Hidden Virtue

No Justice

No Justice

No Escape

No Hope

No Return

No Stopping

No Fear

Once Upon A Crime

Once Upon A Crime

Twice Upon A Lie

Three Times a Murder

Dead For Good

Dead For Good

Left For Dead

Dead Of Night

Wake The Dead

Dead For Life

Stand Alone Novels

Pretty Killer

12

Blown

Miserable Lies

The Target

Secrets We Keep

Close To Home

Heat To Obsession

A Simple Kill

Tell Me No Lies

Red Carpet Black

Fade To Black

Victim